PAWS AND EFFECT

A MAGICAL CATS MYSTERY

SOFIE KELLY

BERKLEY PRIME CRIME
New York

BERKLEY PRIME CRIME
Published by Berkley
An imprint of Penguin Random House LLC
375 Hudson Street, New York, New York 10014

Copyright © 2016 by Penguin Random House LLC
Excerpt from *The Whole Cat and Caboodle* by Sofie Ryan
copyright © 2014 by Penguin Random House LLC

ISBN: 9780451472168

First Edition: October 2016

Printed in the United States of America
1 3 5 7 9 10 8 6 4 2

Cover art by Tristan Elwell

1

The body was lying on the swing on the back deck, the wooden seat swaying slowly back and forth. Definitely dead, I decided. And it had been placed there no more than half an hour ago.

I'd stopped so suddenly Marcus almost bumped into me. He put a hand on my shoulder to steady himself. "What is it?" he asked, leaning sideways so he could see around me. He blew out a breath. "Not another one. Why does she keep doing this?"

Before I could answer, there was a loud meow and Micah, his small ginger tabby, came walking purposefully along the deck railing toward us. I reached over to stroke her fur. "Nice work," I said. I was certain that Micah was the source of that body—a very large, very dead vole.

Marcus pulled a hand back through his hair, a sure sign he was stressed. "Don't encourage her, Kathleen."

"She's a cat," I said. "Cats hunt. It's her nature."

Marcus walked over to the swing and squinted at the dead rodent. "It's the third dead thing this week," he said. "I asked Roma. She said it's her way of showing her affection for me." He looked back over his shoulder at me. "I mean Micah's way of showing affection, not Roma's."

I smiled. "I know. When Roma likes you she takes you to Meatloaf Tuesday at Fern's Diner." Roma Davidson was Mayville Heights's only veterinarian and one of my closest friends. I'd originally come to town to supervise the renovations to the public library in advance of its centenary. Part of the reason I'd signed a contract to stay on as head librarian once the hundredth-anniversary celebrations were over was because of the connections I'd made. Mayville Heights had come to feel like home.

I looked down at Micah, who was intently watching Marcus as I continued to stroke her fur. Like my own cats, Owen and Hercules, Micah didn't give her affection to just anyone. We'd discovered the little cat, abandoned, out at Wisteria Hill, where Roma lived. Although she certainly seemed to like Roma and me now, back then she wouldn't come to either one of us. It was Marcus who had coaxed her out of hiding. Marcus who had picked her up and held her on his lap all the way to Roma's clinic. It was his scarf she'd slept on that first night there. I thought this rash of "gifts" might be Micah's way of showing Marcus she could pull her weight and that she deserved to stay.

Marcus glanced around the deck. I realized he was

probably looking for something he could use to pick up the dead vole.

"Go get your other keys and your boots and I'll take care of that," I said inclining my head in the direction of the swing. Bugs, bats and furry critters didn't bother me. I gave Micah one last scratch behind the ear and headed for the storage shed in the backyard.

I was coming across the grass with a long-handled spade just as Marcus came out the back door holding the extra set of keys to his SUV. The two of us had been headed to Wisteria Hill to feed the colony of feral cats that lived out there. When he'd arrived to pick me up, his SUV had died in my driveway. We'd pushed it out onto the street so I could back my truck out and stopped by his house to get his spare set of keys. Those he'd drop off to Thorsten Hall, who, among his many other skills, was an excellent mechanic.

"Hey, Kathleen, do you really think I need my boots?" Marcus called to me.

"Roma said the path is mud all the way around the side of the carriage house." I stuck out one leg so he could see that I was wearing my old gum-rubber boots. "But don't worry about it. I can feed Lucy and the others."

"It's okay," he said. "My boots are right here." He gestured to a green rubber pair sitting next to the back door, under the small overhang.

Micah jumped down from the railing and padded over to him, rubbing against his leg as Marcus took off his left shoe and shoved his foot into the corresponding boot. And immediately kicked his foot forward, yelling a word he'd never used in my presence. The boot came off and pin-wheeled up and out over the deck toward the back lawn. A second dead vole that had been dropped inside came shooting out of the open end of the boot. Micah leapt into the air and caught the furry corpse with her two front paws like Lynn Swann catching a forward pass from my dad's favorite quarterback, Terry Bradshaw.

At the same time, the boot arced its way toward me. I sprinted forward, holding the spade ahead of me like some sort of medieval soldier with a lance, catching the boot on the end of the wooden handle. I stopped at the bottom of the steps flushed and sweaty, feeling pleased that I'd stopped the boot from ending up in Marcus's rain barrel.

He was still standing by the back door on one foot with a scowl on his face. Micah was sitting in the middle of the deck with a paw on the vole like an African lion with the prey it had just brought down. And I was holding up the boot, impaled on the end of the spade like the leader of some kind of weird processional.

In retrospect it probably would have been better if I hadn't laughed.

Micah wisely picked up the dead rodent, which was easily half as big as she was, and headed for the backyard without making a sound. Silently, I took the boot off the spade handle, crossed the deck and set it next to Marcus. Then I scooped the other vole off the swing with my shovel and followed Micah. It was pretty clear Marcus needed a minute—or maybe several.

By the time I put the garden spade back in the shed he was waiting at the bottom of the steps wearing his old sneakers, I noticed.

We got into the truck without speaking. I cleaned my hands with the sanitizer I kept in the glove compartment, fished my keys out of the pocket of my jeans and started for Wisteria Hill.

"Nice catch," Marcus commented, after a minute or so of silence.

I kept my eyes on the road. "Thank you," I said. "Harrison taught me how to play horseshoes last summer, remember? I think it helped."

Harrison Taylor, aka Old Harry and Harry Senior, figured since I was a good road hockey player I might be good at horseshoes.

We drove in silence again. I chewed the inside of my cheek so I wouldn't laugh. In my mind's eye I could see Marcus sending that boot airborne, Micah leaping to pull the dead vole out of the air and me running with the spade, shouting, "I got it! I got it!" I was starting to rethink that part, too.

"Go ahead and laugh," Marcus said from the passenger seat. "You know you want to."

"No," I said. "It's not funny." I glanced over and he was smiling at me.

"Yeah, Kathleen, it kind of is. You trying to catch that boot. You should have seen your face. It was like you were at the Super Bowl and there were only two seconds left on the clock."

"Well if you'd gotten a little more distance you could have sent that boot right between those two maple trees in the backyard for a three-pointer." I shot him another quick glance and grinned. "You're not the only one who can do a football analogy."

He laughed. Then he reached over and gave my leg a squeeze. "Aren't you going to tell me that I shouldn't leave my boots out on the deck?"

"Uh-uh," I said. "I told you that the time you left them out there and it started to rain. And you gave me a small engineering lecture on how the overhang would protect them."

"Yeah, the overhang didn't really help this time."

I flicked on my blinker and turned into the driveway to Wisteria Hill. "Yeah," I said, mimicking his overly casual tone. "The overhang didn't really help last time, either."

"Wait a minute. You saw me pour the water out that time?"

Out of the corner of my eye I saw him shift sideways a little in his seat so it was easier to look at me.

"Yes, I saw you pour the water out that time," I said.

"You didn't say anything."

I pulled into the gravel parking area to the left of Roma's house and shut off the truck. "We had just started actually dating."

It had taken a while for the relationship between the two of us to get started, even though at times it had felt like the whole town was playing matchmaker. It didn't help that Marcus was a police detective and we'd met when I was briefly a person of interest in one of his cases.

"You volunteered to get up early on a Saturday morning to help supervise a group of teenagers pick up garbage from the side of the road," I said. "I was so impressed you could have tied a couple of plastic bags around your feet and I wouldn't have said anything."

Marcus grinned. "You're only saying that because Maggie made us wear those big orange trash bags with a giant X on the back made of yellow duct tape because there weren't enough safety vests.

I laughed, remembering Mags putting the make-shift vest on Marcus while he stood awkwardly with his arms out at his sides. I think seeing a police officer willing to look a little silly had made points with the kids who were with us.

We got out and carried the cats' food and dishes around to the back of the old carriage house. Because the cats were feral they weren't socialized, although they had all learned to associate Roma's regular volunteers with food. After we put out the food and water, Marcus and I retreated back by the door and waited. I leaned against him and he folded his arms around me. I could have happily stayed there all day.

"Do you think catching mice like that one is how Micah survived out here until we found her?" he asked, keeping his voice low.

"Possibly," I said. "And that was a vole, not a mouse. Probably a meadow vole, *Microtus pennsylvanicus*. They have a short tail and small ears and a chunkier body type."

"Sometimes I picture the inside of your head as a huge room with row after row of filing cabinets filled with information on pretty much everything."

"It used to look like that." I grinned over my shoulder at him. "But everything got digitized last year." I held up my right thumb and forefinger about an inch apart. "It's all on a little computer chip behind my left ear. Really. Librarian's honor."

He smiled, pulling me closer against him.

I turned in his arms and stretched up on tiptoe so I could kiss him. All thoughts of meadow voles and honor among librarians went out the window.

After a couple of minutes Lucy made her way out to the feeding station. She was the smallest of the cats but she was unmistakably the matriarch of the group. "Hi, Lucy," I said softly.

She turned at the sound of my voice. Lucy and I had developed a connection in the time I'd been helping Roma feed the cats. Although I'd never been able to touch her, she got closer to me than she did to anyone else. Now she crossed the wooden floor and stopped a few feet in front of us. I hadn't seen the cats in several weeks. After Roma had bought Wisteria Hill from Everett Henderson she didn't need her volunteers as much.

Lucy cocked her furry head to one side and meowed, inquiringly it seemed to me.

I crouched down but didn't make any move to get any closer. "I'm sorry I haven't been out to see you," I said.

"Mrr," she rumbled softly.

"I promise not to stay away so long next time."

Lucy made the same soft sound again and then turned and headed for the food. After a minute, lured by some unspoken signal I'd never been able to figure out, the rest of the cats joined her. They all looked well, even Smokey, the oldest of the group, who had had to have surgery the previous fall.

"I'm starting to think Maggie is right," Marcus whispered, his breath warm on my neck after I'd straightened up and returned to his embrace. "You are the cat whisperer."

Cat Whisperer was the nickname my friend Maggie Adams had given me because of my rapport with Lucy and the other Wisteria Hill cats. I felt a special connection to the seven cats. Not only was Wisteria Hill where I'd found my own cats, it was also where my friendship with Marcus had been cemented.

"Lucy is special," I said.

"You say that about all the cats from out here." He pulled me in tighter against his chest. He smelled like soap and cinnamon gum.

"That's because they all are."

It seemed more and more that there was something special, something *different* about at least some of the cats from the old estate. I was uncomfortably aware that someday soon I was going to have to talk to Marcus about that.

After the cats had eaten and left, we cleaned up, put out fresh water and gathered the rest of the dishes.

As we came out of the carriage house into the sunny fall morning I couldn't help looking behind the building at the field and the woods beyond it.

"You're thinking about the development, aren't you?" Marcus asked, taking the canvas bag of empty bowls from me.

I sighed softly. "I can't help it. It's all anyone in town has been talking about for the last two weeks."

The development was a proposal that had just been announced to build an upscale hotel and spa on the shore of Long Lake, not far from Wisteria Hill, a place to get away from it all for harried businesspeople. The developers, out of Chicago, had already bought some of the land. The idea had stirred up strong feeling on both sides in town. Those in favor of the proposal pointed out that visitors to the hotel would likely spend time and money in town. Opponents were concerned about cutting down a large section of old-growth forest to build the resort and the chance that the pristine lake would be polluted.

"I know Roma is worried about the cats," I said, as we made our way back to the truck. "If the development goes through, there's going to be a lot of construction traffic out on the main road. She's afraid it might spook them." I sighed softly and looked around. "And I can't help thinking about the cats that get dumped out here."

"What do you mean?" Marcus asked.

I gestured at the carriage house. "People know Lucy and the others are here. It lets them rationalize that it's okay to abandon one out here." I stopped and turned to face him. "Do you know how many cats Roma has rescued just since she started taking care of these cats?"

He shook his head.

"Ten. Ten cats that people left to fend for themselves. Eleven, if you count Micah."

His jaw tightened and anger flashed in his blue eyes. "I had no idea."

"I don't like thinking about how many she didn't find," I said as we started walking again. "If it's busy out here, if there's more activity, more traffic, those cats will be dumped somewhere else."

"We'll figure something out," Marcus said as we reached the truck. "I'll talk to Roma. Either way, no matter what happens with the development, we need to do something about so many cats just being dumped."

I leaned against his shoulder for a moment and smiled up at him. Marcus had a kind heart underneath his play-by-the-rules-detective exterior.

I unlocked the truck and slid behind the wheel, checking my watch as I did so. "Do you have time for breakfast at Eric's?" I asked. "My treat."

He leaned in the open passenger door and a smile pulled at the corners of his mouth. "Are you trying to make amends for laughing at me with coffee and one of Eric's breakfast sandwiches?"

"Yes," I said.

He did smile then. "Well, lucky for you that will work."

I leaned across the seat and kissed him.

"That works, too." He caught my shoulder with one hand and kissed me again.

For a moment I forgot what I was going to do next. His kisses still had that effect on me. He had that effect on me.

I pulled back, *very* reluctantly. "Um, okay, so Eric's. For breakfast."

Marcus pulled a hand over his chin. He cleared his throat. "Right."

Since it was early I had no trouble finding a parking place on the street just down from Eric's Place.

"Do you think it's too early to call Thorsten?" Marcus asked as we started along the sidewalk.

"No," I said, stopping to scrape a clump of mud off my boot. "You could have called him at six a.m. You know the saying, the early bird gets the worm?"

"I get it. Thorsten is the early bird." He pulled his cell phone out of his pocket.

I shook my head. "Uh-uh. He's the guy who wakes up the early bird."

Marcus laughed. "That has to have come from Mary."

I grinned. "Good guess."

Mary Lowe worked for me at the library. She looked like everyone's favorite grandmother with her sensible shoes and decorated sweaters for every occasion. She was also state kickboxing champion for her age and weight class.

"And I think the comment comes from first hand knowledge. Back before Mary was a responsible, married grandmother I think she and Thorsten may have had a thing."

Marcus raised an eyebrow. "What kind of a thing? He's younger than she is."

"I know he is," I said, "which is why I didn't ask any questions. I was afraid she might tell me. I know he's seen her dance."

"Kathleen, a lot of people have seen Mary dance—including you."

I winced. "Don't remind me. It took me about two weeks until I could look her directly in the eye."

I had discovered—very much by accident—that Mary danced on amateur night complete with lacy corset and a feathered fan at a bar up on the highway that featured exotic dancing. I tipped my head in the direction of the café's door. "Try Thorsten and I'll go get us a table."

Eric's was quiet, even for a Friday morning. There were two men at the counter who I knew worked at the marina and a woman and two other men I didn't recognize at a table at the far end of the room.

Eric himself was at the counter. He raised a hand in hello. "Sit anywhere, Kathleen," he called. "Claire will be right out."

"Thanks," I said, heading for my favorite table in the front window. I could see Marcus on the sidewalk. I was guessing he'd reached Thorsten. He was holding his phone to his ear with one hand and gesturing with the other.

I hung my purse over the back of the chair and

pulled off my hoodie, looking up to see Claire approaching with coffee.

"Good morning," she said, as she began to fill the mugs on the table. She didn't ask if we wanted coffee. She knew both of us well enough to know the answer by now.

"Would you like a menu?" Claire asked. "Or do you know what you'd like?

"Two breakfast sandwiches, please." I looked around. "It's awfully quiet this morning."

She nodded. "There's a breakfast meeting about the proposal for Long Lake over at the community center. We catered it for them. Nic is working over there. Eric just came back."

"I thought that was tomorrow," I said, reaching for the small pitcher of cream Claire had set in the middle of the table.

She shot a quick glance over her shoulder to see if anyone needed anything from her. One of the men at the table pointed at his cup. Claire nodded before she turned back to me. "It was," she said. "They changed the date at the last minute. Some environmental group is getting involved." She turned toward the other table. "Your sandwiches won't be very long."

I had just taken the first sip of my coffee when Marcus came though the door of the café. He looked around for me, and then, as his gaze slid by the three people at the nearby table he just stopped, staring at them without moving, as though he'd forgotten about me, forgotten why he was there.

I got to my feet but the woman at the table was

faster. She pushed her chair back and stood up, surprise clear in her wide-eyed expression. "Marcus?"
she said.

The two men with her turned toward the door
when she spoke. They both looked as surprised as she
did. Her astonishment had already been replaced with
a delighted smile. She made her way across the café,
maneuvering quickly around chairs and tables and
threw her arms around Marcus. One of the men was
already on his feet, a smile stretching across his face.
Marcus was smiling, too. And hugging the woman.

I stood at my table feeling lost and confused. I had
no idea who the people were.

2

The man who had just stood up joined Marcus and the woman. He was easily six feet tall with wavy blond hair that looked a little overdue for a haircut, and a rangy build. He and Marcus shook hands and then hugged in the quick way that men do with slaps on the back.

Marcus looked around for me then. I could tell from the half smile he gave me that he was uncomfortable. I felt certain of his feelings for me but even so, I was still learning about him, about his life. There was still a lot I didn't know. Whoever these people were, they were important to him.

The second man walked over to join the little group. He was maybe an inch or two less than six feet, with the wide shoulders and muscled build of an athlete. His dark hair was cropped short and he wore black-framed glasses. He eyed Marcus with curiosity and at the same time seemed to be sizing him up. Nothing in his face or his body language said that he was as happy to see Marcus as his friends clearly were.

He offered his hand. "Marcus, it's been a long time."

"Hello, Travis," Marcus said. I noticed neither man had said "It's good to see you" or anything of the kind.

Marcus saw me approaching and his shoulders seemed to relax, just a little. When I reached his side he took my hand. I was a little surprised. He wasn't one for public demonstrations of his feelings. I gave it a squeeze and smiled at his friends, because obviously that's who they were.

"Kathleen," he said, "I'd like you to meet Danielle, John and Travis. We went to college together."

Danielle immediately held out her hand. "Hi, Kathleen," she said. "Call me Dani." She had long, slender fingers and I felt calluses on her palm. She was beautiful, tall and slender with high cheekbones and green eyes. Her blond hair was pulled back in a messy bun.

The tall, shaggy-haired man was John. He smiled and shook my hand as well. I watched Travis out of the corner of my eye. He was watching me and not trying to be subtle about it.

"Hello, Travis," I said turning toward him. "It's a pleasure to meet you."

"You too," he said. He looked over at their table. "Why don't you two join us? We can catch up and get to know you a little." He looked at Marcus and to me it looked like a challenge in his dark eyes.

I gave him my best librarian-in-charge look. "Thanks, that would be great," I said. I caught Claire's attention and very quickly two tables were pushed together.

They seemed to be good friends, but why had Marcus never mentioned them to me before?

"So what are you doing here?" John asked, turning sideways in his chair and leaning one arm across its back.

"I live here," Marcus said.

"You're still a police officer?"

Marcus nodded. "Detective, yes."

"What are the three of you doing in town?" I asked.

"You know there's a development proposed for Long Lake?" Dani said, propping her elbows on the table.

I nodded over my coffee cup.

"We work for a coalition of environmental groups. We're here to look at the land and see if there's any reason to stop the project." She hesitated. "I'm a geologist, Travis is an environmental engineer—"

"And John's a biologist," I finished.

Marcus covered his surprise at my seemingly psychic abilities very well. Actually, I'd just made a guess based on the *Wildflowers of Minnesota Field Guide* and the copy of *Bird Feathers* that were sticking out of the top of the messenger bag hanging from the back of John's chair.

Dani nodded. "My job is to look at the land to see if there's anything about the soil or the topography that precludes the developers' plans for the site." She gestured at Travis. "Travis will look at what the environmental impact will be on the area."

"Possible air and water pollution, soil contamination, etcetera, etcetera," Travis added.

"And my job is to determine whether there are any rare or endangered plants on the site," John said. "Which reminds me, I heard Mayville Heights has a really extensive herbarium."

"Yes, we do," I said. The library had inherited the herbarium—which was a collection of dried, preserved plants—years before when a government plant research station had consolidated its work in St. Paul.

"Do you have any idea who I'd talk to about looking through the collection?" John pulled a small, hardbound book from his shirt pocket.

"You should talk to the head librarian," Marcus said, turning to smile at me. "Which happens to be Kathleen."

"That's great," John said. He gave me an inquiring look. "So could I?"

"Absolutely," I said. "I can get you set up this morning if you'd like."

"I would. Thank you."

"Kathleen, you're not from here, are you?" Travis asked. He waved a finger by his ear. "I can hear a little of the East Coast in your voice."

I folded both hands around my cup and turned toward him. "You have a very good ear," I said. "And no, I'm not originally from here. I am from back east, all up and down the coast actually, but most recently Boston."

"How did the two of you meet?" Dani asked. She glanced at Marcus and gave him a smile.

"The library had a connection to a case I was working on," he said. Under the table his hand brushed my leg for a moment.

"And he won you over with his charm," Travis commented, a fine edge of sarcasm in his tone.

I nodded, keeping my gaze locked on Marcus. "Yes, he did."

I knew it was wrong to make up my mind about someone I'd just met, but Travis rubbed me the wrong way. I thought of what my mother would say in this circumstance: You can put lipstick on a pig but it's still a pig.

"So did he tell you how we all met?" Travis continued. It was almost as though he knew Marcus hadn't told me about them and wanted to out him on that.

"I don't think I ever asked," I said. Which was true. "So how did a future police detective end up being friends with three environmentalists?"

Dani was sitting next to Marcus. She bumped his arm with her shoulder. "First year bio lab, remember?"

"Biology?" I said. Marcus's undergraduate degree was in criminology with a minor in computer science.

He shrugged. "I was taking the course as an elective because it fit my schedule. The four of us ended up at the same lab bench."

"And?" I nudged, knowing from the sound of his voice that there was more to the story. His face reddened. I raised an eyebrow at him à la *Star Trek*'s Mr. Spock.

"We were staining slides. We had to use a Bunsen

burner for one of them ... and then a fire extinguisher."

"So the four of you bonded when you started a fire in the biology lab and then had to put it out with a fire extinguisher?"

Dani shook her head. "No, it wasn't like that," she said, laughter sparkling in her green eyes. "And technically it was the sprinkler system that put the fire out." She held up a hand before I could say anything. "*And* it wasn't our fault that the sprinkler system activated in the first place. That was because of Dr. Martindale's hair."

"You've lost me," I said. "Who's Dr. Martindale?"

"Bio prof," John said, frowning as though the answer should have been obvious.

"And it was his hair that set off the sprinklers?" I was still lost.

He nodded.

"Because he was wearing a tiki-torch hat?"

"Very funny," he said, "but no. When Travis set his slide on fire with the Bunsen burner he dropped it in the sink. The problem was whoever had been in the lab before us had dumped alcohol down that sink."

"Which was not my fault," Travis interjected.

"I think I get the picture," I said. "But I still don't understand how the professor's hair set off the sprinklers."

"It wasn't exactly *his* hair, if you get what I mean," Dani said with a Cheshire-cat grin.

I nodded. "I'm starting to."

"Dr. Martindale was an excitable kind of guy."

Travis looked toward the front of the restaurant. When he caught Claire's attention he pointed at his cup the same way I'd seen him do earlier.

"Flaming hair will do that to you, I'm guessing," I said.

Claire arrived at the table with the coffeepot then. As she filled my cup I met her gaze and held up one finger. She nodded almost imperceptibly and I felt confident that she knew I intended to take care of the bill.

"Okay, Dr. Martindale's alleged hair was on fire," I said as I doctored my coffee. "Then what happened?" It was impossible to keep my smile contained.

John made a face. "He had on a pair of those big plastic goggles you wear in the lab and when he pulled them off his hair got caught in the strap and it"—he made a rolling motion with one hand—"kind of somersaulted into the sink." He shrugged. "You know, I was never really sure that hair *was* human hair."

"You're making this up," I said, shaking with laughter. Even Marcus was smiling at the memory.

"No, we're not," John insisted. He held up one hand, palm facing out. "I swear it's the truth. There was a lot of smoke, the sprinklers went off and we had to evacuate the building. That was the end of the lab. We all ended up at this bar just off campus." He shrugged again. "That's really how we got to know each other. We all pretty much agreed without talking about it that we weren't going to say a word about Dr. Martindale's hair being the reason the sprinklers went off."

"I can see how it would have been a hot-button issue for him," I said, dissolving into laughter again.

"I think we were probably the reason Dr. Martindale retired at the end of the year." John winked at me and reached for his coffee.

"You mean the field trip," Travis said. The smile on his face was more like a smirk. "Yeah, I think that cemented it for Martindale."

A look passed between Marcus and Dani, so quickly that I wasn't completely certain I'd seen it at all.

Dani stretched one arm behind her head and shifted to look at Travis. "C'mon, Trav, we're probably boring Kathleen talking about the good old days."

Travis was still leaning back in his chair, one hand wrapped around his mug. With the other he sent a knife on the table spinning in a circle. "Are we boring you, Kathleen, talking about Marcus's youthful indiscretions?" he asked.

I could feel the tension in the air, like ozone before a thunderstorm. I knew there was no right way to answer Travis's question. Something had happened between him and Marcus. Maybe that was why Marcus had never talked about any of them.

Under the table I put my hand on his leg. He covered it with his own for a moment. "Talking about Marcus is never boring as far as I'm concerned," I said to Travis. That was true and it was the most neutral answer I could come up with.

Marcus turned sideways in his chair and smiled at me. "The year we took that biology class the administration decided to add some fieldwork to the course."

"It was the only year they did that," John added.

Marcus's gaze flicked to Dani again and she picked up the story. "So, anyway, the college owned a wood-lot and Dr. Martindale decided to take the class camping overnight. We were supposed to collect plant samples all day and then when it got dark we were going to look at the stars. Dr. Hemmings and a couple of grad students from the physics department came with us."

"To foster an atmosphere of interdepartmental co-operation and learning," Travis said, as though he were quoting the words straight from some university press release. He pushed his hipster glasses up his nose with one finger.

"The two grad students had to lug a telescope through the woods," John said, grinning at the memory.

Dani gave me a smile. Her voice didn't betray any tension but I could see it in her shoulders and the way she held her head. "Marcus volunteered to make breakfast."

I glanced at him again and smiled. "He's a good cook."

John almost choked on his coffee. "You're serious? He cooks?"

I nodded.

Dani turned and glared. "Be nice," she said.

He just laughed.

"I didn't exactly volunteer," Marcus said. "I was the only one up."

He looked over at John, who immediately shook his head and turned to look at me. "For the record,

Kathleen, I do not snore and I did not drive him out of our tent."

"Duly noted," I said.

"Dr. Hemmings gave me a bag of oatmeal and a pot," Marcus said. "She told me to make breakfast for my group."

"And you what? Burned the oatmeal?"

John was laughing now. Dani's smile still seemed forced.

"You're a librarian, Kathleen," Travis said. His voice was still laced with a touch of sarcasm. "You probably know the story of Medusa."

I had no idea what a character from Greek mythology had to do with Marcus making oatmeal but I nodded. "Medusa was a Gorgon. According to the legend, the sight of her face was so terrible it would turn anyone who looked at her to stone."

Travis's gaze slid from Marcus to me. "Yeah, well that's pretty much what Marcus did to our breakfast."

"It wasn't quite like that, Kathleen," Dani said. She wore a silver double-infinity-knot ring on the middle finger of her left hand and she twisted it around and around on the finger.

"It was pretty much exactly like that," John retorted.

"My mother always made oatmeal with milk," Marcus said.

"Something you need to know about John is that he always has a few essential supplies when he's out in the field," Dani said. She looked past me, at Marcus, giving him a genuine smile of affection. "Reese's Pea-nut Butter Cups, Pop-Tarts, coffee, powdered milk." She put extra emphasis on the last two words.

"I'm starting to think I know where this is going," I said. "You thought you'd use the powdered milk."

Marcus nodded.

I turned back to Dani. "But?"

"John also had a bag of plaster of Paris in his backpack."

"No," I said.

John's head was bobbing up and down. "Yes."

"You could have put a label on the bag." Marcus leaned forward to look at John.

"Hey, plaster of Paris and powdered milk don't ex-actly look that much alike." John was laughing.

"They do at five in the morning when you're sleep-deprived."

I leaned against Marcus for a moment, feeling the warmth of his body through the fabric of his shirt. "So what happened to the oatmeal?"

Travis spoke up before anyone could answer. "You know how people say stuff like that is good for you because it sticks with you?"

"I do," I said.

"Lucky for Marcus that oatmeal stuck with the pot so nobody actually ate it."

John turned to look at him, waving one hand in the air. "No, that's not true. We actually managed to get it out of the pot. It was like a big cylindrical boulder. We just rolled it into the trees. I think Dr. Hemmings made one of her grad students carry it back to campus so she could use it as a doorstop. She thought it was some kind of unusual rock formation."

"Okay, I know you're making that up," I said, shaking with laughter.

John put a hand over his heart. "Sadly, I'm not."

"So what did you all do for breakfast?"

"Marcus hiked out to the road, thumbed a ride to McDonald's and came back with Egg McMuffins for everyone." Dani smiled at him again.

"Pretty much saved the day," Travis said, an edge of sarcasm in his voice.

"Wait a minute." I gestured at Dani. "You said John had Pop-Tarts in his backpack. Why didn't you eat those?"

John raised a hand skyward as though he were in a classroom. "I know this," he said. "Pick me! Pick me."

Dani rolled her eyes at him. She didn't seem as tense now.

"Go ahead," I said to John.

"When Chef Marcus here was foraging for powdered milk he left my backpack outside the tent and a raccoon took the Pop-Tarts, the Reese's Peanut Butter Cups and two pairs of my socks."

"That was a long time ago," Marcus said with a smile.

I smiled. "And for the record, Marcus is a vey good cook now."

"Back then the problem wasn't a lack of cooking skills," Travis said. "It was taking something you had no business putting your hands on."

The table grew silent. John exhaled and shook his

head, muttering something I didn't catch. Dani closed her eyes, resting her forehead on her hand. Marcus went into police officer mode. He set his cup and then his napkin on the table with precise, economical movements. Then he turned his attention to Travis. "This isn't the time or the place for whatever problem you have with me."

"Trav, don't do this," John said. He stood up. "We should get going."

"I'm just sharing stories with Marcus's girlfriend about the good old days," Travis said. He was talking to John, but his eyes never left Marcus's face.

This was where my mother would say, "Fish or cut bait." Actually, she'd probably use a more colorful expression that involved getting off a pot but the sentiment was the same.

"It was good to meet all of you," I said. "But I have to get going as well." I stood up and reached down to rest my hand on Marcus's shoulder. I was just like Owen with his paw on a kitty treat: I was marking my territory.

"I see the women in your life still rush to your defense," Travis commented, one hand playing with his coffee cup. The snarky edge to his voice was more pronounced.

Marcus pushed back his chair and got to his feet. Out of the corner of my eye I could see Eric over at the counter watching us. I knew all I had to do was raise a hand and he'd be at the table.

"Is this where I'm supposed to go all caveman and take a swing at you?" Marcus asked.

"C'mon, Trav, don't be a tool," John said to his friend.

Travis got up as well. "Did you tell Kathleen how you stabbed your best friend in the back?" Feet apart, shoulders squared, I could see confrontation in his body language as well as his words. He was a big man and his anger made him look even bigger

"Don't do this," Dani said.

"Defend him the way you always do." Sarcasm dripped off of Travis's words.

What could have happened that he felt so wronged after so many years? I didn't have to wait long to find out.

Dani sighed and pushed a stray strand of hair back off her face. She looked tired all of a sudden. "Fine, then," she said. "Kathleen, Travis and I were a couple in college, until Marcus and I met." She swallowed hard. "And we started seeing each other . . . behind Travis's back."

My first thought was why hadn't she just broken up with Travis if she wanted to date Marcus, but I hadn't always made good decisions when I was in college, so who was I to judge? "We do dumb things when we're in college," I said. "I know I did things I'm sorry for now."

I looked at Travis. He hadn't made a very good first impression, but I couldn't help feeling sad that he hadn't been able to let go of something that had happened so many years ago. He seemed to be wearing his hurt like a hair shirt. Why on earth was he still working with Dani?

Travis's dark eyes flashed. "First of all, we were

more than a couple. We were engaged. And second, I caught them together in—what's the polite term? A compromising situation? It was more than a dumb thing, Kathleen."

His words hit Dani like a slap. Her face reddened and she bit her lip.

I could feel the tension vibrating in Marcus like a plucked violin string. "Leave," he growled, his voice low and harsh with warning. "Stay away from Dani. Stay away from Kathleen and stay the hell away from me. If you think my badge means I won't defend the people I care about you're very, very wrong."

John grabbed Travis's arm. "Let's go, man," he said.

Travis glared at Marcus, who met his gaze seemingly calmly. I think only I could feel the hum of anger his body was giving off.

John caught the neck of Travis's shirt with his free hand and pulled. "We're going. Now!" he said, sharply.

Marcus's jaw was tight with tension. I knew he was grinding his teeth together and I was impressed with his restraint.

Travis shook off John's hands, shoved his chair out of the way and headed for the door.

John closed his eyes for a moment and blew out a noisy breath. When he opened them again he looked at us and gestured in the direction of the door. "I should go . . . check on him." He shrugged and gave me a wry smile. "Kathleen, it really was good to meet you. I'm sorry about . . ." He made a helpless gesture in the air. " . . . everything." He reached for his wallet but Marcus shook his head silently.

John rested his hand on Dani's shoulder for a moment. She seemed to shrink inside herself as though she were cringing with embarrassment.

Dani said nothing until the door closed behind John. Then she sighed. "I'm sorry," she said.

"It's not your fault." I said. "I'm sorry that Travis got hurt and I can see you both are, too."

"You probably think I'm a—"

I shook my head. "I think I'm glad I got to meet you, Dani. And I hope I'll see you again while you're in town."

She nodded, swatting at a stray strand of hair. "Thank you, Kathleen. I'm very glad I got to meet you. And I'm glad Marcus has you."

"I'll get this," I said to Marcus, gesturing at the table. "Stay here with Dani. I'm going to head over to the library."

He hesitated for a moment and then leaned over and kissed my cheek. "Thanks," he said. "I'm sorry about this."

"It's not your fault," I said. "I'll talk to you later."

I headed over to the counter. Eric held up his largest take-out coffee cup and raised an eyebrow.

"Please," I said.

"Everything okay?" he asked quietly as he picked up the coffeepot.

I glanced back at Marcus and Dani. He was sitting down facing her, elbows resting on his thighs, hands with fingers interlaced hanging between his knees. Dani was listening as he talked, still twisting her ring around her finger.

"I uh . . . I think so," I said.

Eric handed me my coffee and the bill. I glanced at it and pulled enough money out of my wallet to cover the total plus a tip.

"Guy's crazy about you, you know." Eric inclined his head in Marcus's direction.

I gave him a smile. "Thanks, Eric," I said. "Have a good day."

When I stepped outside John was alone on the sidewalk.

"Hi, Kathleen," he said, giving me a wry smile. "My plans for the day have changed. Any chance I could get a look at your herbarium? Or have you had enough of us?"

I gave him a smile that was probably more professional than friendly. "I was going to walk over to the library. Would you like to come with me right now?"

He looked back at the café. "Yeah, why not?"

We started down the sidewalk. I took a sip of my coffee. John looked out toward the water. The sky was a deep, seemingly endless shade of blue. "This is a nice place," he said.

I nodded. "Yes, it is."

We walked a bit farther in uncomfortable silence and then John stopped. He turned to face me. "Does this feel as awkward to you as it does to me?"

I nodded and took another sip from my cup.

"Look, I'm sorry about Travis," he said. "This whole thing with Marcus and Dani happened a long time ago and ended pretty quickly." He gave an off-handed shrug. "And it's not like they were going to do

the whole happily-ever-after thing anyway. It's just . . .
I think working together for the past few weeks
brought up some old feelings for him. Dani made it
pretty clear she wasn't interested and I think seeing
Marcus, well, it was just easier to blame him than face
the fact that it was never going to happen with Dani."

"So they don't work together all the time?" I said.

John shook his head. "No. The engineer who was
working with us on this project dislocated his shoulder and broke his arm rock climbing. Travis came on
board at the last minute." He held out both hands.
"And now I'm going to change the subject. How did
you end up in Minnesota? Was it the librarian's equiv-
alent of running off to join the circus?"

I laughed. "I wanted to do something different. The
library board was looking for someone to supervise
renovations to the building." I held up my cup. "And
here I am."

"How the heck did you end up with an herbarium?
I don't think I've ever come across one in a library before." We started walking again.

"That happened before I got here. It's a small town.
We have a lot of things people don't expect to find in
a library—a collection of documents with the history
of this area, high school yearbooks going back almost
a hundred years." We stopped at the corner to let two
cars go by before we crossed the street.

"Basically we inherited the herbarium when the
government plant research station consolidated all its
work in St. Paul."

John made a face. "I've already been through the

endangered species database. I'm hoping there might be something in the herbarium records, some rare plant we didn't know was native to this area. Plants don't always follow the rules about where they grow." He held out both hands and shrugged. "It's a long shot."

It occurred to me then that maybe it would help John if he talked to Rebecca. "I have a friend who's been making herbal remedies all her life," I said as we approached the library. "She knows a lot about the plants that grow in this area. I could call her and see if she has any suggestions, I mean, if you think it would help."

"It couldn't hurt," he said. "Thanks. If we're going to stop this project or at least get the proposal modified we don't have a lot of time."

"So all three of you work for the same environmental group?" I asked.

John shook his head. "Dani and I do. Not Travis. There are four different groups working together right now. They're all opposed to the resort proposal. It just made more sense for us to pool our resources." He stopped in front of the old brick building. "This is your library?"

I nodded.

"Very nice," he said approvingly. "How old is the building?"

"Over a hundred years." I led the way up the steps. I noticed John eye the wrought-iron railings and the heavy wooden doors.

Mary Lowe was at the circulation desk when we

stepped inside. "Good morning, Kathleen," she said. "You're early."

"A little," I said. "Is Abigail around?"

Mary tipped her head in the direction of the stacks. "She's shelving in the children's section." She looked past me and gave her best grandmotherly smile to John. "Welcome to the Mayville Heights Free Public Library."

"Thank you," he said. "It's a beautiful building."

Mary beamed. "We think so."

I touched John's arm. "I'll introduce you to Abigail Pierce. She can get you set up."

We found Abigail arranging picture books on a low shelf, forehead furrowed in concentration. Abigail was also a children's author and I was hearing lots of great buzz about the new book she had coming out in early winter, just a couple of months away.

She straightened up and smiled when she caught sight of us. I made the introductions and explained what John was looking for.

"I can get you set up in our small meeting room," Abigail said. A pensive look crossed her face and she tucked a strand of hair absently behind one ear. She looked so different without her long braid. "We also have some sketchbooks that might be helpful. One of the botanists who worked at the research station was also an artist. He drew some of the plants he saw and there are maps and notes as well."

John pulled a hand back over his neck. "That sounds terrific but I think I'm going to need an extra set of hands to go through all that."

"I think I can get those for you," I said.

"They're not going to come ripping out of my chest like in that *Alien* movie, are they?" he asked.

Abigail looked at me, narrowing her eyes. "Are you thinking of Maggie?"

"Yes," I said. "Rebecca taught her a lot about plants in this part of the state and I know she took a look at those sketchbooks." I turned back to John. "My friend Maggie Adams is an artist. If you think it would help I could call her and see if she could stop by and go through those sketchbooks."

"It would help," John said. "But are you sure she's available?"

"I can ask. Maggie is very much on the no side when it comes to the development. I think she'd be happy to help if she can."

Abigail—who I knew was also opposed to the development—smiled. "Why don't I show John the herbarium while you call Maggie?"

I nodded. "Thanks."

John picked up the leather messenger bag he'd set at his feet and gave me a warm smile. "Thanks, Kathleen. I appreciate all your help."

I smiled back at him. "You're welcome."

I went upstairs to my office to call Maggie. "I can walk over right now," she said once I explained about John and the sketchbooks.

I swiveled in my chair and looked out the window over the water. There were a few clouds, like puffs of white cotton floating high in the sky. "I'm not taking you from anything important, am I?" I asked.

"I've been staring at a bunch of photos on my computer for the last twenty minutes and I still don't know which ones to print," she said. "And stopping the plans for the lakefront is more important than anything else right now as far as I'm concerned. I'll see you in a little while."

I ended the call and leaned back in my chair. I didn't want the development—at least the way the plans were at the moment—to happen, either. But more than that I wanted the whole debate settled. It was beginning to affect the town. Rebecca and Everett were on different sides of the issue but they had somehow found a way for that to not affect their relationship—probably because in the end Everett would do anything for her if she asked. But they were the exception. Even at the library we'd agreed to disagree. Abigail and I were in the no camp, but Mary was for the proposal, pointing out that Mayville Heights would benefit from more tourists so close by.

"I grew up swimming in Long Lake, picking blueberries and getting a Christmas tree out there every year," she'd told me one morning about a week and a half previous, standing in the upstairs hallway. "And in a perfect world none of that land would ever be developed. But it's far from a perfect world." She'd brushed a stray bit of lint from the front of her blue sweater, which was decorated with huge yellow-and-brown sunflowers. "Time only runs in one direction, Kathleen. Forward," she'd continued, her expression serious, which was rare for Mary. "I believe it's because we're supposed to keep moving forward, not live in the past."

I hadn't argued with Mary's reasoning—but I knew that Harrison Taylor had had a fairly heated conversation on the subject with her. Harrison and Mary had been friends for years and I felt sure their friendship would withstand this disagreement, but I still hated seeing them squabble instead of blatantly flirting with each other the way they usually did.

When Maggie arrived I took her in to meet John and promised I'd bring her back lunch from Eric's.

"I'm going home to change," I told Mary. "I shouldn't be long." Generally I didn't start until lunchtime on Fridays.

Mary nodded. "The young man who came in with you, he's looking for something to stop the plans for the resort, isn't he?"

I turned back around to face her. "Yes, he is," I said. "Will that be a problem for you?"

The moment the words were out I regretted saying them. I held up my hand. "I'm sorry, Mary. I shouldn't have asked that. I know that you don't let personal feeling interfere with your work."

She gave a snort of laughter. "Yes, I do. All the time. But I promise you I won't go into the meeting room where he's working loaded for bear."

I smiled. "I appreciate that."

When I got home I found Hercules in the backyard sitting on the wide arm of my favorite Adirondack chair. "What are you doing out here?" I asked. He looked in the direction of the gazebo in Rebecca's backyard. *Rebecca and Everett's backyard*, I mentally corrected myself. Rebecca had been my neighbor since I'd moved to Mayville Heights. She'd been the first person to welcome me. Then I'd met Maggie and Roma when Rebecca invited me to try her tai chi class. She was one of my favorite people. Both Owen and Hercules adored her and not just because she spoiled them with kitty treats.

Now that Rebecca and Everett were married Hercules had taken to joining Everett for coffee—and the occasional (I hoped) slice of bacon in the gazebo a couple of times a week.

"So have you solved all the town's problems?" I asked, scooping up the little black-and-white cat and heading for the back door. Hercules pretty much came and went as he pleased. That was because he had a very unique ability. He could walk through the door—walls, too. The first time I'd seen him do it—at the library while it was under construction—I didn't know if I was hallucinating or having a stroke. I wasn't sure what it said about me that seeing my cat walk through an otherwise solid wooden door or an equally solid brick wall was pretty much commonplace for me now.

I unlocked the back door and set Hercules on the porch floor. At least Owen didn't walk though walls. I opened the kitchen door, letting Hercules go ahead of me. "Owen," I called. "Where are you?"

Hercules cocked his black-and-white head to one side and looked toward the cats' food bowls next to the refrigerator. Owen winked into view, materializing like Captain Kirk getting beamed onto the bridge of the starship *Enterprise*.

No, Owen couldn't walk through walls and doors the way his brother could. His superpower, as it were, was the ability to make himself invisible. Which he generally did at the worst times for me.

He made his way across the kitchen floor toward me, making disgruntled little murps.

I crouched down and stroked his fur. "I'm sorry it took so long. I took Marcus out to breakfast." That got me a louder dissatisfied murp.

"I need to change and head back down to the library." My regular workday would be starting soon anyway and I wanted to see how John was doing in the herbarium. "And I need to call Rebecca," I said aloud.

Owen immediately headed for the back door. "No," I said. "She's not coming over for tea." Owen stopped in his tracks and looked over at his brother. They exchanged a glance and then Herc nudged his food dish with his head, pushing it several inches across the floor. He looked over at me, his green eyes wide and unblinking. I didn't need to turn toward Owen to know his golden eyes were also fixed on me.

"Neither one of you knows the meaning of the word 'subtle,'" I said as I got the container of sardine crackers out of the cupboard.

"Merow!" Hercules said, which may have meant he did in fact know what the word meant, but in reality was probably his way of saying "Hurry up."

I gave each cat a small stack of the homemade crackers and a fresh drink of water and then went upstairs to change.

When I came out of the bathroom after brushing my teeth I found Hercules in the hallway. Because Owen could be kind of finicky I knew it would take him a lot longer to finish his snack.

Hercules followed me into the bedroom and poked his head in the closet. I sometimes got the feeling he'd been some sort of fashionista in a past life. He eyed every item while I was picking out my clothes as though he had an opinion on everything—which it sometimes seemed to me that he did.

"Marcus has friends from college," I said as I pulled the elastic from my hair and ran my fingers through it.

"Mrrr," Hercules said.

"They're here, three of them. In town, I mean."

I talked to the cats. A lot. For a long time I'd rationalized it by telling myself it helped me to work out things out loud—to hear what I was thinking. And that was true, but I also believed they understood most if not all of what I was saying. Given their other "skills," it wasn't that far-fetched.

I told Hercules all about meeting Travis, John and Danielle. At one point in the conversation I looked over to see Owen in the doorway, carefully washing his face. He looked up at me when I stopped talking and meowed—cat for "Keep going," perhaps?

"It's not like Marcus," I said. Hercules leaned against my leg and I reached down and picked him up. If he shed any fur on my charcoal sweater it wouldn't show. "He slept with his best friend's girlfriend. Does that sound like Marcus to you?"

The cat wrinkled his nose as though he was actually considering my question. "I know it was a long time ago, but . . ." I let the end of the sentence trail off because I didn't know what else to say. Marcus hadn't told me anything about these friends that he'd been very close to at one point in his life—in the case of Dani, extremely close. He was a very private person but this felt wrong, even for him.

It had been hard for Marcus, who was accustomed to keeping things to himself, to share his life with me. And it had been hard for me, used to my let-it-all-hang-out family, to give him time to let me in. "I really do love him," I said to Hercules.

"Mrr," Hercules said. It may have seemed silly, but I was glad both cats liked Marcus. I remembered the first time he had told me he loved me. He'd had a furry Greek chorus urging him on.

"There's some reason he didn't tell me about them," I said. "Something more than he slept with his friend's girlfriend."

"Merow!" Owen chimed in from the doorway, one paw in the air as he paused in his fur care routine.

"Owen agrees with me." Hercules made a sound a lot like a sigh and nuzzled my chin. It seemed he was going to take more convincing.

Before I left I called Rebecca. She readily agreed to come by the library and share what she knew about the area's plant life with John. I called Marcus but the call went to voice mail. "I just wanted to check in," I said after the beep. "I'll be at the library if you need me."

Down in the kitchen I put a container of chicken soup and one of Rebecca's rhubarb muffins in my insulated lunch bag. I grabbed my purse and the messenger bag that had been doubling as a briefcase and looked around for the boys. There was no sign of either furry face. "I'm gone. See you tonight," I called. I waited but there was no answering meow from either one of them.

There was a stray dried leaf on the windshield of the truck. Harry Taylor had been over earlier in the week to clean up my flowerbeds. He'd covered the two new bushes he'd planted the previous summer and some of the dried, wizened leaves that had been caught at the base of the shrubs had blown around the yard, much to the delight of Owen, who had chased them like he was a kitten again.

I leaned over and brushed the crumpled maple leaf off the windshield before climbing into the truck and setting my various bags on the passenger floor mat.

I adjusted the rearview mirror, looked around to make sure I had everything and said, "I know you're here, Owen."

Nothing. No murp, meow or hiss. I folded my hands in my lap and waited. A minute went by— maybe—it seemed longer but I knew it couldn't have been, given Owen's impatience.

"I have the rest of the morning," I said, a warning edge creeping into my voice. Both cats may have been smarter than the average feline, but neither one of them could tell time as far as I knew. I looked at the "empty" bench seat beside me and in a moment Owen winked into sight. I had no good words to explain what it was like, suddenly seeing the little tabby in a spot that had previously appeared to be empty. It seemed to me that there was the softest of pops as he appeared, but I wasn't even certain that it wasn't just my mind filling in a blank because I thought there should be a sound. Owen fixed his golden eyes on me and tried to look innocent. That was a waste of time. We both knew he was trying to sneak down to the library, probably because he'd heard me say Maggie was there.

Owen adored Maggie. Like Rebecca she spoiled him with catnip chickens. In return Owen could be counted on to dispatch any small, furry vermin that made the mistake of intruding in Maggie's life. Maggie was one of the kindest people I'd ever met. I'd seen her rescue a seagull with a broken wing and carefully carry a spider out of her studio, but she was terrified of any kind of rodent. She wouldn't see the humor in the dead vole in Marcus's boot at all.

I stuck the key in the ignition and reached for my seat belt. "Buckle up," I said to Owen.

To my delight he actually scanned the seat. Then he took a couple of steps toward me and meowed, studying me with narrowed eyes.

I backed out onto Mountain Road. "Didn't see that coming, did you?" I said with a grin.

3

Owen continued to eye me with suspicion, even looking back over his shoulder as though he expected me to pull back into the yard, tuck him against my elbow like a football and sprint for the house.

The cat sneaking into the truck had happened more than once. I'd put him back in the house and then try to squeeze into the truck again without leaving any space for him to slip by me.

It didn't work. He was fast, more than a little devious and his ace in the hole was being able to make himself invisible. I couldn't win, so this time I wasn't even starting the contest.

"You may come to the library on two conditions." I held up a finger. "One, no wandering around the building. And two"—I held up a second finger—"after you see Maggie you stay in my office."

Owen's whiskers twitched.

I waited and tried not to think about the fact that I was negotiating with a cat.

"Mrr," he finally said.

We were agreed, I decided.

I started down the hill, braking suddenly for a soccer ball that came out of nowhere, bouncing into the street. One of the Justason boys—my up-the-hill neighbors—came out of a yard, waved at me when he recognized the truck, retrieved the ball and disappeared around a dense cedar hedge.

Owen looked out through the windshield, a sour expression on his face. He'd almost landed on top of my messenger bag when I jammed on the brakes.

"Are you all right?" I asked.

He shook himself, stretched out on the seat and grumbled the rest of the way down the hill. I stopped at Eric's Place for a chicken salad sandwich and a cinnamon roll for Maggie. Owen sniffed the takeout bag when I set it on the seat between us but otherwise he ignored me.

I parked at the far end of the library lot and before I did anything else fished my phone out of my bag. Marcus hadn't called. I kept a couple of cloth bags under the seat of the truck in case I needed them for groceries—and wayward cats. Owen climbed in without complaint. Maggie was inside. I think he would have climbed in a container of garbage if it meant he'd get to see her.

"Not a sound," I warned sternly. "Not. A. Sound."

I gathered up all my various bags and headed for the steps, loaded like a Sherpa guide headed up the side of Mount Everest.

Abigail was at the circulation desk, talking to someone on the phone. She raised a hand in hello as I passed her on my way to the stairs.

"I'll take you up to my office and then I'll go get—" I didn't get to finish the sentence. The cloth bag squirmed against my hip and Owen leaped out. He bolted across the mosaic tile floor and disappeared around a shelving unit. I looked around. The library was quiet. *Maybe no one will see him. Maybe I can just give chase, corral Owen and no one will be the wiser.*

Wishful thinking on my part.

I dropped everything but Maggie's lunch on one of the low tables in the children's department and gave chase. Owen wasn't on the other side of the shelves. In fact I didn't see so much as a twitch of whisker or a flick of his tabby tail.

I headed for the meeting room where Abigail had gotten John settled. That's where Maggie was, so that's where Owen would be.

And he was, already sitting on a chair, head cocked to one side while Maggie leaned down, talking to him in a low voice. Rebecca was seated on the other side of the long table next to John. Several of her mother's journals were spread in front of them. John looked up and raised a hand in hello before dropping his gaze back down to the open notebook he'd been studying.

I took a deep breath and exhaled slowly. Maggie caught sight of me in the doorway and grinned. "Hi, Kath," she said. "I see you brought us some help."

"I'm sorry." I pinched the bridge of my nose. "He snuck in the truck and I wanted to see how you were all doing. I should have turned around." I glared at

Owen as I said the last sentence. As soon as I got my hands on that furry little sneak I was taking him back home.

And the furry little sneak knew that. He jumped up onto the table and walked across it to Rebecca, sitting down next to her elbow.

"Hello, Owen," she said, beaming at him. "You're looking very handsome today." She looked up at me. "Hello, Kathleen," she said.

"Hello, Rebecca," I said. I handed Maggie the takeout bag with her lunch and started around the end of the table after Owen. "I'm sorry for the disruption."

"Owen's not a disruption," Rebecca said. The cat gave me a smug look and nudged her pencil with his paw.

"Owen," I said sharply. "Leave that alone!"

The pencil rolled across the tabletop. Owen walked behind it to the table edge and watched as Rebecca caught it before it ended up on the floor.

I tucked a strand of hair that had fallen in my face back behind my ear. "He may not be a disruption but he has no business being here, either," I said, trying and failing to keep the frustration I was feeling out of my voice. "I thought I could take him up to my office and he'd stay there."

"I think the cat's out of the bag," Rebecca said, eyes twinkling.

Behind me Maggie gave a snort of laughter. I turned to look at her.

"I'm sorry, Kathleen," she laughed. "Rebecca's right."

"Both of you are a big part of why that cat is so

spoiled." I had to stop myself from shaking my finger at them.

John, who had been watching everything with a bemused expression on his face, reached over to stroke the cat's fur.

"You can't pet him," I said, sticking my arm in front of his hand.

John looked confused. "I'm not allergic, if that's what you're worried about."

"Owen was feral," Maggie said.

The cat turned at the sound of her voice and she smiled at him.

"He isn't good about anyone other than me touching him," I explained.

"So what does he do if someone else touches him?" John asked.

"Have you ever seen any old Looney Tunes cartoons?" I said. While Owen was busy giving adoring kitty eyes to Maggie, I moved around to Rebecca's side of the table.

"Sure," John said. "There was a local station that used to run them every Sunday morning when I was in college."

"Remember the Tasmanian Devil?"

John looked at Owen, who was now sniffing the stack of books in front of Rebecca while she smiled indulgently at him. "You're kidding?" he said.

I shook my head. "No, I'm not." *I should have walked down the hill*, I thought. When Owen finally materialized on the seat of the truck I should have grabbed him and made like a running back.

"Some people don't like to be touched by someone they don't know," Rebecca said.

I could have pointed out that Owen was a cat, not a person, but it would have made me a bit of a hypocrite given that I was the one who most often treated him like he was anything but.

Meanwhile, the little tabby had moved closer to the pile of journals. He poked them with a paw. He was going to damage something if I didn't get him out of the room. I reached across the table to pick him up, but Owen was having none of it. He tried to leap over the stack of notebooks but misjudged his launch. One paw caught the books, knocking them over, the top one flopping open and skidding like a curling rock across the table to Maggie, who caught it before it fell off the edge.

Owen looked around, not at all shamefaced, and this time I did manage to grab him, mentally crossing my fingers that he wouldn't "disappear" on me.

"I'm sorry," I said. I let out an impatient breath and glared at Owen. "Cats do not belong in the library."

He gave me the typical cat stare, cool and unblinking.

"There's no harm done, dear," Rebecca said.

Beside her John grinned at me. "You weren't kidding when you said you had a lot of interesting things at your library."

Maggie—who was usually quick to leap to Owen's defense—was silent, her blond head bent over the open journal in front of her and a furrow forming above the bridge of her nose. "I think I found something," she said slowly, looking up from the page.

John's laughing expression immediately grew serious. He pushed his chair back and moved around the table. "What is it?" he asked.

Mags tapped the open page with her index finger. From my side of the table everything was upside down but I could see a drawing of some kind of flower and about half a page of writing in Rebecca's mother's neat script.

"Leedy's roseroot," John said. "Rhodiola integrifolia."

"I'm almost positive I've seen it," Maggie said.

"Recently?" I asked. Owen's golden eyes flicked away from her face for a moment to give me a look that was . . . smug?

A completely preposterous idea began to spin in the back of my brain. I looked at the little gray tabby, who was back to watching Maggie with full kitty adoration. No. *No.* I was wrong.

"Couple of weeks ago," she said, leaning forward to study the drawing again.

John put both hands flat on the table and, like Owen, gave her his full attention. "Are you absolutely sure?"

She looked up again and nodded. "You know where the brook goes from Roma's property to Ruby's land?"

I nodded.

"Brady and I climbed up the embankment on the

right side. I know I saw that plant." She glanced at John. "It has thick leaves that come off a center stem."

John nodded, all his attention on the drawing.

"That's good, isn't it," Rebecca asked, phrasing her words as more of a statement of fact than a question.

John scanned the page again. "Maybe," he said slowly. I could see the beginnings of a smile pulling at the corners of his mouth and eyes. "Maggie, can you describe the plant you saw?"

"Of course," she said. "The leaves are waxy and the plants grew in clumps." She gestured elegantly in the air, almost as though she had a paintbrush in her hand. "I've seen the plants before. The flowers are a deep red."

"And where did you see the plant? You said some kind of an embankment?"

"Out at Wisteria Hill," Maggie said. "There's a field behind the house and the old carriage house. Beyond that there's woods and a brook. That's where I saw it."

John turned to look at Rebecca. "Wisteria Hill is where your mother worked?"

"Yes, it is," she said. "She knew those woods as well as she knew the inside of that house." She gestured at Maggie. "Look on the back of that page. There should be a description of where she found that plant. Not all the landmarks are going to be the same, of course, but it should give you an idea if you saw the plant in the same place."

Maggie turned the page and began to read, nodding slowly as she did.

"Does this help?" I asked John.

"Maybe," he said, pulling a hand over the back of his neck. "I'm pretty sure I saw Rhodiola integrifolia on the federal endangered species list. That could work in our favor." He glanced at the journal again. "I know it grows in Minnesota."

"It doesn't grow anywhere else?"

"New York State. The plant has a very specific habitat. It only grows in crevices on north-facing cliffs where there's groundwater coming through the rock. Maggie's description of the leaves sounds exactly like Leedy's roseroot." He glanced at her again. "Because she's an artist she's going to be more aware of color shading and proportion than a lot of people would be. The big issue is was she on Wisteria Hill land or land that's part of the proposed development?"

Maggie pulled a hand back through her blond curls. "I don't know for sure. Once you get back there, nothing's marked. I could have been on Roma's property. I could have been on the little bit of land Ruby owns."

John held up a finger. "Hang on a sec," he said. He moved back around the table and rummaged through the messenger bag he'd hung over the back of his chair. He pulled out a folded map and spread it out on the table. "Okay, here's Long Lake." He pointed to the middle of the map. "This area bordered in yellow is the area proposed for the resort. Can somebody show me exactly where Wisteria Hill is?"

I leaned over to get a better look, keeping a firm hand on Owen. He craned his neck for a look as well, reaching out to touch the creased paper with one paw before I could stop him.

Rebecca pushed her glasses up her nose and stood up, moving closer to John for a better look. "Let me see," she said. "It should be a little southwest of the lake proper."

"It's right there where Owen is pointing," I said.

Rebecca squinted at the map. "Well so it is," she said. She beamed at Owen. "You are such a big help today." The same impossible idea I'd had before began to spin in my head again.

"Pretty smart cat you've got there," John said, grinning up at me.

"He certainly thinks he is," I muttered.

Owen made an indignant murp as though he'd understood every word I'd said—which I felt confident he likely had.

"I'm going to put the furry genius in my office," I said. I looked at Owen. "Say good-bye to Rebecca and Maggie."

"Merow," he said.

John laughed at the cat's perfect-as-always timing.

"You are a very smart cat," Rebecca told Owen. She looked at me. "He really should get some kind of treat for helping us," she said. Owen tipped his head to one side and licked his whiskers. If he'd been a person I would have said he was gloating.

"I'm sure you and Maggie will take care of that," I said to her with a sweet smile.

Mags and John were still bent over the map. I touched her arm. "I'll be in my office," I said.

She nodded. "Thank you, Owen," she said, giving him a smile. In my arms the little tabby began to purr.

I carried him back through the library, crossing my fingers that we wouldn't meet anyone—and luck was with me because we didn't. I put Owen back in the canvas tote, gathered my things and headed up the stairs, careful to keep my hand on the top of the bag—something I should have done the first time.

Once we were inside my office, with the door closed, I set the carryall on the floor. Owen jumped out, shook himself and hopped onto my desk, where he looked expectantly at me.

I folded my arms over my chest and tried to keep my expression stern. "Just because Rebecca thinks you should have a treat doesn't mean I do."

He continued to eye me without making a sound.

"You were supposed to stay in the bag."

He blinked but nothing else changed.

"You were lucky," I continued. "Instead of finding that drawing you could have damaged those journals."

Once again I was arguing with a cat and it was a completely one-sided argument. I really should have known better.

I sat on the edge of the desk next to him and stroked his soft, gray fur. And gave voice to the incredibly ridiculous idea that had been buzzing in my brain. "Did you know that drawing was there?" Those journals had been part of a display at the library and they'd been at my house before that. No. It was too far-fetched to believe that Owen had remembered something he'd seen in one of them.

I closed my eyes for a moment and shook my head.

Yes, Owen seemed to understand most if not all of what was said to him. And there was his ability to become invisible, which was far-fetched by anyone's definition of the word, but for him to be able to remember what had been in that book would mean he had some kind of incredible memory and had understood what had been going on.

I opened my eyes to find Owen looking quizzically at me. I couldn't really explain why the idea of a cat with an almost photographic memory seemed ridiculous but one who could disappear at will was a lot more believable. It just was.

I got the cat settled in my office, brushed his hair off my sweater, grateful that it was dark gray so the bits I missed wouldn't show, and decided to go back downstairs to see what was going on. My cell phone buzzed then, making Owen, who had jumped down onto my desk chair so he could poke his nose inside my bag, jump back and almost end up on the floor. He did a little undignified dance before righting himself.

I retrieved my phone and the little bag of cat crackers I kept in one of the inside pockets of the tote. I was guessing that was what he'd been after.

It was Marcus calling. "Hi, I got your message," he said, an edge of weariness in his voice.

"Are you all right?" I asked. I leaned against the desk and fished two crackers out of the bag, handing them over to Owen, who immediately set them on the seat of my chair so he could examine them because that was what he did with his food.

"I'm sorry about this morning, about Travis, for not telling you about them." I heard him blow out a breath. "I'm sorry about everything."

"It's okay," I said. "Really."

"Could we have supper tonight since you don't have tai chi? I could fill in some of the blanks for you."

"I'd like that but I switched my shift, remember?"

He groaned. "I forgot. You're working late." I heard voices in the background. "Hang on a second, Kathleen," he said.

I waited for maybe thirty seconds and he was back. "Did you bring any dinner with you?" he asked.

I hadn't, I realized. The soup and the muffins were my lunch. "No," I admitted.

"I could get something from Eric's and stop by for a few minutes. That way I could at least see you."

I wanted to see him. I wanted to make sure he knew Travis's words hadn't changed how I felt about him. It didn't matter what had happened between him and Dani all those years ago. "That would be wonderful," I said.

"Did you see John when you left?" Marcus asked. "I was wondering where he went."

"He's here. He's downstairs checking out the herbarium with Maggie and Rebecca."

He laughed. "You work fast. I should have guessed you'd help him. Thanks."

"I don't want this development to happen any more than your friends do," I said. "And John actually might have found something."

"That would be good."

After we ended the call I decided to go back downstairs and see what was happening. "You're staying in here," I told Owen, who had moved from the chair to the desk, where he sat carefully washing his face. "If you so much as stick a whisker outside the door there will be consequences." He paused for a moment with a paw in midair, seeming to consider my words, and then he went back to his ablutions. It was hard to make consequences seem like more than an idle threat to someone who could become invisible on a whim.

Maggie was just coming up the stairs. "Hi," she said. "I'm heading over to the shop for a little while." The artists' co-op that Maggie was past president of had a small store and workspace a few blocks over.

She looked at my office door. "How's Owen?"

"He's fine," I said. "Sitting in the middle of my desk as though it's his office."

She smiled. "I can't believe he knocked over the one journal with the one drawing that might be able to stop this whole development."

"Me neither," I said.

Maggie narrowed her green eyes at me. "So Marcus went to school with John and a couple of other people who are working with this environmental coalition?"

I nodded, hoping she couldn't read anything in my face. Maggie knew me well. "Dani—Danielle—and Travis."

"John is looking to see if there's a sample of that plant in the herbarium. Abigail found the index. Either way, I'm going to talk to Roma and tomorrow I'll take him out to Wisteria Hill." She smiled at me. "Everything is going to work out. I have a good feeling."

"I hope you're right," I said as we started down the stairs. I didn't share that feeling.

It was a busy day at the library. John and Abigail found a sample of Rhodiola integrifolia preserved in the herbarium, more evidence, hopefully, that he and Maggie were on the right track.

John left the library mid-afternoon. I was putting away magazines in the children's section after updating the software on our public access computers when he came to tell me he was done for the day.

"I'll be back in the morning, if that's all right," he said. "I need to make some calls and do a little more research. Rebecca has a couple more books for me to look at." He hesitated. "And I want to check on Travis."

"If there's anything else we can do, please give Abigail or me a call," I said. "I'll be here until closing."

"I will for sure." He shifted the strap of his messenger bag higher on his shoulder. "Thank you for everything, and I don't mean just for letting me look at your herbarium. You introduced me to Maggie and Rebecca and it may be a little unorthodox, but thanks to your cat I might have a way to stop the resort in its tracks."

I gave him a wry smile. "Maybe we could keep the cat thing just between us."

He laughed. "No problem, Kathleen. I'll see you tomorrow."

I had a quick meeting over at Henderson Holdings late in the afternoon. The library had been awarded a grant to be used on books and programs for our children's department. I wanted to go over my plans for the money with Everett's assistant, Lita, before I made my presentation to the library board at their November meeting.

When I got to the office Lita was standing in her open doorway, talking to a man I didn't recognize. I hung back, waiting for her to finish the conversation. She smiled when she caught sight of me and waved me over. "I'll give Everett the new figures," I heard her say as I joined them.

"I appreciate that," the man said, giving her a wide smile.

"Kathleen, this is Ernie Kingsley," Lita said.

Ernie Kingsley, the main investor and driving force behind the development proposal for Long Lake.

She gestured at me. "Ernie, meet Kathleen Paulson. She runs our library."

Kingsley was a heavyset man of average height with a ruddy complexion and keen brown eyes behind his horn-rimmed glasses. He had a strong handshake and a TAG Heuer stainless steel watch on his wrist. "Nice to meet you, Kathleen," he said.

"You as well, Mr. Kingsley," I replied.

"Tell Everett to call me," he said to Lita. He glanced at his watch. "I need to get going. I have another meeting to get to."

"I'll pass on the message," she said.

Kingsley nodded and left.

"C'mon in," Lita said. "Would you like a cup of coffee? I would." She moved toward the credenza where she kept a coffeemaker and several pottery mugs.

"So that's the man who's either the worst or the best thing that's ever happened to this area," I said, dropping my briefcase on one of the chairs in front of Lita's desk.

"Yes, that's Ernie," she said, reaching for the coffeepot.

"What's he like?" I asked.

She didn't answer right away. Instead she poured two cups of coffee and handed one to me. I raised my eyebrows questioningly.

"I'm trying to think of an answer that won't incriminate me," she said, wrinkling her nose at me.

I smiled at her. "Never mind," I said. "I think you've answered my question."

Abigail was at the circulation desk when I got back to the library. She held up a middle-grade chapter book. "What is this?" she asked, pointing to something sticky on the front cover.

"Marshmallow Fluff," I said. "Tommy Justason brought it back, didn't he?"

"I'm not sure," she said. "Let me look." She turned to the computer. After a minute she smiled. "How did you know that?"

I raised an eyebrow. "It's my librarian superpower."

"Oh, I want one of those," Abigail said.

"You already have one," I said. "Writing great books is your superpower."

She smiled as her cheeks got pink. "I hope you're right."

"Set it aside. I'll talk to his mother. This is not the first time Tommy returned a sticky book. Our deal was that if it happened again he had to give me a Saturday morning of work here."

Abigail set the book on the counter. "What are you going to make him do?" she asked.

"I thought I'd have him help me repair those two boxes of books we have in the workroom." Tommy Justason was an eight-year-old who loved to read, something that made me very happy. But he treated books like they were disposable. His mother had paid for a chapter book that had ended up in the bathtub, two reference books that had been left in the rain and multiple graphic novels that had been run over by Tommy's bike. "He's not a bad kid," I continued. "I think a lot of the time his mind is just somewhere else."

Abigail nodded. "Let me know if I can help."

"I will," I said. "Thanks."

"I almost forgot," she said, reaching for a pad of paper next to the phone. "I have a message for you. Detective Gordon called." She gave me a sly smile and wiggled her eyebrows at me.

"Don't tell me he's not bringing my supper after all," I said.

Abigail just looked at me the way Owen did when we were having a staring contest.

I waited but she didn't say anything. "Umm, aren't you going to give me the message?" I asked.

"I would," she said, "but you told me not to tell you

that he's not bringing your supper. He said to tell you he's sorry. He has a meeting with the prosecuting attorney." She handed me the piece of paper. "He sounded sorry." She wiggled her eyebrows again. "I'm sure he'll make it up to you."

"No comment," I said, feeling my cheeks get warm.

"I have hummus," Abigail offered, grinning at me. I would eat pretty much anything but hummus—which she knew.

"I have sardine cat crackers in my bag," I countered.

Abigail had once stopped at my house while I was making a batch for Owen and Hercules. "That's a . . . powerful smell," she'd said, blinking several times as she stood in the middle of my kitchen.

Mary came bustling behind us with an empty cart. "Crackers and dip," she exclaimed. "Sound's delicious. I'll go up and put the coffee on."

"Is she messing with us?" Abigail asked as Mary headed up the stairs.

"Probably," I said with a grin. "But she's also making coffee, so if she wants a sardine cracker who am I to say no?"

I was in my office, working on a list of books I wanted to buy for the children's department with the grant the library had been awarded, when Maggie called just before five. Our tai chi class had been canceled because Oren was painting the studio space. "Are you taking a dinner break?" she asked. "I'm not making a lot of progress here and I don't feel like going home to cook."

Maggie didn't do a lot of cooking, although she did make incredible pizza. However, every pot, pan and dish in her apartment would be dirty by the time it went in the oven.

"Yes, I'm taking a dinner break," I said. Owen, who was snoozing in the middle of my desk, lifted his head when he heard me say "dinner." "I can meet you at Eric's in about an hour."

"I'll see you there," she said.

Owen had gotten to his feet and walked over to me. He rubbed his face against the phone. I had no idea how he knew it was Maggie on the other end, but the only time he did that was when I was talking to her.

"Owen sends his love," I said.

Maggie laughed. "Right back at him."

Mia, who worked after school and on the weekends was at the front desk when I came downstairs, checking out a couple of teenagers with a stack of graphic novels and a reference book about the Vietnam War. One of the history teachers at the high school insisted that her students use as many books as they did online references for any essays they wrote. For some of the kids it would be the first time they'd been in the library since story time when they were four.

I left the truck in the lot and walked over to Eric's. My timing was perfect because Maggie was just coming up the sidewalk from her studio as I got to the restaurant. I hugged her. "You smell like patchouli," I said.

"I was in Ruby's studio," she said. "She was making bath salts."

Ruby Blackthorne was the new president of the artists' co-operative. She had multi-pierced ears, Kool-Aid–colored hair and a collection of funky T-shirts. She was also whip-smart and a talented artist, getting some much-deserved attention for her large pop-art paintings.

"You should see what she's done to her hair," Maggie said, picking a clump of cat hair off my jacket. It seemed pretty clear Owen had been doing some roaming around during the afternoon.

"Did she shave one side of her head again?" I asked. "Or do her bangs navy blue? I liked that."

Mags shook her head. "No. It's brown, light brown." She made a motion in the air with one hand near her chin. "And she cut it about to here."

"No lime green or neon orange?"

"No."

"That is odd," I said.

"That's what I thought." Maggie led the way into Eric's. "Do you want to eat at the counter for a change?" she asked.

I could see two empty stools at the far end. "Sure," I said.

Nic was working. Like Maggie and Ruby, Nic was an artist. He worked with found metal and paper and also did some photography.

"Hi, guys, what can I get you?" he asked. He was about medium height and stocky, with light brown skin and deep brown eyes.

"Tea, please," Maggie said. She looked at me. "Hot chocolate?" she asked.

I nodded.

Nic gave us each a menu. "I'll be right back," he said with a smile.

I slipped off my jacket and got up to hang it on one of the hooks on the end wall. "What are you having?" I asked as I sat down again.

"The special is a polenta bowl with roasted vegetables."

"That sounds good." Everything on Eric's menu was good. He was a great cook and since his wife, Susan, also worked for me at the library I often got an advance taste of new additions to the menu.

Nic came back then with my hot chocolate and Maggie's tea. They talked for a moment about an issue she was having with one of her cameras and then he headed to the kitchen with our order.

Maggie began the little ritual she did with her tea. She reminded me of the way Owen insisted on checking his food before he ate it.

"I called Roma," she said, lifting the lid of the pot of hot water and dropping in the tea bag. "She said it's okay to take John out there tomorrow."

"That's great." I took a sip of my hot chocolate, topped with a couple of the Jam Lady's homemade marshmallows. It was chocolaty and not too sweet with a hint of vanilla from the marshmallows. In other words, perfect.

"Hey, is Dani about my height, a little bit thinner with long blond hair?" Maggie asked.

"Uh-huh," I said. "Did you meet her?"

She opened the lid of the little pot again and poked

the tea bag with a spoon. "No, but I just saw someone I guessed was her with Marcus heading into the bar at the hotel."

"When?" I asked swallowing hard against the lump that was suddenly stuck in my throat.

"When I was walking to the studio," Maggie said. "Three hours ago I guess." Then she looked at me. "Wait, you don't think that . . ." She let the end of the sentence trail away.

No I didn't, I realized. I trusted Marcus and I wasn't going to be jealous and suspicious. "No," I said aloud. I hesitated. "But something happened earlier, when Marcus and I had breakfast with his friends. Did John mention Travis to you?"

She peered into the little pot for the third time before finally pouring her tea. "The environmental engineer?"

I nodded. "Uh-huh. When they were all in school together Travis and Dani were a couple."

"I take it they're not a couple anymore."

"No." Nic came back then with our polenta bowls. Once the steaming dishes were in front of us and he'd gone to take someone else's order I told Maggie what had happened at breakfast. I knew I could count on her to be discreet.

"So he's still angry after all this time?"

"Very," I said.

She reached for her tea. "It's painful to hold on to that bitterness for such a long time."

That was Maggie, always taking the compassionate viewpoint. She was unrelentingly kind.

"You know, it doesn't really sound like the kind of thing Marcus would do," she said.

"That was my thought," I said, chasing a mushroom around the side of my bowl with a spoon. "But why would you admit to sleeping with your best friend's girlfriend if you didn't?"

"The only reason I can think of is you wanted to hurt him, and I know *that's* not Marcus."

We finished supper and Maggie went back to her studio while I headed back to the library. It was quieter than usual and Owen and I were on our way home by eight fifteen. Over the summer and early fall I'd been experimenting with the library's closing hours.

Owen disappeared—not literally—down the stairs headed for his basement lair as soon as we were in the house. I hung up my things and made a cup of hot chocolate. The one I'd had at Eric's had left me craving more of the Jam Lady's homemade marshmallows.

I took my cup and wandered into the living room. Hercules was curled up in the big chair. He at least looked guilty.

"That's not your chair," I said. To my amusement instead of jumping down he moved over as though he was inviting me to join him. So I did.

Once I was sitting down with my feet up on the footstool Hercules climbed onto my lap and eyed my mug, whiskers twitching.

"Marshmallows are not cat food," I said.

"Mrr," he grumbled.

I swiped my little finger in the creamy vanilla foam

and held it out to him. "Do not tell Roma I did this," I warned. "Or your brother."

The moment the words were out there was an indignant meow from the kitchen doorway. Owen was standing there, glaring in my direction.

"How do you do that?" I asked.

The little tabby stalked over in high indignation, jumped onto the footstool and looked pointedly at the cup. I swiped another finger through the melted marshmallow and held out my hand so Owen could have a taste. That meant jostling Hercules just a little, which got me an annoyed look from him as well. Finally everyone, including me, had tasted the marshmallows and, in the case of the boys, licked the stickies off their whiskers. Hercules stretched out on my lap. Owen sprawled across the footstool with his head on my legs. And I told them about Maggie seeing Marcus with Dani.

Neither one of them seemed the slightest bit interested. I realized that I didn't really want to talk to them. I wanted to talk to Marcus. I put one hand on Hercules so he wouldn't be disturbed and reached over for the phone with the other.

Marcus answered on the fourth ring. "Hi," he said. "I was just going to call you."

"I was going to come out for a few minutes, if that's okay," I said. I could tell by their ears that both cats were interested now.

"It's more than okay," he said. "Are you leaving right now?"

I smiled. "As soon as I get the cats off of me and put on some shoes."

"I'll see you soon, then," he said.

Hercules sat up of his own volition, murped at me and jumped down to the floor. Owen, being a little contrary, rolled onto his back and looked at me. I picked him up and set him down on the floor next to the footstool, where he rolled on his back again, paws moving lazily in the air as though he was doing a very low-energy workout.

I leaned down and stroked the top of his head. "You're very goofy," I told him.

Marcus was waiting on the back deck when I walked around the side of his house. He looked tired. I could see lines around his mouth and his hair was mussed as though he'd been pulling his hands back through it, which is what he did when he was stressed.

He wrapped me in a hug. "I'm glad you're here."

I stretched up on tiptoes so I could kiss him. "Me too," I said.

He gestured at the swing and we sat down, his arm around my shoulders. "I'm sorry about dinner," he said.

"I got your message," I said, thinking how good he always smelled. Sitting so close, it was easy to get distracted.

"I had a meeting with the prosecuting attorney that ended up being rescheduled at the last minute." He paused and cleared his throat. "And I talked to Dani again."

"Is she okay?" I asked.

He exhaled, his breath stirring my hair. "She's upset about Travis and a little embarrassed that you found out about the two of us that way, but she's okay."

We rocked slowly back and forth in silence.

"It was Dani who made the oatmeal with the plaster of Paris, not you, wasn't it?" I said.

He laughed softly in the darkness. "How did you know?"

I laid my head against his shoulder. "Because you're more careful than that and I don't think that's a quality that's just happened since you graduated."

He kissed the top of my head.

"And I was watching Dani," I continued. "She was embarrassed. I could see it in her face."

"I came out of the tent and she was sitting on a rock next to the camp stove holding this big pot of oatmeal, which was more like a big pot of concrete."

I stretched up intending to kiss the line of his jaw, but he turned his head and I ended up kissing the side of his mouth instead.

"Umm, what was that for?" he asked. "Not that I'm complaining."

"That's for being so kind to Dani—then and now."

He put his other arm around me. "She's a good person, Kathleen. Things haven't always gone so well for her."

As it got darker I could see the first stars overhead. "You mean Travis," I said.

"I thought he was past it all, I really did," Marcus said. "I haven't spoken to him since graduation and all he said to me then was that he was never going to forgive me." He shifted on the seat of the swing so he was facing me. "I'm sorry Travis dropped all of that on you and I'm sorry I didn't tell you about them."

"I have to admit, it didn't sound like you—sneaking around with someone else's girlfriend, I mean."

"I'm not trying to make excuses," he said. "But Dani did try to break it off with him. And for the record, the compromising situation Travis caught us in was me—without a shirt—kissing her just outside her dorm room. We weren't in bed together."

"I don't understand," I said, trying not to sound judgmental. I didn't see why Dani couldn't have ended things with Travis before she got involved with Marcus. "What do you mean she tried?"

Marcus made a face. "Travis was—still is, as far as I can tell—extremely persistent."

"You're saying he wouldn't take no for an answer." I leaned back and the swing began to sway gently back and forth again.

"Now I realize that's a sign of a very controlling person. We'd call it obsessive or harassment. But back then . . . And it didn't help that Dani's family was crazy about Travis. They put a lot of pressure on her to try to work things out." He blew out a breath. "We were kids. It . . . uh . . . it was complicated."

There was more to what had happened between him and Dani. My instinct wasn't wrong. "What do you mean by complicated?" I asked.

Marcus's cell phone rang then. "Hang on," he said. He leaned sideways and reached for his phone on the small table next to the swing. The only thing he said was, "Hello." He listened and then his body went rigid.

I saw him nod even though the person on the other end of the call couldn't see the movement. "I'll be right there," he said finally, ending the call.

But he didn't move. He just sat there, one hand still holding the phone.

I touched his shoulder. "What's wrong?" I asked.

He turned his head toward me and cleared his throat before he spoke. Even so, his voice was husky with emotion. "That was Hope," he said.

Hope Lind was also a detective with the Mayville Heights Police Department.

"It's . . . it's Dani. She fell off an embankment out by Long Lake."

"Are they taking her to the hospital in Red Wing or going to Minneapolis?" I wondered if John knew yet. And what about Travis?

Marcus shook his head. And then I knew. I didn't need to see his face. I could see it in the slump of his shoulders and the way his hands just hung between his knees. "No," he said. "She's . . . she's dead."

4

Marcus left to meet Hope, and I drove home. Before I got into the truck I wrapped my arms around him and gave him a hug. "I'm so, so sorry about Dani," I said. "If you need me call or just come by. It doesn't matter how late it is."

He nodded. "Drive carefully."

I did drive home just a little more attentively, thinking how fragile life can be. I barely knew Dani but I had liked what I did know. As I headed around the house to the back door I stopped to look up at the stars overhead and hoped that wherever Dani was now she was at peace.

Marcus showed up just after six a.m. I'd had a restless night. I was leaning against the counter waiting for the coffee when he tapped on the back door. He had dark circles like sooty smudges under his eyes and he needed a shave. The half smile he gave me didn't make it anywhere near his blue eyes. He propped an elbow on the table and leaned his head on his hand. I got a cup of coffee and set it next to him.

"Thanks," he said.

I sat next to him at the table. "Could I get you some breakfast?"

He put a hand over mine. "Just sit with me for a bit."

We sat like that for maybe a couple of minutes and then Marcus said, "I have to tell John." He stared down at the table. "And I have to find Travis."

"I'm coming with you," I said. "Maybe John will know where he is."

"You don't have to come," Marcus said.

"I'm coming," I repeated. He gave my hand a squeeze.

I scrambled eggs with the last sausage patty I'd gotten from Burtis Chapman and served them with toasted English muffins and more coffee. Marcus ate every bite on his plate but I think I could have cooked the eggs shells and toasted the bag the muffins had been in and he wouldn't have noticed.

"Hope's taking the lead on this one," he said, pushing his plate back and folding his hands around his cup. "I just thought it would be easier for everyone if I was the one who broke the news to John and Travis." He shook his head. "I don't know. Maybe I'm wrong."

"No, you're not." I put my arms around him. "I liked Dani. I'm sorry I didn't get to know her better. Would you, maybe later, tell me more about her?"

He nodded. "I'd like that. I think maybe the two of you would have been friends."

"I'm sorry we didn't get the chance," I said, and

even though I'd barely known Dani I had to swallow down a sudden lump in my throat.

I went upstairs to finish getting ready for work, leaving Marcus with Hercules, who had been sitting next to his chair in silent sympathy from the moment he'd arrived. When I came back down Marcus was talking to the cat in a low voice, not the first time I'd seen that kind of thing happen.

"John is staying out at the Bluebird Motel," I said.

Marcus slipped something to Hercules, trying to be surreptitious about it. I let it pass. I could get a hint of the unmistakable aroma of stinky crackers and I knew one or two wouldn't hurt the little tuxedo cat.

"I texted Maggie," I continued. "She was planning on taking John out to Wisteria Hill. Don't worry, I didn't tell her why I was asking."

Marcus pulled a hand over the back of his neck. "Thanks. Hope is looking for Travis." He got to his feet.

"Are you ready?" I asked.

"No," he said. I linked my fingers though his and we left anyway.

A red SUV was parked in front of John's room at the Bluebird Motel. There was a rental company sticker in the top right corner of the windshield. The tailgate was open, which told me that John was up, getting ready to start his day. Marcus knocked on the door and then lifted my hand and kissed it before letting it go.

"I should be out of here in about ten minutes and you can—" John opened the door as he stuffed papers into his messenger bag. He looked up, surprised to see Marcus and me instead of the maid he'd probably been expecting. "Hi," he said. He looked at us and his expression grew serious. "What did Travis do?" he asked. "Is he all right? I swear I'm going to kick him when I see him. He didn't come back last night and I had to rent a car this morning so I can get everything done. Lucky for me I found a place that opened at seven thirty."

I felt my chest tighten as though a giant hand were squeezing me. This was part of Marcus's job and I wondered how he did it over and over again.

"Marcus, is Travis all right?" John asked a lot more insistently.

"As far as we know," Marcus said. He was in police officer mode. His voice was strong and steady.

"What do you mean as far as you know?"

Marcus ignored the question. "John, it's Dani."

John grinned. "Let me guess. She got nabbed for speeding again." He looked at me. "Dani has a lead foot."

"Could we sit down for a minute?" Marcus asked.

"Sure." John took a couple of steps back. "C'mon in."

I followed Marcus into the room. It looked just like any other motel room I'd ever been in: bed, nightstand, dresser, flat-screen TV above the desk. There was a large duffel bag on the end of the bed.

John gave Marcus a puzzled smile. "So what's up?"

"Dani was out looking at the land around Long Lake," Marcus said.

"Yeah, I know. I talked to her yesterday afternoon.

She said she might stay in town last night. She didn't want to run into Travis out here."

"John, she had an accident," Marcus said. I could see the tension in his shoulders and the stiff way he held his body.

John's gaze darted between the two of us. I stuffed my hands in my pockets because they suddenly felt huge and clumsy. "What kind of an accident?" he asked slowly.

"She fell. There was an embankment not that far from the lake. It looks like she was taking core samples."

John swore. "Is she in a hospital here or back in Minneapolis?"

For a moment Marcus didn't say anything, and when he did it was just a single word: "Johnnie."

John closed his eyes. I could see from the set of his jaw that his teeth were tightly clenched together. He let out a shuddering breath. "When?"

"Last night," Marcus said. His right hand moved sideways and I caught it, giving it what I hoped was a comforting squeeze before letting go again.

John opened his eyes again. "This wasn't supposed to happen," he said. "Not to Dani." He looked at me. "You didn't know her, Kathleen, and I know this is the kind of thing people always say when someone dies, but she was special."

"I'm sorry I didn't get to know her," I said, feeling more than a little helpless in the face of both his and Marcus's grief. "I liked what I did know. I'm so sorry."

He gave me what passed for a smile for him right

now. "Thank you." Then he turned to Marcus. "We have to find Travis. He can't hear about this from a news report or from some stranger."

"I'm working on that," Marcus said. "Do you know where he is?"

John shook his head. "Like I said, he didn't come back here last night. I got the maid to check his room. The bed hadn't been slept in. I just assumed he'd stayed in town . . . like I thought Dani did."

Marcus's phone buzzed then. He pulled it out. "It's Hope," he said. "She might have something." He stepped just outside the door.

"Hope is Marcus's partner," I explained to John. "She'll be in charge of the investigation. Don't worry. She'll find Travis."

John put a hand over his mouth for a moment. "I know what a jerk he was yesterday but he shouldn't have to hear this from a police officer, a *stranger*."

I shook my head. "He won't."

"I should go with him." He meant go with Marcus to give Travis the news, I realized.

"I think you probably can." I hesitated, and then laid my hand on his arm for a moment, hoping there would be some comfort in the gesture.

"It wasn't supposed to end like this," John said, glancing toward the door. "We were supposed to be friends again. Why don't things work out the way they're supposed to?"

He was talking to himself, not me, which was good, because I didn't have any answers.

Marcus came back in with the news that Travis was in Red Wing.

"I'm going with you," John said. He looked at me. "Kathleen, could you . . . explain to Maggie. Please tell her I'm sorry. And I was going to call Rebecca." He made a helpless gesture with one hand.

"I'll take care of all of that," I said. "Don't even think about it."

Marcus put a hand on my shoulder and leaned down to kiss me. "I'll call you or I'll come in to the library when we get back. I don't know how long this is going to take."

I nodded. "I wish this hadn't happened."

"Me too," he said.

I'd driven my truck up to the Bluebird Motel. Marcus and John got into his SUV and turned in the direction of Red Wing and I headed back to town. I had my things so I just went to the library even though it was early. I parked at the far end of the lot, the way I usually did, and as I walked across the pavement to the front entrance I couldn't help thinking that it felt wrong somehow that it was such a beautiful day given what had happened to Dani. Once I got inside I put on a pot of coffee and while I waited for it I called Maggie. This wasn't something I could do in a text.

"I'm so sorry," she said. "Is John okay? And Marcus?"

I leaned against the counter. "They're all right. Sad. Shocked."

"What can I do?"

I sighed. "I don't know. I have to call Rebecca, but other than that, I don't think there is anything we can do. She was out there by herself, so there'll be an investigation. Hope's in charge given that Marcus knew Dani."

"What if Brady and I went out to Wisteria Hill? I could try to find that plant again. Brady knows that whole area, too."

"That's a good idea," I said. I had no idea what effect Dani's death would have on the work of the coalition of environmental groups. I wasn't sure how John and Travis would feel about staying in the area and continuing their work without her. I knew they felt strongly about stopping the development.

Maggie promised to take pictures of anything that seemed promising and we said good-bye. I knew she was right about Brady. He and his brothers had grown up in the woods in and around Wisteria Hill. His father, Burtis Chapman, had worked for Idris Blackthorne, Ruby's grandfather and the one-time area bootlegger. A lot of things had happened at the old man's cabin on his stretch of land adjacent to Wisteria Hill, but the trees told no tales.

I called Rebecca and explained what had happened to her as well. She expressed her sympathy and I promised to be in touch if she could help in any way. "John was out here last night after supper," she said. "I'd found two more of my mother's books. He spoke about his friend. It sounded like she was a nice person."

"I think she was," I said.

* * *

Marcus came into the library just after eleven. He'd been home to shower and change. He was wearing a white shirt with dark trousers, he'd shaved, and the ends of his hair were still damp.

"C'mon up to my office," I said. Susan was at the circulation desk. "I need a few minutes," I said to her.

"Take your time," she said. As usual, there had been a reporter from the *Mayville Heights Chronicle* out at the scene of Dani's accident. The story was already online at the paper's website.

Once we were in my office Marcus hugged me. "How are you?" I asked, leaning back to study him. He still looked tired but he was in police officer mode and his emotions were firmly in check.

"We found Travis," he said.

I waited, holding both of his hands in mine. There wasn't anything I could say to erase the pain in his eyes. I would have given anything to be able to do that.

It was then that I noticed the beginning of a bruise on the left side of his jawline. I let go of his hand and touched it gently with two fingers.

He winced.

"He hit you," I said softly.

Marcus nodded. "He still has a pretty good right cross."

"You let him?" Marcus was strong, with fast reflexes. He'd clearly taken the punch instead of avoiding it.

He looked away for a moment and a flush of color came into his cheeks. "I don't expect you to understand, Kathleen," he began, "but he needed to."

"I do understand," I said. "Do you want some ice?"

"No, I'm okay." He worked his jaw from side to side. "It looks worse than it feels." He let out a slow breath. "He cried, Kathleen. He swung at me and then he started to cry."

I felt the prickle of tears myself but I swallowed them away because this wasn't about me. "What do you need?" I asked.

He let go of my hand so he could rake his own through his hair. "They're both coming over to the house tonight. We, uh, we want to do something—I don't know, maybe some kind of memorial service for the people she worked with and her friends. I thought maybe we could plan something."

"That's a nice idea," I said. "What about Dani's family?"

"There's just an older brother and her grandmother. John is going to try to contact the brother."

"So how can I help?"

"Will you come tonight?" he said. "I know you didn't really know Dani but—"

I cut him off before he could finish the sentence. "I would be honored."

He smiled and I saw some of the stress ease in his face. "I have to get to the station," he said. "Hope is waiting to find out when we can expect the medical examiner to be finished."

"All right," I said. "I'll see you tonight. If you need me before then—"

"I'll call, I promise."

I laid my hand gently against his cheek. "I love you," I said.

He swallowed hard, pushing down some emotion. "I love you, too," he said.

I walked Marcus downstairs and after he left Susan came around the desk to me. "I heard about Marcus's friend," she said, touching my arm. "I'm so sorry. If there's anything you need to do we can hold down the fort here. I can call Mia in."

News spread quickly in Mayville Heights, but I could see the genuine concern in her eyes and once again I realized how lucky I was to be in the small town with people who genuinely cared about me. As much as I sometimes missed my family back in Boston, Mayville Heights was my home now.

I had to clear my throat before I could answer her. "Thank you, Susan," I said. "There isn't anything I can do right now, but I might take you up on your offer later."

She nodded and then wrapped me in a quick and unexpected hug before going back to the desk. I went upstairs to my office and once the door was closed didn't even try to stop the tears from sliding down my face.

I drove out to Marcus's house about four thirty with a crock of soup and two dozen of Rebecca's wholewheat donuts. Hercules had had another gazebo "meeting" with Everett, and Rebecca had walked him home. "Please tell Marcus we're thinking about him," she'd said. "Everett asked me to pass on his sympathies and to tell you that if Marcus or his friends need anything please let him know."

"Thank you," I said, wrapping her in a hug and thinking how such a simple gesture made me feel a little better, giving or receiving. "I think they just need some time."

Rebecca nodded. "It isn't just that they all lost a friend—which is devastating enough—they've also lost another connection to a time in their lives when everything seemed possible."

"How did you get so smart?" I asked her.

Rebecca laughed. "I've been around long enough to pick up a thing or two—plus I drink a glass of warm water with lemon every morning."

"I'll keep both of those in mind," I said.

Micah was sitting on the swing on Marcus's back deck when I came around the side of his small house. She jumped down and meowed as though she'd been waiting for me, all her attention fixed on the bag of donuts. Owen had been the same way, clearly disgruntled because I wasn't leaving any of them behind for him. To express his displeasure he'd disappeared from the kitchen—literally—and I'd been extra careful when I got in the truck in case he decided on another stealth ride.

"Donuts are not for cats," I said firmly. Micah wrinkled her whiskers at me. She was much politer about expressing her unhappiness with me than Owen was. "I did bring you something, though," I said, patting the pocket of my sweater.

She made a soft sound of happiness and rubbed her face against my leg. The back door opened then.

"Hi," Marcus said. "I thought I heard someone out here." He'd changed into a gray sweatshirt and jeans.

"Hi," I said. "Micah and I were just talking about donuts."

"Cats aren't supposed to eat donuts," he said.

"And you've never broken that rule with my cats," I said. I handed him the canvas bag I was holding. "These are from Rebecca. And Everett offered his help if there's anything you or John and Travis need."

"That's really nice of them," he said as Micah and I followed him inside. "I don't think there's anything that needs to be done. Once the medical examiner releases her . . . body, the family is planning a service. And I think there's also going to be another one in Chicago for the people she worked with." He put the donuts on the counter and took the soup crock from me. "John talked to Dani's brother. He'll get in touch when their plans are finalized."

"That's good," I said.

Marcus looked around the kitchen. "I feel I should be doing something."

"Like what?" I asked. I took off my sweater and hung it on the back of one of the kitchen chairs.

"That's the thing," he said, swiping a hand over his neck. "I don't know. Hope is taking the lead on this."

"So let her," I said, reaching for his hand and pulling him toward me. "Let the world turn without you for a little while."

Marcus and I had half the soup for supper and I put the rest in his refrigerator. John and Travis showed up about seven o'clock.

"Hey, Kathleen," John said. He'd changed into a white shirt with his jeans. He looked tired but his emotions seemed to be under control. I gave him a quick hug and he managed a small smile.

Travis, on the other hand, looked broken. There was dark stubble on his cheeks and his face was drawn as though he'd lost weight in the brief amount of time since I'd last seen him.

"Travis, I'm so sorry," I said.

His mouth moved but at first no words came out. Then he said, "Kathleen, I owe you an apology. The last time I saw you I . . . I was an asshole."

"You don't need to apologize," I said. His behavior at the restaurant didn't seem like such a big deal now.

His eyes met mine. They were sad behind his glasses, and there were lines on his face I hadn't noticed yesterday. "I do," he said. "I can't apologize to Dani. Please let me say the words to you."

I nodded. I couldn't speak. My throat was tight.

"I'm sorry," he said. "If I could do it again . . ." He closed his eyes for a moment. "I'd behave . . . differently. Better."

I managed to find my voice. "Thank you," I said.

Marcus made coffee and I put half of Rebecca's donuts out on a plate. The conversation was strained and awkward at first. I filled John in on what Maggie and Brady had found, which was nothing so far.

"Dominic called me back," John said. "That's Dani's brother," he added as an aside to me. "The service will probably be the end of next week. It will be by invitation only. I told him all three of us wanted to come." He let out a breath. "He said he'd put us on the list."

We sat in silence for a moment. Then Travis spoke. "She'd hate it. It'll be all pomp and circumstance and nothing that she wants."

Marcus nodded.

John looked down at the table. "She wanted 'Livin' La Vida Loca,' remember?"

"It's her favorite song," Travis said. He managed what I was guessing passed for a smile for him at the moment. "That night she got us drunk she said that's what she wanted played at her funeral and she wanted us to come and dance with our walkers." He put both hands flat on the table and stared down at them.

They needed to talk about her. They needed to remember and grieve and do it together. I needed to keep the conversation going.

"She got *you* drunk?" I asked.

"Yeah," John said. "*She* got us drunk." He shifted in his chair to look at me. "She could drink a lumberjack under the table."

"And not be hungover the next day," Marcus added. "I don't know how she did it."

"So why exactly did she get you drunk?" I said.

"It was a bet." John looked in his mug and Marcus immediately got to his feet and reached for the coffee-pot. "Dani bet all three of us that she could match us beer for beer and still walk a straight line."

"She did, too," Travis said, joining the conversation for the first time. "She has some kind of freaky metabolism. Alcohol never affects her the same way it does most people. None of us could walk that line." He looked up at Marcus, who was topping up my cup. "*He* kept insisting the line was moving, so he sat on it."

"It felt like it was moving," Marcus said, making a face.

"Wait a minute," I said. "Were you on some road?"

Travis shook his head. "We were at the drive-in. It was this retro place. It's not open anymore." He gestured at the others. "The three of us worked there one summer. Bowling shirts and slicked-back hair."

"Are there pictures?" I asked, looking directly at Marcus.

"No," he said.

"Yes," John said.

Marcus shot John a look. "No," he repeated.

"Do you still have your key chain?" John asked. He patted his pocket. "Or am I the only one?"

Travis pulled a set of keys out of his pocket and held up the fob. It was a stylized black crescent moon with a dotted white line down the center and a gold star at the top point of the crescent.

Marcus had the same thing on his spare set of keys. "I didn't know that meant something," I said.

"So you still have it?" John said.

Marcus nodded. "Uh-huh. On my extra keys in the bedroom. I think I have the shirt somewhere as well." He gestured at the key chain Travis was still holding. "Stuckey's Drive-In. Don't drive by."

"Drive-in," all three of them said.

They all smiled at the memory.

"Blast from the Past," John said. "Remember that?"

Marcus sat down at the table again. "The night before the drive-in closed for the season they did this thing they called Blast from the Past. You could get in for half price if you came in costume, and they showed *American Graffiti* and *Grease*."

John nodded. "Dani came in a poodle skirt and a pair of those black cat's-eye glasses with the rhinestone things on the ends." He smiled. "This guy in a leather jacket and a beer belly hanging out kept hitting on her."

"He asked her, 'Where have you been all my life, Sweetlips?' She patted his cheek and said, 'Washing bodies in the cadaver lab.'"

John leaned back in his chair and laughed at the memory. "I'm surprised the guy didn't get whiplash backing away from her."

We finished our coffee and moved into the living room. The three of them spent the next hour and a half telling me stories about Dani and their college days and I found myself wishing I'd had the chance to get to know her better. When John and Travis left, Travis extended his hand and Marcus shook it. I hoped that the rapprochement between them would continue.

*   *   *

The investigation into Dani's accident continued. Marcus took a day off and went to Chicago for the memorial service held by her friends. John and Travis came back to Mayville Heights with him. They had decided to continue their work against the development.

"It was important to Dani," John said, standing in the middle of the library, still dressed in the suit he'd worn to the service. "There isn't anything else we can do so we'll do this."

For the next week it seemed as though nothing was happening. John alternated spending time at the library with wandering around out at Wisteria Hill. Travis was back and forth between Red Wing and Mayville Heights.

Marcus was frustrated by the slow pace of Hope's investigation. "I don't understand why she's shutting me out," he said as we cleared the table after supper Wednesday night.

We'd had spaghetti and meatballs. Marcus had snuck a meatball to each cat and I'd pretended not to notice.

"The only thing she said is there's some kind of backup at the medical examiner's office."

"Maybe that's all it is," I said. "Or maybe she's not telling you anything because Dani was your friend and you really shouldn't be involved in the investigation."

"That doesn't mean Hope wouldn't tell me what's

going on." He shook his head. "I know her. The last couple of days she's been avoiding me."

"Maybe she's just trying to spare you from some of the details of how Dani died."

"I don't want her to keep that kind of thing from me," he said. I recognized the stubborn set of his jaw.

"Hope cares about you," I said.

He dropped a glass in the soapy water I'd filled the sink with.

"I know that," he said. "I do, but I don't like being shut out. Why can't she just tell me what she knows so far?"

"Whatever it is, she has her reasons, I'm sure."

He studied me for a few silent seconds. "This is what it's like for other people, isn't it?" he asked.

"I don't know what you mean," I said.

"About three years ago a young man was killed on the train tracks down by the old warehouses. There isn't any traffic on them now, but there was back then. It turned out he'd been drinking and lost his balance and fell. His mother called me every day of the investigation. Every single day at quarter after nine. And every time I'd tell her that as soon as I had something to share I'd call her." He looked up at the ceiling for a moment before meeting my gaze again. "And the next morning at nine fifteen my phone would ring. I didn't get it, but I do now."

I gave him a hug. "You'll get your answers. And you and John and Travis will be able to say a proper good-bye to Dani."

*   *   *

Thursday turned out to be busier than usual at the library, so I was already running a little late when I pulled into the driveway at home. I discovered Hercules waiting for me on the back steps. He had a black feather in his mouth, the fur on his head was standing on end and his right ear was turned half inside out.

"Did you and that grackle get into it again?" I asked as he followed me into the house.

He spit the feather on the mat where I kept my shoes and gave me what could only be described as a self-satisfied look.

"Let me check the top of your head," I said. I didn't think he was wounded. The cat and the bird had some kind of arch-nemesis thing going. It was more WWA wrestling fighting than the real thing.

Hercules shook his head. Translation: "I'm fine." He made a move to go up another step and I leaned down, putting one hand on his back so I could use the other to part the fur on the top of his head and check for any bird-inflicted injuries and then fix his ear. He grumbled while I looked but didn't try to squirm away. "You're fine," I said. He shot me a look that seemed to suggest he was insulted I had ever suspected otherwise.

Hercules was more than capable of taking down the big black grackle mid-flight and the bird could have easily injured the cat with its long beak. They both seemed to enjoy the battle. If someone won, the whole thing would be over and it didn't seem as though either one of them wanted that.

In the kitchen I discovered that Owen had decapitated yet another catnip chicken. There were bits of catnip all over and a limp yellow chicken head in the middle of the floor.

Hercules immediately sneezed and jumped in the air at the sound. He always managed to scare himself when he sneezed, as if he couldn't seem to grasp the small explosion was coming from him.

"Owen!" I yelled. When he didn't appear—literally or figuratively—I called his name again. "I'm putting Fred's head in the garbage if you don't get in here right now."

I heard a meow from the living room and after a moment Owen appeared in the doorway. He made his way across the kitchen and took the chicken head from my hand.

Rebecca and Maggie kept the cat in a steady supply of the little yellow catnip toys known as Fred the Funky Chicken. Owen in turn destroyed them almost, it sometimes seemed, on some kind of schedule of his own.

"Why do you do this?" I asked pointing at the bits of dried catnip all over the kitchen floor. He looked up at me, blinked twice and headed for the basement, the yellow chicken head firmly in his teeth. I couldn't exactly make him go get the vacuum and clean things up. Behind me Hercules sneezed again. He had never been enthralled by catnip the way his brother was.

By the time I cleaned the kitchen floor, ate supper and changed, I was running very late for tai chi class, so Maggie was announcing "Circle," as I walked into the studio. She worked us hard and it wasn't until class was finished that we got a chance to talk. "Nice job, everyone. See you on Tuesday," she called as she walked over to me.

I blotted sweat from my neck with the edge of my T-shirt, which was damp with perspiration in places.

"Your Push Hands are looking better," she said. "Remember to think about your weight and where your center is."

I nodded. "Aren't you going to tell me to bend my knees?" It was a running joke in the class that Maggie told me to bend my knees at least once per session.

"You're getting better at that," she said with a smile.

I bumped her with my shoulder. "See?" I said. "I do listen to you."

"I told Owen to remind you when you practice."

I started to laugh.

Mags frowned. "What's so funny?"

"I was working on the form a few days ago and Owen kept making these little murping noises the entire time."

"Did any of those noises sound like 'Bend your knees'?" Maggie asked.

"No," I said, stretching one arm over my head. "They sounded more like 'Where's my breakfast?'"

We walked over to the table where Maggie kept supplies for tea. I gestured at the wall behind the table. "I like the color." Oren had painted the walls in the studio a very pale yellow.

Maggie smiled. "Me too. I probably looked at two dozen colors but I kept coming back to this one. She leaned over to plug in the kettle then reached for a box of chamomile tea bags. "Was John in the library today?" she asked.

I shook my head. "He went back to Red Wing with Travis to check on something." I studied her face. "Did you find the plant?"

She nodded. "I think so. Brady and I went out to Roma's yesterday after supper. I took some photos to show John but I'm pretty sure it is Leedy's roseroot."

"And you found the plants on Roma's land, didn't you?" She would have been more excited if they had been growing anywhere else.

Maggie dropped the tea bag in a cup and reached for the kettle. "Yes. Brady said we were definitely on Roma's land."

I let out a sigh. So there wasn't going to be any way to stop the development after all. Then I noticed that Maggie was humming to herself as she finished making her tea.

"Wait a minute," I said. "You don't seem that upset. What's going on?"

"When we went out to Wisteria Hill we walked around that little piece of land that Ruby owns. I asked her first and she said it was okay."

Considering that Ruby stood to benefit from the development I thought it was generous of her to tell Maggie she could look around her property.

"Did you know there's a cave just beyond that old cabin that Ruby's grandfather owned?"

Goose bumps puckered my skin. I didn't like small tight spaces. I'd been that way since I was a kid. Owen and I had been trapped in the dark, damp basement of a camp in the woods not that different from the old building on the Blackthorne property a couple of winters ago. The experience hadn't made my claustrophobia any better.

"I was going to say I didn't know that, but I think maybe Marcus told me about it." He'd spent a lot of time checking out those woods after a body had turned up at Wisteria Hill a year and a half ago when an embankment collapsed after a week of seemingly endless rain.

"We were dive-bombed by a bat," Maggie said with a shudder. She felt the same way about small, furry animals as I did about small dark spaces.

"Oh, Mags, I'm sorry," I said. "You're all right?"

"I'm fine." She took another sip from her tea. "Brady said the bat was more afraid of me than I was of it but I don't think that's true. The bat did not hurl itself at Brady and pull his jacket over its head."

"Are you sure you're okay?" I said, reaching out to give her arm a squeeze.

"Yes, I'm okay," she said, "because I think the bat may help us stop the development."

"How?" I asked just as Rebecca came across the floor to join us.

She looked at Maggie, curiosity in her blue eyes. "Did you have any luck last night?" she asked.

"I was just telling Kathleen," Maggie said, leaning over to plug the kettle in again. She related her story about being bat-bombed while Rebecca looked at the selection of teas and made her choice.

"Bats have gotten a bad reputation thanks to all those myths about vampires," Rebecca said. "Did you know that just one little brown bat can eat up to a thousand mosquitoes an hour? They provide pest control without all those nasty chemicals. And during World War Two the US government considered using bats to drop bombs on the enemy."

"How do you know these things?" I asked as she reached for the now steaming kettle.

"I visit my public library," she said primly and then laughed, a mischievous twinkle in her eyes. She turned her attention to Maggie. "So tell me about the bat cave. Did you find Alfred there?"

Maggie gave her a blank look. She wasn't into comic book heroes.

"Batman's butler," I explained exchanging a smile with Rebecca. "Tell us what you found."

"Brady thinks the bat may have been a long-eared bat. I didn't know because I didn't get a very good look at it."

Rebecca paused with her cup in midair. "Wait a minute, wasn't the long-eared bat on one of those lists John had?"

Maggie nodded.

"So it's endangered?" I said.

"Threatened," Maggie said.

"White-nose syndrome," Rebecca interjected. "It's killing bat populations all over North America." She glanced at me. "That's from PBS, not the library."

"So if Brady is right about the type of bat and if they're living in that cave—" I began.

"It might be enough to at least slow the proposal down for a while," Maggie finished. "Brady said there is some precedent for protecting the bat's habitat."

"That's wonderful news." Rebecca smiled. "Have you told John yet?"

"He was in Red Wing all day, but I know he's planning on being at the library in the morning," I said. "There are a couple of things he wants to check in the herbarium again."

"I could text him," Maggie said, setting her cup down on the table. "But I really wanted to talk to him face-to-face."

"Come over about ten," I said. "I'll be there. I changed shifts with Abigail."

Rebecca touched my arm. "How's Marcus?" she asked.

"He's all right," I said. "Thank you for asking. Dani's family is waiting to have a funeral service until the investigation is wrapped up so Marcus—and John and Travis—are still hanging."

"They need to say a proper good-bye," Rebecca said. "That's understandable. I'm sure Detective Lind will have things wrapped up very soon." She glanced down at her watch. "Oh, I better get going," she said. "I have a date with my husband and some Tubby's frozen yogurt."

"Have fun," I said, leaning in to give her a hug. She reached for Maggie's hand and gave it a squeeze. "Will you call me, dear, after you speak to John?"

"I will," Maggie promised.

I stretched both arms up over my head. "I have to

go, too," I said. "Owen chewed the head off another chicken and I don't think I got all the bits of catnip off the kitchen floor."

"Does that mean he's out of chickens?" Maggie asked.

"No," I said firmly, narrowing my eyes at her. "Owen does not need any more chickens. He has enough assorted parts to put about half a dozen of them together. He's the Dr. Frankenstein of funky chickens." I glared at her. "No new chickens."

"I heard you," she said. She leaned over to give me a hug. "I'll see you tomorrow."

I headed for the coat hooks, knowing there was at least one new Fred the Funky Chicken in Owen's immediate future.

It was dark when I got home. I was unlocking the back door when something furry wound around my leg. I jumped, almost falling off the step. It was Hercules.

"You scared me," I said, reaching down to pick him up. "What are you doing out here?"

He gave a non-committal murp but his green eyes darted to the big maple tree in the backyard. "Were you stalking that bird again?" I asked.

Hercules suddenly got very interested in the bag with my tai chi clothes hanging from my shoulder. "That grackle is tucked in his little bird nest right now. You can terrorize each other tomorrow," I said. I gave the top of his head a scratch and started again to unlock the door.

"Kathleen," a voice said behind me.

I jumped and swung around. Hope Lind was standing there. "I'm sorry," she said, holding up one hand. "I didn't mean to startle you. Do you have a few minutes?"

Hope was wearing her dark hair a little longer and the curls looked a little windblown, like she hadn't had time to look in a mirror for a while. She was dressed in black trousers and heels that brought her to my height instead of the couple of inches shorter she was in flats.

"Of course," I said. "C'mon in."

Hope followed me inside. I set Hercules on the kitchen floor and he cocked his head to one side and eyed her.

I indicated the table. "Have a seat. I'm going to have a cup of hot chocolate. Would you like one? I have tea as well."

She seemed distracted. "No," she said, "hot chocolate is fine." She glanced down at the cat. "Hello, Hercules."

"Mrr," he answered.

Hope looked around the kitchen. "This is a nice little house."

"It actually belongs to Everett Henderson." I put two mugs of milk in the microwave. "It was one of the perks he used to woo me to Mayville Heights."

"I'm glad it worked," she said, propping her elbows on the table.

We were both stalling, her in saying whatever it was she'd come to talk to me about and me in hearing her out. I could feel my pulse thumping in the hollow below my throat. This had to be about Dani's death.

When the hot chocolate was made I set a cup in front of Hope and joined her at the table.

She cleared her throat. "Kathleen, I need to keep this conversation just between us."

"I'm sorry, I don't like keeping secrets from Marcus, Hope," I said, wiping a hand over the back of my neck. "It's gotten us into trouble in the past."

"This has to do with Marcus. And I wouldn't be here if there was anyone else I could talk to."

I couldn't miss the intensity in her voice. It matched the look in her eyes. I felt my chest tighten. I sighed. "All right."

"Danielle McAllister's death wasn't an accident," she said. "There's evidence that she didn't fall over that embankment."

That was why the investigation had been taking so long. That was why Hope had been avoiding Marcus. "Did someone push her?" I asked. Had someone killed Dani because of the development? Would someone go that far?

Hope played with her cup, turning it in slow circles on the table. "The medical examiner thinks she was hit by a car, then the body was moved and she was . . . dropped over."

An image of Dani, sitting at the table at Eric's, laughing as she told the story of their first meeting in the biology lab flashed into my mind. I felt the sour taste of bile at the back of my throat. "That's horrible," I whispered.

"It gets worse," Hope said. "We found her phone. It was a little way away from her body. It had probably fallen out of her pocket when . . . when she went over. At first, I wasn't sure what we were going to be able to get from it." She looked down at the table and then met my eyes again. "The last text Dani sent was to Marcus. She wanted to talk to him. He texted back a yes."

"They did meet," I said. "Over at the hotel."

"I know," Hope said. "This was after that."

"Wait a minute," I said. "He *texted* back a yes?"

She nodded silently.

"That . . . that doesn't make sense." Because of his dyslexia Marcus rarely sent texts. He called people. Everyone who knew him knew that. "Why didn't he call Dani back?"

Hope sighed softly. "I don't know," she said. "I haven't asked him. I haven't told him about any of this. I haven't told anyone, except now, you."

"Maybe someone else sent that text," I said.

"C'mon, Kathleen, you know Marcus. He doesn't leave his phone lying around. And even if he did, you think what? That someone else at the station answered that text and now doesn't want to admit it? Seriously?"

Okay, so it didn't really make sense that someone else had answered Dani's text, but it didn't make sense to me that Marcus had, either.

Hope raked a hand back through her hair. "Look, I

know he doesn't text very often but he does sometimes. He sent me one this afternoon. Two words: *Anything new?* He wants to know what's going on with the case. I'm guessing he didn't call because he didn't know where I'd be and he didn't want anyone to know he's asking."

I nodded slowly. Hope was probably right. Marcus wouldn't want to get Hope in trouble for keeping him in the loop.

Hope looked down at Hercules, still sitting next to her chair, his green eyes fixed intently on her as though he were following the conversation. I knew there was a good chance that he was. Her eyes met mine again. "I think you're missing the point," she said. "Marcus may have seen Dani the night she died. Why didn't he say so?"

I stared at her. "Hope, you don't think that Marcus . . . ?" I couldn't finish the thought.

"No," she said. She cleared her throat. "No."

I felt Hercules lean against my leg. I studied Hope's face. "There's something you're not telling me."

She took a deep breath and let it out slowly. She still didn't say anything.

My heart was pounding so hard in my ears that my own voice sounded like I was underwater when I spoke. "Tell me!"

Hope looked at me for a long moment as though she was deciding what to do. Then she reached into her pocket and pulled out a plastic bag. She dropped it onto the table.

I leaned over for a closer look. For a moment I

couldn't speak. I couldn't breathe. The bag held a small, round metal disc. On the front was a stylized black crescent moon bisected by a white line. There was a small gold star at the top point of the moon.

"It was underneath her body," Hope said. "And before you tell me it's not the only one in existence, I know that, but this one was wiped clean of fingerprints."

"How did you get that out of the police station?" I asked, gesturing at the bag.

Her eyes slid off my face and she picked up her cup and took a drink.

"Hope, you broke the chain of evidence."

"No, I didn't," she said. "It was never logged in as evidence."

I just stared at her and finally, when I didn't speak, she lifted her head and looked at me again. "You and I both know Marcus didn't have anything to do with Danielle McAllister's death. But he was the last person she had contact with and part of his key chain was found with her body." She closed her eyes for a couple of moments and took several breaths. "And before you ask, John Keller and Travis Rosen both have theirs." She had obviously uncovered the backstory of the key chains at some point in her investigation.

"You can't hide evidence," I said. A bubble of panic had settled in just under my breastbone and I pressed my fist there as if somehow I could hold it in place and keep it from overwhelming me. "I know how it looks, but you're putting yourself at risk and if it comes out this will just make things look worse for Marcus."

Hope opened her eyes again. "They were old friends, Kathleen, old friends who were involved in some kind of disagreement in a public place. And then one of them is dead. How much worse could it look?"

"It could look like Marcus asked his partner to hide evidence of a crime. You could lose your badge. You could go to jail. Both of you could."

My voice was getting louder. Hercules pressed his furry body against my leg. I stopped talking and swallowed a couple of times to get my emotions under control.

Hope looked away again, her expression a mix of guilt and defiance.

"I know you care about him," I said. "But you have to turn that key chain in, because you and I both know it doesn't belong to Marcus so it has to belong to whoever killed Dani."

"All right," she finally said. She still wouldn't look at me. "You know what will happen."

"Uh-huh," I said. "You'll be taken off the case and Marcus will be called in for questioning."

"And then what?" Hope said, finally looking in my direction.

I shook my head. "I don't know."

5

The key chain fob was logged in as evidence. I didn't ask Hope how she explained the time lag. We agreed that I would tell Marcus what she'd uncovered so far, that way she'd be able to truthfully say that *she* hadn't shared any information with him. It was splitting hairs but it protected both of them and that was enough for me.

I tossed and turned most of the night. I woke up in a tangle of blankets with an arm and a leg hanging off the bed. It made me think of all the mornings my mother had insisted that sharing a bed with my dad was like being on the channel ferry.

I missed them. They were both on the West Coast at the moment while my mother did a two-week guest stint on *The Wild and Wonderful*. She was hugely popular with fans of the racy soap opera, who had been clamoring since her previous visit for a return performance.

I looked at the clock. It was too early to call. My mother hated mornings. I couldn't tell her what was going on, anyway. I pulled on a long-sleeved T-shirt and a pair of sweatpants and went down to the kitchen to make coffee. That's where I was when Hercules came through the door. "Through" as in the bottom left panel almost seemed to shimmer and then he was standing in the kitchen.

"Merow?" he said, looking like he was surprised to see me. He'd probably been sitting out on the porch. He liked to do that, look out the window at the world and not have to get his feet wet in the early morning dew on the lawn.

"Couldn't sleep," I said.

He stretched, arching his back and yawning. "You too?" I asked.

He gave an offhand murr that might have been a yes.

I poured a cup of coffee and sat down at the table, curling one leg underneath me. Hercules launched himself into my lap. He craned his neck to look in my mug.

"It's coffee."

He sat back on my leg and looked around the kitchen.

"I'll get breakfast in a minute," I said. I pushed up the sleeves of my shirt and took another drink of my coffee.

Herc bumped my free hand with his head and I stroked his fur.

"How am I going to tell Marcus that he could be a suspect in his friend's death?' I asked the cat. I set my cup down and massaged the back of my neck. "How do I tell him her death wasn't an accident?"

My plan had been to invite Marcus for dinner, but now that seemed like such a long time away. "Hope said she thought the medical examiner's official report would be ready on Monday, but what if she's wrong? I don't want him to be blindsided."

Hercules hopped off my lap and walked over to the back door. He didn't go through it; he just sat down and stared pointedly at it, then looked over his shoulder at me.

"I don't want to have coffee on the porch," I said. "I don't have any socks on and I don't have a fur coat like you do."

He made a sound in the back of his throat, which could have best been described as an expression of exasperation. I didn't know what he was trying to tell me. I was tired and trying not to give in to the worry gnawing at my insides.

Hercules came back across the floor to me. I'd left my purse and keys on one of the chairs the night before. He stood on his hind legs and swept the keys to the floor. Then he sat down, shot me a look and started to wash his face.

Door. Keys. I was supposed to make the connection and I likely would have, if I'd had more sleep. I needed to talk to Marcus before I could deal with anything else.

Marcus.

Door.

Keys.

"You think I should go talk to him right now," I said.

Hercules looked up at me, his white tipped paw paused in midair. "Merow," he said. It was about as close to "Well, duh," as a cat could get.

I got to my feet, put my cup in the sink and got four stinky crackers from the cupboard. I put the crackers at his feet. "You're a very smart cat," I said.

I went upstairs, brushed my hair and teeth and found a pair of socks. I didn't bother with makeup and I didn't call Marcus, either. I went back downstairs and put out breakfast for both cats. There was still no sign of Owen but I found Hercules in his favorite spot on the bench in the porch.

I sat down beside him for a moment. He put two paws on my leg and I stroked the white fur at the top of his nose.

"I won't be very long," I said.

He lifted his head and nuzzled my chin.

"I love you, too," I said.

There was no traffic on Mountain Road and very little all the way to Marcus's house. I pulled in behind his SUV and walked around the house. The light was on in the kitchen. He must have heard the truck pull in, because the back door opened as I stepped onto the deck.

Marcus was barefoot and shirtless. He hadn't

shaved yet and his dark hair was still damp from the shower. "Kathleen? Is everything all right?"

I nodded, crossed the distance between us and wrapped him in a hug. He hugged me back, then took a step back, hands on my shoulders. "It's not that I'm not happy to see you but it's six thirty in the morning. What are you doing here?"

"I need to talk to you and I couldn't wait."

"All right," he said. "Come in. It's cold out there."

We went into the kitchen and I sat across from him at the table.

"So what do you need to talk to me about?" he asked, pulling on a T-shirt that had been over the back of his chair. His blue eyes were narrowed with concern. "Is it . . . Are we okay?"

I reached over and put both my hands over his. "No, no, no. It's not us." I made myself smile at him. "We're fine. We're better than fine."

I saw him relax a little. Then a shadow seemed to pass over his face. "It's Dani, isn't it," he said.

I nodded. "I'm so sorry. She . . . didn't fall off that embankment by accident."

His mouth twisted to one side. "I probably shouldn't ask you how you know that."

"It would be better if you didn't," I said.

"What happened?"

I told him what Hope had shared with me. He had to know that she was the source of the information, but neither one of us said her name.

"She didn't text me, Kathleen," he said. "I gave her

my number and I told her she could call me, but she
didn't."

"That's good," I said. "You can show them your
phone."

He shook his head. "Even though I don't text I still
get some spam. I clear it out once a week."

My heart sank.

Marcus was meticulous and organized and I knew
he would have a system in place to deal with those
unwanted texts, just the way he did with so many
other things.

"You deleted them all," I said. Inside I groaned.

He gave an almost imperceptible nod. "Last Friday."

Anyone who knew Marcus would know it was
completely in character for him to do something like
that.

"If this were my case I'd think it was suspicious," he
said. "But I give you my word that Dani didn't send
me any texts the day she died. She didn't ask me to
meet her."

The only thing I could think of was that someone
else must have answered that text, and then, realizing
it was Marcus's phone, deleted the original message
and the reply out of embarrassment. Maybe it had
been someone at the station who had mistaken his
phone for their own. It seemed far-fetched but what
other explanation was there? I knew Marcus generally
kept his cell in his pocket but it was possible he'd set it
on his desk for a moment and gotten distracted.

"I don't need your word," I said. "I know you. And

everyone else who knows you knows that you had nothing to do with Dani's death."

"Thank you for the vote of confidence," he said, "but you know that police investigation is based on following the evidence, and from what you've just told me that evidence leads to me."

"You told me once that an investigation is a little like putting a jigsaw puzzle together. First you have to make sure you have all the pieces. Then you have to start putting them together to form a picture and sometimes you can't be sure how one piece fits until you get some of the others in place."

He laughed, which was the last thing I was expecting.

"What?" I said.

"Kathleen, when I said that to you I was trying to impress you. I was trying to make what I do sound more like an art than just the facts, ma'am." He got to his feet, touching my shoulder as he moved behind me.

"Yes, police work is a process, but it's also an art," I pointed out. "It's as much instinct and feeling as it is observation and fact-finding."

"I think instinct and feelings are how *you* figure things out," he said as he poured a cup of coffee for each of us, "not me."

He was right. The conflict between feelings and facts had been the major source of turmoil between the two of us. It had taken a case that was very personal to Marcus for us to start to see things from the other's perspective.

He came back to the table with our coffee. He waited until I had taken a sip, then he spoke. "What else do they have? There has to be more than just those texts. You wouldn't have come out here this early just for that."

"Marcus, where are your extra keys?" I asked.

"In the bedroom on my dresser."

I got up and went down the hall to the bedroom. The keys were in a pottery bowl that he'd told me his sister, Hannah, had made when they were kids. I snagged the keys with one finger. The round metal fob from the drive-in wasn't attached. Somehow I'd known it wouldn't be.

I went back to the kitchen.

"What is it?" Marcus asked, turning in his seat to look at me.

I dropped the keys on the table in front of him. He got it immediately. He pressed his lips together for a moment. "Where was it?"

"Under her body," I said softly.

His face twitched. "I wasn't there. I didn't—"

I wrapped my arms around his neck and pressed my cheek against his hair. It smelled like baby shampoo. "I know," I said.

"It must have gotten lost when Thorsten had my keys."

"That's possible."

"And someone picked it up."

I didn't say anything.

Marcus eyed me slowly, shaking his head. "You don't think John or Travis . . . ?"

"No," I said. My stomach did a queasy flip. "They have theirs."

His forehead creased. "You think it's a setup?"

It was the conclusion Hope and I had come to. Someone—the real killer—wanted to make it look as though Marcus had murdered Dani. "Nothing else makes sense," I said. "We just have to figure out who's behind it."

He twisted around to look at me. "No. I don't want you involved in this in any way."

I took a step backward and folded my arms over my midsection. "I'm already involved. I'm not going to sit around twiddling my thumbs or making stinky crackers for the boys while someone sets you up for murder, so if we're going to argue about this let's hear all your arguments now because I have things to do." I made a beckoning gesture with one hand and waited for him to tell me this was a police matter and I had no business getting involved.

Instead, he stood up, pulled me against him and gave me a kiss that made me forget—for a moment at least—what we'd been talking about. "I love you," he said.

I laid my head against his shoulder. "I love you, too," I said. I tipped my head back to look up at him. "If this is our new way of fighting about things, I like it."

He smiled and kissed me again, on the forehead this time, so I didn't temporarily lose all my senses. "Somebody is trying to make it look like I killed Dani, Kathleen. This is dangerous."

I was starting to see the kisses were more about distracting me than anything else. I broke out of the embrace and took a couple of steps backward so the counter was at my back and there was some air space between me and his broad, muscled shoulders.

"It was dangerous when Ruby was a suspect in Agatha Shepherd's murder," I said. "Remember what happened when Owen and I got locked in the basement of that old cabin?" I felt a fleeting rush of panic as an image of that small dark cellar flashed into my mind.

"I remember exactly what happened," Marcus said. He narrowed his blue eyes. "You could have been killed in that basement or you could have died from hypothermia. It was dangerous." He enunciated each of the three words, biting them off as though they left a sour taste in his mouth.

"I know that," I said, struggling not to raise my voice. "I went out there for Ruby, and for Harrison because the papers about Elizabeth's adoption were out there. I went because I care about both of them."

I could see from the stubborn set of his jaw that he wasn't going to be easily dissuaded. "Ruby is my friend and Harrison is like family. I went out there because I cared . . . care about them." I was having a hard time keeping the emotion out of my voice. "But what's between you and I"—I gestured from me to him—"is a lot . . . stronger. I was willing to take a risk so Ruby wouldn't go to jail for a crime she didn't commit and so Harrison could meet his daughter. You can't ask me to do any less for you." I felt the prickle of tears and I blinked several times so they wouldn't fall.

"That's when I knew," he said, his eyes locked on my face.

"Knew what?" I said.

"That I was crazy about you."

"Way back then? You knew then?"

He nodded. "Uh-huh. I was afraid you were . . ." He cleared his throat. "I was making all sorts of ridiculous bargains with God and when I saw you and Owen through the trees, wading through the snow almost up to your waist, I wanted to dance. I wanted to jump up and down like a kid and high-five everyone in sight."

I felt myself tear up again and I had to swallow down the emotion or I wouldn't be able to say the things I needed to say to him. "I'm trying to imagine you dancing in that big parka you were wearing and all that snow," I said with a small smile.

"I came pretty close." He swiped a hand across his mouth. "I don't want anything to happen to you, Kathleen. You understand that, right?"

I nodded. "I do. I really do. And I feel exactly the same way about you. The difference is that you're trying to protect me from something that's up here." I tapped my temples with the knuckles of each hand. "From something you think might happen. The threat, the danger you're in is real. Here. Now. And I won't stay out of it. I can't."

"I know," he said.

There really wasn't anything else to say.

The medical examiner officially ruled Dani's death a homicide on Monday. Marcus was put on leave—with pay—and Hope was removed from the case. The chief had decided, given Marcus's connection to the victim, to bring in an outside investigator. A detective from Red Wing, Bryan Foster, took over the investigation.

"It could be worse," Hope said that evening, sitting once again at my kitchen table with Hercules ensconced next to her chair. He seemed to like her and she him.

"Foz and I go way back. We went to the academy together. He won't shut me out completely. I can keep tabs on what's happening in the investigation under the table."

"You trust him?" I asked, pulling up one knee and tenting my fingers on top of it.

She nodded. "I do. He won't cut any corners and he won't make any assumptions. He's going to gather the evidence and follow the facts." She shrugged. "And so am I."

"The chief took you off the case," I said.

"Foz is a good cop and he'll be fair, but we both know that all the evidence so far points at just one person."

"Marcus."

Hope picked up her cup, took a drink and set it down again. "I can't sit on my hands and do nothing, Kathleen."

"Neither can I," I said.

We looked at each other across the table. "Are you sure you're in?" she asked. "You know what Marcus would say?"

I nodded slowly. "I know what he would say and yes I'm sure I'm in."

"Merow," Hercules said from his place next to Hope's chair.

We were all in.

6

"So who could have wanted Dani dead?" Hope asked.

I tucked my hair behind one ear. "That's the thing," I said. "I don't know. I met her one time."

"Is John Keller still at the library going through those dried plant samples?"

"Wait a minute. You don't think . . . ?"

Hope waved the question away. "No. I don't think either of Marcus's friends killed Dani. They both have alibis. Keller was with Rebecca." She gestured in the direction of the backyard. "And Travis Rosen was in Red Wing at a meeting with someone from the Department of Natural Resources."

"That's good to know," I said. "John should be at the library tomorrow, but he's pretty much done."

Hope propped both forearms on the table. "Could you talk to him? See what you could find out?"

"Okay," I said. "What do you want to know?"

"Anything you can find out about her family. We know she has a brother—Dominic McAllister. I spoke to him, and a grandmother. Did they get along? Is there any other family?"

"What are you going to do?"

"See what I can find on Ernie Kingsley."

"The majority shareholder in the development company."

"Yes," she said. "How did you know?"

"Lita," I said, getting to my feet. "More coffee?"

Hope shook her head.

The basement door opened then and Owen appeared. He had the end of a red plaid scarf in his mouth. He passed through the kitchen, giving a muffled meow as he headed for the living room.

Hope watched the whole thing with an amused look on her face.

"I have no idea," I said in answer to her unspoken question.

She laughed. It was a good sound to hear after the tension of our previous conversation. "I thought maybe you'd taught him to put the laundry away for you."

I laughed as well. "I did very briefly wonder if it was possible to teach him how to push the buttons on the washing machine so he could do a load of towels."

"Merow!" Hercules interjected loudly.

Hope looked down at him. "I'm sure you could do laundry, too," she said.

After Hope left I got my laptop and went into the living room, curling up in the big chair. Hercules followed, jumped onto the footstool and looked expectantly at me.

"Yes, you can help," I said.

Hercules and I spent the next hour researching Danielle McAllister and her family. Dani's parents had been killed in a plane crash when she was twelve. She'd been raised after that by her brother, Dominic, almost ten years older, and her paternal grandmother. The McAllisters were very wealthy and very conservative. The family fortune began with shipbuilding, massive wooden boats that took to the sea during the age of sail.

Dominic McAllister ran McAllister Enterprises, which was made up of, by my best guess, at least half a dozen different businesses including several hotels. I found it interesting that Dani was listed in the company's annual report as being on the board of directors but, unlike the other members, there was no mention of what she did for a living.

After a bit of digging going all the way back to her college years, I found some photos of Dani with her brother and her grandmother at several charity events sponsored by her family's company. I noticed Dani was usually dressed down just a little—no elegant black dresses with four-inch heels for her. And the truth was she was stunningly beautiful in a flowing, gauzy skirt and flat sandals.

"I'm starting to think Dani's environmental work may have been her way of rebelling a little. It looks like she may have been the black sheep of her family.

"Mrr?" Hercules asked, his black-and-white head tipped to one side—mostly so he could view the computer screen without having to move from the spot on my lap where he'd settled.

"No, I don't think being a black sheep is anything like being a black-and-white cat," I said. I had no idea what he'd actually been asking me, but my answer seemed to satisfy him.

John came into the library just after ten o'clock the next morning. Tuesdays were busy, so I'd been keeping an eye out for him and I met him at the door.

"Hi, Kathleen," he said. "Is the meeting room free? I just need to go though a few more plant samples that look promising."

"The room is still yours," I said. "I just made a cup of coffee. Do you have time for one?"

He nodded. "That sounds good."

I took John up to the staff room. He sat at the table while I poured coffee for both of us. I thought about all the cups Marcus and I had shared in the same space.

"Cinnamon roll?" I asked, bringing over the plate Mary had brought in with her. "They're wonderful, I promise. Mary made them and she has some sort of secret ingredient I haven't been able to wheedle out of her."

I hoped that the combination of coffee and one of Mary's sweet cinnamon creations would put John in a talkative frame of mind.

"Hey these are good," he said, taking a large bite.

He chewed and swallowed, gesturing with one hand. "Was Abigail serious when she told me that Mary is a kickboxer, or was she pulling my leg?"

"She was serious. Mary has been regional and state champion more than once for her age and weight class."

"But she looks like Little Red Riding Hood's grandmother."

I laughed. "And she could take you down faster than the Big Bad Wolf."

"I'll remember that next time I ask to use the printer." John grinned, then his expression grew serious. "Kathleen, how's Marcus doing, really? It's ridiculous that the police are even looking at him as a suspect. He hadn't talked to Dani—or any of us, for that matter—in years. It was just that we met that morning the two of you walked into the restaurant. And then he kills her? C'mon!"

"It doesn't hang together because Marcus didn't do it." I hesitated. "John, was there anyone who had a problem with Dani, maybe a conflict over a project or some kind of environmental issue?"

He slumped back in the chair. "You always get a few crackpots who call us tree-hugging hippies or crunchy granola space cadets but that's all it's ever been—words and a couple of times protestors with signs."

"What about with this project?"

He made a face. "When the different groups banded together to stop the Long Lake project Ernie Kingsley requested a meeting. He offered to make a large donation to every group if we'd all drop our opposition to the project."

I raised an eyebrow. "I take it that didn't go well?"

"No, it didn't. But my point is that Kingsley is a businessman. He solves problems by throwing money at them. Not by throwing a body over an embankment."

"What about her family? Could someone have gone after Dani as a way to get to her brother or her grandmother, maybe?"

John brushed crumbs off the front of his shirt. "I don't know that much about her family's business dealings. They own three or four fancy hotels. They're the largest manufacturer of sails in the world and they also run several wind-turbine farms. Not a whole lot of controversy or reasons to kill anyone there. She was very close to her brother and her grandmother. They were really proud of her work. And if there was any problem I think Dani would have said something to me. We were pretty close." He held up a hand. "As friend, nothing romantic."

I remembered Dani's bio in McAllister Enterprises' annual report. If her family was so proud of her work why wasn't it mentioned? "What about since you all got here?" I asked. "Did you have any run-ins with anyone about the resort plans?" I rubbed the space between my eyebrows with one finger where a headache was forming. "I'm sorry for putting you on the spot with all these questions."

John leaned forward, putting both hands flat on the table. "Don't apologize. You're worried about Marcus.

I get that." He hesitated, opened his mouth and closed it again.

"What is it?" I said.

"I don't want to offend you or give you the wrong impression."

"But."

"Is it possible someone from around here killed Dani?" Before I could say anything both of his hands came up off the table. "I don't mean on purpose, Kathleen. I mean by accident. He—or she, I guess—came across Dani working out there, they got into some kind of an argument and things just got out of hand. This kind of project can stir up strong feelings on both sides. I've seen it before."

I couldn't tell him what Hope had shared, that Dani had been hit by a car and her body moved. Even though there were strong feelings on both side of the development proposal I just couldn't believe that anyone in Mayville Heights felt so strongly that they'd run Dani down over it and then dump her body. I knew these people. I knew what they were capable of and it wasn't murder. Not over this.

But I didn't say any of that. All I did was nod and say, "You're right. It has stirred up a lot of complicated feelings."

"I need to get to work," John said, pushing back his chair and getting to his feet. "Look, from what I've seen the police here seem to know what they're doing. Let them do their job, Kathleen. It'll work out."

He headed for the stairs and I put the dishes in the

sink. I hadn't learned that much about Dani except that based on what John had said, the conclusions I'd made after my online research seemed to be wrong.

I took my lunch outside to the gazebo and called Hope. I told her what I'd discovered. It didn't take very long.

"I didn't find out much about Ernie Kingsley, either," she said. "Nothing that isn't part of the public record. His grandfather started Kingsley-Pearson. They made their money with car dealerships. They own fifty-six of them. But other than saying Ernie is a shrewd businessman, no one will say anything else about him." I heard her sigh. "At least not to me."

The breeze off the water blew my hair against my face. I brushed it back. "How about you see if you can find anything more about the McAllisters' and let me see if I can learn more about Ernie Kingsley?" I said.

"Why not?" Hope said. "You couldn't do any worse than I have so far." She said good-bye with a promise she'd call me with whatever she found out about Dani's family.

So how could I find out more about the developer? Everett? I knew he liked Marcus and if I went to Rebecca she'd nudge her husband to help. Then I remembered Rebecca telling me that Everett was going to Japan on business for a few days. Who else could I talk to? Lita? I didn't really want to put her on the spot.

I broke my brownie in half and ate it, hoping somehow inspiration would find me. And then it drove into the parking lot in the form of a delivery truck bringing two boxes of easy readers for our Reading Buddies program.

"Simon Janes," I said aloud. There were no cats to murp their agreement to my idea and the robin in a nearby tree didn't seem very interested.

Simon Janes was the father of Mia Janes. She'd come to the library as a student intern and worked out so well that I'd hired her part-time. I knew Simon's company was involved somehow in commercial real estate. Maybe he could tell me something, anything, about Ernie Kingsley. It was worth a try.

I finished my lunch and went back inside. "I just have to make a call and then I'll be down to take over," I said to Susan, who was at the desk sorting books.

"Take your time," she said. It looked like she'd secured her updo today with a couple of demitasse spoons. I'd learned a long time ago that there was always going to be a sense of whimsy to Susan's fashion choices.

Upstairs in my office I looked up the number I wanted and after a moment of hesitation punched it into the phone. The phone at the other end rang twice before it was answered. "Good afternoon, Simon Janes's office," a polished, professional voice with just a hint of huskiness said.

"Hello," I said. "It's Kathleen Paulson from the library calling."

The professional voice got a little warmer. "Hello, Ms. Paulson. Mia works for you. She's told me how good you've been to her. Is everything all right?"

"Everything is fine," I said. "Mia has been a wonderful asset to the library. She's a hard worker and everyone from the preschoolers at story time to the seniors book club adores her."

"I'm not at all surprised," the woman on the other end of the phone said. "So how may I help you?"

"I was hoping to get about ten minutes of Mr. Janes's time," I said. "It doesn't have anything to do with Mia."

I'd met Simon Janes the previous winter at a fundraiser for the library's Reading Buddies program. He was outspoken to the point of being rude, in my opinion—very different from his quiet, soft-spoken daughter. However, Mia had clearly inherited some of her father's confidence. When the expansion of the Reading Buddies program had been put at risk because we hadn't raised enough money, Mia—according to her father—had called him on his brash behavior and pointed out that he could easily afford to fund the program, which he did, with a check from his personal account.

I'd seen Janes several times since then when he came into the library to pick up his daughter. And more than once I'd caught him watching me, a bemused look on his face. He didn't look away and he didn't seem the slightest bit embarrassed at being caught.

"Would eight o'clock tomorrow morning work for you?" the woman with the lovely voice asked.

"Yes, it would. Thank you," I said, relieved that she hadn't asked me why I wanted the meeting. I got directions to Janes's office, thanked her again and hung up.

Abigail and I were in the workroom, late that afternoon, opening the boxes of readers when Susan poked her head around the doorway. "Call for you, Kathleen," she said.

"Thanks," I said, getting to my feet and brushing bits of paper and packing materials off my hands. I went into my office to answer the phone.

"Hello, Kathleen, it's Simon Janes," the voice on the other end said.

"Good afternoon, Mr. Janes," I said, wondering why he'd called. Was he going to cancel our appointment or did he just want to know why I wanted to see him?"

Luckily, he got right to the point. "We have an appointment scheduled for tomorrow morning and I have to make an unplanned trip to Minneapolis."

My heart sank.

"But if you'd like to join me for an early supper at the St. James Hotel we could talk then."

I didn't want to lose the chance to pick the man's brain. "Yes, thank you. I would," I said.

We agreed to meet at the hotel bar at five thirty. I didn't doubt that Simon Janes had a meeting in Minneapolis, but I also suspected that changing the time and place of our meeting was a way for him to control it. That was fine with me. As Harrison Taylor would say, I'd been around the block a time or two and recognized the scenery.

I left the library at the same time I would have left if I'd been going home to have supper and change for tai chi class. I'd already sent Maggie a text letting her know I might miss class. I parked the truck on a side street near the hotel. I was early but as I walked into the hotel bar I discovered I wasn't as early as Janes. He was leaning back in his seat at a small table in the center of the room, legs crossed. As I approached he got to his feet and pulled out the other chair for me.

"Hello, Kathleen," he said. He was tall with a firm handshake and direct gaze, and once again I thought he didn't look anywhere near old enough to be the parent of a seventeen-year-old.

Since he'd referred to me by my first name I did the same. "Hello, Simon," I said as I sat down. "Thanks for fitting me into your schedule."

He took the chair opposite me again. "When Mia's working at the library I generally eat alone." He shrugged. "I like my own company but sometimes it's good to have someone else's. I've heard all my stories." He gave a practiced, self-deprecating smile.

"Well, I promise to listen attentively and nod and smile in the appropriate places."

He laughed. "Then it should be a good meal."

He turned his head and a waiter materialized beside us. He handed each of us a menu.

"Are you driving, Kathleen?" Simon asked.

I nodded.

"Sparkling water, then?"

"Please," I said.

"Two please, Michael," he said to the waiter.

The young man nodded. "Right away, sir."

Simon leaned back in his chair, the menu untouched on the table in front of him. "How do you feel about pizza?" he asked.

"I like pizza," I said.

I noticed he had a crescent-shaped scar that ran from the end of his right eyebrow to just below the eye. "Mia says that my habit of suggesting what to order when I'm with a woman is condescending and patriarchal. So I'm just going to say that they have great pizza here and would you like to share one? Of course you don't have to say yes." He raised an eyebrow. "I think that covers all the disclaimers."

I couldn't help smiling back at him. I'd seen his arrogance and I had no doubt that he could be condescending and patriarchal, but he could also be charming. "I've never had the pizza here," I said, "but I've heard good things about it, so yes, let's split one."

Michael, the waiter, returned with our sparkling water. I squeezed a little lime into mine and took a drink while Simon relayed our order, taking the opportunity to study the man. He wasn't wearing a tie, but his dark suit was expensive and expertly tailored. He was somewhere below six feet, rangy, with his hair buzzed close to his head. He certainly looked the part of the successful businessman but something about the way he carried himself made me think he'd started at the bottom. He reminded me of Burtis Chapman, I realized. I wouldn't want either man for an enemy.

Once the waiter left Simon turned his attention to me. "So what do you want to ask me about first?" he said. "The Long Lake proposal or Ernie Kingsley?"

I think my mouth fell open in surprise. "How did you know?" I managed to get out.

"I knew this meeting had nothing to do with Mia," he said. "I know she's happy working for you and I've picked her up enough times to feel confident that you're all happy with her."

I nodded. "We are."

"From what Mia's told me the reading program is going well and you don't have any papers with you, so you didn't want to meet with me to hit me up for money."

He'd approached our meeting the same way I might have. "You're right again," I said.

One forearm rested on the edge of the table. The other was on his leg. He didn't have any fidgety tics that I'd picked up so far. "You and Detective Gordon are a couple."

It wasn't a question, so I didn't say anything.

"He has a connection to the woman who was killed—the geologist with that environmental group."

I nodded again. "They were friends in college."

"You're looking for information."

The conversation was beginning to feel like a tennis match. Serve and volley. Serve and volley.

"Yes," was all I said.

"So what? You think Ernie could have killed that woman?"

At least I wasn't going to have to play any games. "I don't know. I don't know the man—he doesn't have a library card. But you know him. What do you think?"

He laughed. "I don't have a library card, either. Does that mean I'm flawed as a human being in your eyes?"

Out of the corner of my eyes I caught sight of our waiter, coming from the kitchen. "You're generous when it's a good cause, like Reading Buddies, but you don't like to waste money. I don't see that as a flaw. Also, you're a big fan of Vin Diesel and you wanted to be a lawyer."

I'd timed it perfectly. Michael arrived then with the pizza and our plates. Simon waited until we each had a slice before he spoke.

"Very good," he said. "How did you do that?"

I took a bite of my pizza before I answered. It was good, with a thin, crispy crust, tomatoes, onions, salami, fresh herbs and wonderfully stringy mozzarella. "This is good," I said.

Simon didn't say anything but "I told you so" was written in the expression on his face.

I set my fork down. "So how do I know so much about you? I'm observant. You don't have a library card, but you do borrow things on Mia's card. You've watched every movie in the Fast and the Furious franchise more than once."

"Maybe Mia's the fan," he said.

I shook my head. "She likes fantasy and Japanese anime. So it has to be you who likes Vin Diesel. You could have bought those movies or downloaded them but you didn't. That would be a waste of money when you can borrow them for free. But you did give us money for Reading Buddies. That says you're frugal but not cheap."

"And law school?"

"Scott Turow and a lucky guess. You've read everything we have that he's written and requested two books we didn't have. And I know Mia wants to be a doctor."

For a moment he didn't say anything. Then he laughed. "Very good, Kathleen. I'm impressed. And I'm not easily impressed."

I cut another bite from my pizza. "I answered your question but you didn't answer mine."

"Do I think Ernie could have killed that woman?"

I nodded.

"Ernie Kingsley is a junkyard dog who would sell out his own mother to make a deal. But I don't think he'd *kill* someone to make a deal." His expression turned serious. "He does have a temper, though. Last year he was at some business lunch at a restaurant in Minneapolis. I don't know any of the details, but things got a little heated, some punches were thrown, the police were called. Then it all went away." He held up his left hand and ran his thumb over the end of his middle finger, implying, it seemed to me, that money had made everything go away.

"Have you considered that squatter?" Simon asked. He glanced in the direction of the bar and once again the waiter seemed to appear out of nowhere, this time with another glass of sparkling water for Simon. "Could I get you another?" he asked me.

I shook my head. "No, thank you. I'm fine." I turned my attention to Simon. "What squatter?"

"There's a guy living in the woods out there, close to the lake. He claims his family owned that land a hundred years ago and it was taken from them illegally. I don't think there's anything to his claims. In fact it looks like he's nothing but a deadbeat dad trying to avoid supporting his kids." He didn't try to hide the contempt in his voice.

"I know the natural-resources people have had a couple of run-ins with him and I heard that the guy came after Ernie with an ax. Guy has this old truck with some kind of camper thing on the back that he's living in."

Hope's words came back to me: *"The medical examiner thinks she was hit by a car, then the body was moved and she was . . . dropped over."*

Maybe this was the answer. Maybe this man, this squatter living in the woods, was the person who killed Dani. Maybe he'd hit her by accident and panicked.

"Thank you, Simon," I said. The knot that had been in the pit of my stomach since the night Hope showed up at my door loosened.

"I'm glad I could help," he said.

We spent the rest of the meal talking about Reading Buddies. He seemed genuinely interested and once again I thought that behind the somewhat arrogant exterior there was a pretty nice guy.

Before we parted ways in front of the hotel Simon

took out a business card and scribbled something on the back of it before handing it to me. "My cell phone number. If I can help with anything else."

I headed back to the truck and drove up Mountain Road. A furry-faced committee of two was waiting in the kitchen.

"I'm sorry I'm late," I said, dropping my briefcase and shoes under the coat hooks. "I was talking to Mia's father. I may have something that can help find whoever killed Dani."

I bent down to pet them both. Hercules sniffed my hand and then narrowed his green eyes in suspicion. Owen's whiskers twitched and he gave a loud and somewhat huffy meow.

"Yes, I had supper with him." The cats exchanged a look.

"Mrr?" Hercules asked. I knew what that meant. I'd heard it enough times.

"Pizza," I said.

Hercules made a sound a lot like a sigh. Owen, on the other hand, put on his indignant face and made a point of turning his head and looking away from me.

"It was the only time he had available and it's not as though I could call you."

Hercules tipped his head and looked in the direction of the living room, where the phone was.

I put my face close to his and scratched the spot where the white fur of his nose met the black fur from the top of his head. "You don't have opposable thumbs," I said.

Beside him Owen gave an audible sigh. I reached

over with my free hand and scratched behind his left ear. Then I leaned closer to him. "I'm sorry," I said. He still wouldn't look at me.

I got to my feet, got the stinky crackers and put a stack of four in front of each cat. Hercules looked up and smiled at me. Clearly all was forgiven. Owen sniffed the crackers as though he hadn't eaten hundreds if not thousands of them by now. He eyed me briefly, then nudged the pile over with his nose and began checking the crackers one by one.

Poet Alexander Pope wrote, "To err is human; to forgive divine." In my experience a few sardine crackers helped getting to the divine.

7

I made it to tai chi just as Maggie formed the circle. I hurried across the room, hopping on one foot as I pulled on my shoes, and slid in next to Roma. She smiled a hello, already swinging her arms along with Mags and the rest of the class.

It was good to set aside everything else that had been on my mind and just concentrate on the form and my Push Hands for the duration of class.

"How are you?" Roma asked after we'd finished the form at the end. "And how's Marcus?"

Roma had been out of town at a convention for several days. Marcus and I—along with Harry Taylor—had taken care of the cats while she was gone.

"We're both okay," I said, patting my face with the edge of my shirt. "There's something I wanted to ask you. Do you have a second?"

"Sure. What is it?"

I led her over to the windows at the end of the

room. "Do you know anything about some guy living in an old truck somewhere near Long Lake?"

Roma nodded. "His name is Ira. He's been out there for the last five or six months. Do you think he had something to do with what happened to Marcus's friend?"

"I don't know. Maybe. How has he managed to stay out there for so long?"

"He claims his family owns some piece of land out there—nothing that's part of the development. I heard there's some kind of court case and that's why he hasn't been forcibly evicted." She reached over and picked a clump of cat hair off the front of my shirt. "You could try talking to Oren. I think the guy is related to the Kenyons somehow."

"I'll do that," I said. "Thanks." I studied her face for a moment. "How are you, really? Rebecca told me that Eddie is going to be working with Everett."

Eddie was Eddie Sweeney, former all-star player for the Minnesota Wild hockey team, now retired, and Roma's former boyfriend. Their relationship had ended when he proposed and Roma turned him down. She was older than Eddie and that, plus the fact that it was too late for her to have children, was the reason she'd said no. Eddie was crazy about Roma and he wasn't giving up.

Roma sighed softly and played with the wide silver ring she wore on the index finger of her right hand. I could see part of the chain from her rose gold locket peeking out from the neck edge of her long-sleeved T-shirt. Eddie had given her that locket. "It's harder than I thought it would be, having him here in town."

Eddie had retired at the end of the season and moved to Mayville Heights just a couple of weeks earlier.

"You could say yes and put both of you out of your misery," I said lightly.

She gave me a sad smile. "You know I can't do that."

I leaned over and gave her a hug. I knew that she could do it. I just didn't know how to make her see that.

I called Hope when I got home and told her what I'd learned from both Simon and Roma. "Nice work," she said. "Marcus said you had a way of getting people to tell you things."

"I think it's just because I ask a lot of questions," I said. "I'll try to talk to Oren tomorrow. I'll let you know what I find out."

"Sounds good," she said. "How's Marcus?"

I was sitting in the big chair in the living room, rubbing a knot in my left calf with one hand. "You know him, Hope. He doesn't say a lot. He's been helping Eddie do some work on his new place the past couple of days. I think it's making him crazy that he can't investigate."

"Maybe we'll get lucky and find something and this will all be over."

"I hope so," I said. I didn't add that in my experience things rarely went that easily.

I woke well before my alarm Wednesday morning and since I was up so early, decided to drive out to Long Lake to see if I could find Ira the squatter and his truck. There was no sign of him or the vehicle. Instead of going back home I stopped at Eric's for a breakfast sandwich and coffee, which I took to the library and ate at my desk, my chair turned around to the window so I could look out over the water.

I was halfway up a ladder with a set of pumpkin lights when Eddie Sweeney walked into the building after lunch. He was six-four with broad shoulders and muscles in all the right places, the walking definition of tall, dark and handsome.

"Kathleen, what are you doing?" he asked, grinning up at me.

"Getting ready for Spookarama," I said. I draped the lights over the top step of the ladder and climbed down so I was at Eddie's level, more or less.

"That has to have something to do with Halloween."

"It's a party for the little ones. It's safer than them being out on the streets on Halloween night."

"Could I help?" Eddie was good with kids. It was part of the reason Roma insisted he needed to marry someone who could give him more children. Eddie had a daughter, Sydney, who lived with her mother, Eddie's ex. I knew that part of the reason Eddie had bought the loft that Marcus was helping him work on was so that Syd could spend more time with him now that he wasn't playing.

I leaned back and studied him, squinting my eyes and trying to see him with green skin and neck bolts. "How would you like to be Frankenstein? I'm thinking more Herman Munster than Mary Shelley."

"Sure. Why not?"

"Abigail will call you." I gave him a hug. "Thank you. The kids are going to love this."

He nodded and his smile faded. "Kathleen, how's Roma?"

"She misses you."

He nodded. "I miss her. I went out to see her. She said I was just rubbing salt in the wound. I told her I wanted to be friends."

"Do you?" I asked even though I knew the answer.

Something flashed in Eddie's dark eyes. "I want to be her husband." He took a deep breath and blew it out slowly. "You know she's staying in touch with Syd."

I smiled. "It doesn't surprise me. That's Roma." I knew that Roma and Sydney had bonded over their shared love of animals. Roma would never cut the child out of her life. I also knew that Sydney was all for her father marrying Roma and was probably pleading his case.

"Syd's working on her," Eddie said as if he could read my mind. "She's crazy about Roma and so am I. And I know she still loves me."

"She does." It was written all over her face whenever his name came up.

He jammed his hands in his pockets. "I'm not going to get all weird and follow her around town. I'm just going to camp on the edge of her life until she figures out that we're better when we're together."

"I hope that happens," I said.

Eddie smiled then. "Don't tell anyone, because it

would blow my tough-guy hockey-player image, but I kinda believe in all that happily-ever-after stuff."

I thought about Everett and Rebecca, who had spent a big part of their lives apart but who had gotten their happily ever after in the end. I hoped it wouldn't take Roma and Eddie that long.

I was crossing the parking lot at the end of the day when my cell phone rang. It was Hope. "We need to talk," she said.

"All right," I said. "Where are you?"

"In the parking lot at the marina."

"Stay there. I'm standing beside my truck. I'll be there in five minutes."

Hope was parked at the far end of the marina parking lot. I pulled in next to her car. I could see her standing by the rock wall that ran from the wooden dock around to the point. Just from her body language I could tell that she didn't have good news to share. I walked over to join her.

"Hi," I said. "What's up?"

"I talked to Foz—Bryan—a little while ago," she said. The breeze off the water tousled her dark curls and she pushed them impatiently back from her face. "He was pretty close-mouthed but I did find out that they've found more evidence that seems to implicate Marcus."

My throat tightened. "I don't understand. He didn't do this. How can they find evidence of something that didn't even happen?"

"I don't know," Hope said. "This whole thing is off."

"Did he tell you what this so-called evidence is?" I couldn't help the sarcastic edge to my voice.

"Someone—I have no idea who—saw Marcus and Dani arguing outside the motel."

I shook my head. "That's not new evidence. We already knew they were there. Maggie saw them."

Hope pushed her hair away from her face again. "Motel, Kathleen," she said. "Motel. The Bluebird Motel, where all three of them were staying."

"Whoever saw them is wrong," I said flatly. "If Marcus had been out there arguing with Dani he would have told us."

Hope didn't answer me right away. Her mouth moved as though she was trying out the feel of what she wanted to say before she said it.

"Are you sure?" she finally asked.

"Of course I'm sure," I retorted. "Why aren't you?"

"You know better than most people how private a man Marcus is."

I nodded.

"And you know how important trust and loyalty are to him."

"I know," I said. They had almost derailed our relationship before it got started.

"There's something he hasn't told us in all of this."

My stomach clenched as though some giant hand had grabbed it and started squeezing. "Hope, he's what you two like to call a person of interest in his friend's death and you think he's keeping secrets?"

She exhaled softly. "I think he's protecting someone— I don't know who—that he cares about." She looked down at the ground for a moment and kicked a rock, skittering it across the grass. Then she met my eyes again. "Can you tell me with one hundred percent certainty that Marcus has told us everything? Absolutely everything?"

The hand on my stomach squeezed harder and harder. Because I realized that I couldn't. That little niggling feeling that had been burrowing in the back of my brain wouldn't let me.

"I don't know what he's holding back," Hope said. "But we need to find out."

All I could do was nod. I wasn't sure what felt worse: the thought that Marcus didn't completely trust me, or the thought that I didn't completely trust him.

I cleared my throat. "I'll talk to him."

"I'm sorry to put you in this position," Hope said. I believed her. I could see the sadness in her eyes and the downturn of her mouth. "I can't let Marcus be arrested for something we both know he didn't do."

She pressed her lips together and it suddenly hit me that she loved him. Not as a partner. Not as a friend. She *loved* him. Why hadn't I seen it before? Or maybe I had and I just hadn't wanted to admit it.

"It has to be done," I said. I looked past her to the lake. The water looked rough and troubled—exactly how I felt. "What else did you find out?"

"I didn't get this from Bryan," she said. "I have a . . . contact in the prosecuting attorney's office—he's keeping a close eye on this—and anyway, it looks like Marcus doesn't have an alibi for the time that the medical examiner thinks Dani was killed."

I held up a hand. "Wait a minute. The prosecuting attorney's office is where he was. Remember? He went for a meeting. The prosecutor had been held up. He went to talk to Dani and then he went back to the prosecuting attorney's office."

"Where the meeting lasted all of about five minutes," Hope said. "Which means there's an hour unaccounted for."

"Did you ask Marcus where he was?"

"Uh-huh. He was evasive. Finally he said he went for a walk. He said he had a lot on his mind and just wanted to figure some things out. When I asked him what things he said they had had nothing to do with the case." She looked past me, at the water, and for the first time I saw a flicker of fear in her eyes. "Keeping secrets is the worst thing he could be doing right now."

The words hung in the air between us. "I'll find out where he was," I said, working to keep the emotions that were swirling in my chest from getting out. "I'll find out all of it."

Hope looked away again for a moment. "I don't want this to come between the two of you."

I believed her. She loved him and I should have seen that a long time ago but I could also see that she wanted him to be happy.

"It isn't going to come between us."

"I have to go," Hope said abruptly.

"Wait," I said. "Did you find anything more about Dani's family?"

"I've got a line on someone who might be able to give us some inside information."

I nodded. "Good. I'm going to out to see Marcus and I'll stop and talk to Oren about the guy in the truck."

"Okay, I'll talk to you later, then," Hope said. She walked back across the grass to her car. I was about to head back to the truck when my phone rang. It was Marcus. He had been planning to make dinner for us. I had thought I might stop to talk to Oren on the way out to Marcus's house. If I left now I could still do that.

"How do you feel about spaghetti at Eric's?" he asked.

"Okay, but what happened to spaghetti at your house?"

"My stove won't work. Larry Taylor is coming to take a look at it in the morning. I told him it wasn't an emergency."

I started for the truck. "Okay," I said. "I'll meet you at the café in about an hour. There's something I need to do first."

Oren's house was a renovated farmhouse not a lot different from mine, with the same steeply pitched roof and bay window. His house had an addition on the left side, set back from the main house. A covered veranda ran along about half of the front of the main house and all the way across the front of the extension.

I could see his truck in the driveway as I got close to the house. He was on the veranda painting what looked like a long wooden bench with a hinged seat.

I pulled my truck in behind his and got out. Oren waved his paintbrush in greeting and got to his feet. He was tall and lean, in his mid-fifties, with sun-bleached sandy hair. He minded me of actor Clint Eastwood with a little quiet farm boy thrown in.

"Hello, Kathleen," he said. "It's good to see you."

"It's good to see you, too, Oren," I said with a smile. I craned my neck to get a closer look at the bench. "Is that going in Roma's porch?"

He nodded. "It gives people somewhere to sit down and take off their boots in the winter time and it gives Roma some storage space."

The bench was about five feet long and he was painting it a pale gray that reminded me of foggy mornings down by the water. "You've done a beautiful job," I said.

Oren was a very talented carpenter. He was an even better musician. He could have been a famous concert pianist but it wasn't the life he'd wanted for himself. He could play the piano by the time he was four and he'd started composing music at six, using his own method of notation because he hadn't learned to read music at that point.

As he had once explained to me, "I could—I can—make music with almost any instrument: piano, guitar, bass, mandolin. If I look at a piece of music, just once, I can remember it and play it. Years later I can play it."

As someone whose musical ability was limited to making sounds with my armpit and not very well at that, I was in awe of his talent.

"Roma showed me the bench you and Maggie found for the upstairs hallway," he said, reaching down to set his brush on the edge of the painting pail. "You did a beautiful job on that."

"Thank you," I said. "All that took was paint and sandpaper. You built this."

He smiled again and ducked his head. "My father was a good teacher."

I cleared my throat. "Oren, I need to talk to you about something."

He didn't ask me what, he just nodded. "All right. I just need to put the paint back in the can and wash the brush."

He put one more stroke of paint on the front of the bench seat, then bent down and picked up the plastic pail.

"It'll only take me a minute," he said. "C'mon in."

The extension attached to the main house was Oren's workshop. The space was completely open from floor to ceiling. There were high windows on the back wall that flooded the room with light even on the darkest winter days. More windows on the end of the room overlooked the long workbench. There was a counter with cupboards underneath and a sink at one end over on the other side of the room. Everything in the room was neat, clean and perfectly organized.

I stood in the doorway and remembered the first time I'd seen the space. My mouth had literally gaped open. Oren's father, Karl Kenyon, had worked as a carpenter and a house painter. But he had the soul of an artist. In his spare time he made massive metal sculptures. The first one I'd ever seen was an enormous metal eagle with a wingspan of at least six feet. It had been suspended, in flight it seemed, from the ceiling beams at the back half of the room. Even though the sculpture was nothing more than pieces of metal welded together somehow I'd felt I could see the bird flying, its powerful chest muscles making those huge wings slice through the air. Now the beautiful bird, along with another of Karl Kenyon's pieces, was touring museums on the East Coast.

Oren looked over his shoulder at me. "It still looks a little empty when I come out here," he said.

"Those pieces deserve to be seen," I said.

"It's happening because of you." He shook the wet brush in the sink before setting it in an empty ice cream container on the counter.

"Actually it's happening because of you," I said. "I'm glad you said yes to letting them be exhibited."

Oren poured the paint back into the can, hammered the lid back on and set the pail in the sink. He walked back over to me, wiping his hands on his overalls.

I looked around the room. Something else was missing besides the metal eagle.

"What happened to the harpsichord?" I asked.

Oren looked down at his feet for a moment. "I sold it," he said. "I'm going to build a guitar. Burtis is clearing part of his woodlot. He promised me first choice of the wood."

I smiled. "I'm looking forward to seeing and hearing it."

"Would you like a cup of coffee, Kathleen?" he asked.

It felt awkward being here to ask Oren if he had a cousin living in the woods who just might have killed a woman. It would be good to have something to keep my hands occupied. I nodded. "Yes, I would."

Oren indicated the two stools at the counter, then poured a cup for each of us. There was a carton of milk and a little bowl of sugar cubes on a tray by the coffeemaker. After we'd both doctored our coffee, he folded one hand around his mug and looked at me. "I heard about Detective Gordon's friend," he said. "I'm sorry. Does what you want to talk to me about have anything to do with that?"

"In a way," I said.

He nodded, took a drink from his mug and set it on the counter again. "Ira. He's been living in his truck out by the lake. That's who you want to talk to me about."

"Yes."

For a long moment Oren didn't speak, didn't move. Then finally he said, "You think he might have been the one who hurt that woman."

I wanted to reach out and somehow push the words away but I couldn't. Because that was why I was there.

"I want to know if you think he could have."

Oren studied his own hands for a moment. "I want to say no," he said. "But the truth is, I don't know."

I nodded, hoping he'd keep talking.

"The thing is, Kathleen, that piece of land out there. It doesn't belong to the Kenyons anymore. It hasn't for a long time, but Ira can't seem to get his mind around that. He's managed to find more than one lawyer who takes his money and starts a lawsuit that isn't going to amount to anything. I don't think Ira would have hurt Detective Gordon's friend on purpose . . ."

He left the end of the sentence hanging.

"Do you know where he might have gone?" I asked.

"You mean he's not out there anymore?"

I shook my head. When I'd driven out to Long Lake before work, I'd checked out every dirt road in the area where Roma had said the squatter's truck had been parked. There had been no sign of him.

Oren sighed. "He could be anywhere. The last time Ira disappeared he turned up in Clearwater Beach in Florida but for weeks no one knew where he was. I go out to check on him every couple of weeks and he was talking about Clearwater the last time I saw him. That's all I know."

I hadn't touched my coffee and now took one long drink and then set the cup back on the counter. "I better get going," I said. "Thank you for talking to me."

Oren got to his feet. "If I hear anything about Ira, I promise I'll call you."

"Thank you," I said. I walked back to the truck thinking that I was no closer to answers in Dani's death and I really had no idea what to do next.

Marcus was already at our favorite table in the front window when I got to Eric's Place. We gave Nic our order—spaghetti and meatballs—and after he'd headed back to the kitchen Marcus smiled across the table at me. "How was your day?" he asked.

"All right," I said. "Owen climbed in the laundry

basket and got cat hair all over the towels again. At least this time it wasn't the clean ones. And we started decorating for Spookarama. I think Eddie is going to be Frankenstein."

He laughed. "I'm looking forward to seeing *that*."

I couldn't do it. I couldn't sit there and make small talk while we both pretended everything was fine when it wasn't. "Do you trust me?" I said.

His blue eyes widened. "Where did that come from?"

If I'd had even the tiniest bit of doubt that Hope was right that Marcus was keeping something from us it disappeared like a balloon popping.

"That question only has two answers," I said, struggling to keep the maelstrom of emotions I was feeling from sneaking into my voice. "Yes or no."

"Why would you think I don't trust you?"

I didn't say anything. I just continued to look at him. Finally, he sighed softly. "Of course I trust you, Kathleen," he said in a low voice.

My heart was pounding so hard it felt like there was a steel band playing in my chest. "Then tell me what it is you've been holding back. I know it has to do with Dani."

To his credit he didn't pretend he didn't know what I was talking about. He reached across the table for my hand. "I can't. Not because I don't trust you, because I do. I trust you with my life. But I gave my word and it's not my secret to tell."

"Whatever this secret is could get you arrested," I

said, this time not even trying to keep the emotion from my voice.

"It doesn't have anything to do with Dani's death. And I don't know if it will make any difference to you, but this . . . information goes way back to before you and I got together. If it was now, I would say no to anything I had to keep from you." He had that look on his face that told me it wasn't going to be easy to change his mind.

"How do you know it doesn't have anything to do with Dani's death?"

The muscles along his jaw tightened. "I gave my word, Kathleen," he said again. "If I don't honor my commitments or keep my promises, what kind of a man am I?"

Love is not love which alters when it alteration finds. The words of Shakespeare's sonnet came unbidden into my mind. In this case nothing about Marcus had changed, I realized. He'd always been a man of principles, a man of his word. He hadn't changed and how I felt about him wasn't changing, either.

I took a deep breath and exhaled slowly. "Okay."

"Really?" he asked.

"I think this is a bad idea, but for now I'm not going to push."

"It doesn't have anything to do with Dani getting killed. I swear," Marcus said, giving my hand a squeeze before letting it go.

"I hope you're right," I said.

Out of the corner of my eye I saw the door to the

café open. I didn't recognize the man who walked in but I knew he was a police officer. It was clear in the way he stood, in the way he surveyed the room before walking over to us.

"Marcus," I said softly.

He turned and his face hardened.

The man stopped at our table. "Hello, Marcus," he said.

Marcus gave him a tight smile. "Bryan," he said with a nod.

This had to be the detective from Red Wing, Bryan Foster. He was about average height, a couple of inches shorter than Marcus. He had smooth brown skin and dark hair clipped close to his head.

"We need to talk," the detective said. "I need you to come to the station."

Marcus shifted in his seat, propping one arm on the back of the chair. "Sure," he said. "We just ordered. I can be there in"—he looked down at his watch—"about an hour."

The other detective shook his head. "I'm afraid it can't wait that long."

"Like I said, I can be there in about an hour." Marcus raised his voice slightly. I'd seen the challenge in his blue eyes before.

"I don't want to make this embarrassing for either one of us," Detective Foster said, keeping his voice low. "Don't put me in that position."

Marcus pushed back his chair and stood up. I could feel the anger coming off him.

At the other end of the room Eric came around the counter.

"C'mon, man," Foster said softly. "Just come with me." His eyes flicked in my direction for a moment. Behind us the door to the café opened again and I caught a glimpse of a white-haired man.

"I'm sorry about dinner, Kathleen," Marcus said. His eyes never left the other man's face.

"It's all right," I said, my voice suddenly hoarse. "Go."

"My client isn't going anywhere," a voice said. It belonged to the white-haired man who had just walked in. The color drained from Marcus's face. "Don't say a word," the man told him.

"And who might you be?" Detective Foster asked.

The smile he got was a mix of arrogance and condescension. "Elliot Gordon, attorney at law. What do you want with my son?"

8

"Kathleen, meet my father," Marcus said.

"Is my son under arrest?" Elliot Gordon asked the detective as though Marcus hadn't spoken. He either didn't see or ignored the hand I held out.

"I just need to ask him a few questions," Foster said. He stood with his hands in the pockets of his jacket, feet apart, and though he was a bit shorter in stature than Marcus and his father, his solid frame seemed to command more of the space.

"I'm fine," Marcus said. His face gave nothing away but one of his hands was clenched tightly into a fist. "This is just routine."

Elliot Gordon continued to keep his eyes fixed on the Red Wing detective, who met his gaze with what seemed to me to be just a touch of amusement. This staring thing seemed to be a Gordon family trait. "Doesn't matter. You still need a lawyer."

"Then I'll get a lawyer," Marcus said. He pulled out his cell phone and punched in a number. "Brady, it's Marcus," he said. "Can you meet me at the police station?" He listened for a moment. "Now." Then, "Thanks," and ended the call. He looked at Detective Foster and shrugged. "Let's go."

The detective turned to me. "I'm sorry for disrupting your dinner," he said. He inclined his head in Elliot Gordon's direction. "Mr. Gordon."

Marcus stretched out his hand and caught mine. "It's okay, Kathleen," he said. "I'll call you later."

I nodded. "Okay."

They started for the door. "Go home," I heard Marcus say softly to his father, the words tight and clipped as he moved past the older man.

If the words hurt, and I didn't see how they couldn't have, nothing in Elliot Gordon's expression gave it away. Detective Foster and Marcus headed for the door and as soon as they stepped outside Elliot Gordon followed. I was left standing by our table alone.

Eric walked over and put a hand on my shoulder. "You all right, Kathleen?" he asked.

"I'm okay," I said, nodding slowly. I turned my head to look at him. He looked skeptical. "No, I am. Really. And I'm sorry all of this happened here." I gestured with one hand.

"It's none of my business, but Marcus isn't under arrest, is he?" Eric glanced back at the counter. "I know the woman who was killed at Long Lake was a friend of his."

Eric had had a couple of run-ins with the police in his younger days, back before he stopped drinking.

He would have realized that Bryan Foster was a police officer

"No," I said, not feeling one hundred percent certain I was right. "Just questions."

"Try not to worry about it," he said. "No one who knows Marcus is going to believe he killed anyone."

"Thanks," I said. I wasn't exactly sure what to do next. I looked over at our table.

"Want me to get your food and box it up for you?" Eric asked.

My appetite had disappeared. "No thanks. Just give me the bill."

He gave me a small smile and shook his head. "It's on me."

"No, Eric, you can't," I said.

The smile got a little bigger. "Yeah, I can," he said cocking one eyebrow at me. "I own the place."

I made myself smile back at him. "Thank you."

He glanced over at the counter again and held up one finger to Nic, who nodded. Then he turned back to me. "If you need anything you call, got it?"

"I got it," I said. I grabbed my jacket and purse and headed out to the truck.

I didn't know what to do next. I tried Hope but all I got was her voice mail. Clearly her "friend" hadn't told her what he planned to do, otherwise Hope would have warned Marcus.

And what was Marcus's father doing in town? I knew Marcus would never have called him. The two of them had a strained relationship. Marcus didn't have a single photo of his father in his house, which is why I hadn't realized who Elliot Gordon was when he walked into the café.

More questions without any answers.

There was no sign of Owen or Hercules when I got home. "Hello," I called. After a minute I heard an answering meow. Owen. I put a mug of milk in the microwave and a piece of bread in the toaster. I knew the sound of the toaster would bring him.

"Mrr?" he said, crossing the floor to me. I stretched one arm behind my head. "Long story," I said. I bent down and picked him up.

He leaned in close to my face and peered at me. The microwave beeped then. "Give me a second," I said, scratching the top of his head and then setting him down on one of the kitchen chairs. Once I had a cup of hot chocolate and some toast with lots of peanut butter I scooped up Owen, sat down and settled him on my lap.

He looked pointedly at my plate. "Fine," I said, breaking off a tiny bite for him, because I really was trying to heed Roma's admonition about not feeding either cat people food.

I told Owen what had happened at Eric's Place while we ate. Then I filled him in on my visit with Oren. "I have no idea what to do next."

There was a knock at the back door. Owen leaned sideways, looking toward the porch, then looked pointedly at me. "Yes, I suppose I could go answer the door," I said.

I set him on the chair again and headed for the porch. Hope was standing on my back steps. "I got your message," she said. "What's up?"

"Detective Foster came into Eric's and took Marcus down to the station for questioning."

She closed her eyes for a moment and swore softly. "I'm sorry, Kathleen," she said. "I didn't know."

"It's not your fault," I said. I gestured at the kitchen door. "Come in."

"I can't," she said. "Remember I told you Marcus said he went for a walk during that hour he can't account for?"

I nodded.

"He said he was down on the waterfront. Thorsten says a couple of those old warehouses have security cameras. I'm hoping to find some footage that'll show Marcus was where he says he was."

I told her what Oren had told me about his cousin. "Did Oren say where the guy went the last time he took off to Florida?" Hope asked.

"Clearwater Beach."

"I'll see if I can get the local police to keep an eye out for his van."

"You're supposed to be off the case."

She shrugged. "I'm supposed to make my bed every morning and not drink so much coffee and neither one of those things is going to happen, either." There was something defiant about the way she stood there, hands jammed in her pockets, shoulders squared.

"Just don't put your own career in jeopardy, please," I said.

"Don't worry about me, Kathleen," she said.

But I was worried about her.

Hope jingled her car keys in her pocket. "So I'm guessing you didn't find out what Marcus has been holding back, then?"

I shook my head. "I didn't."

"I can't believe Foz did this," she said. "You're certain he said it was just questioning? He didn't arrest Marcus?"

"I'm positive. And Marcus has a lawyer with him. Brady Chapman."

"Brady?" she shot back. "Why not his own father?"

"Wait a minute," I said. "You knew Elliot Gordon was in town?"

She nodded. "I knew he was coming."

I think my mouth fell open just a little in surprise. "Marcus didn't know. How did you know?"

She looked at me like I was dense as a block of wood. "I called him."

I bit the end of my tongue so I wouldn't say anything that later I'd wish I had kept to myself.

"You disapprove," Hope said.

Everything I knew about Elliot Gordon came from Marcus. He'd been a mostly absent father, building his career as a criminal defense attorney while Marcus and his sister, Hannah, were growing up, and when he was present, he'd set impossibly high standards for his only son. "I think getting in touch with his father was Marcus's call," I said, taking a deep breath and exhaling slowly.

"He never would have done it, Kathleen. I had to. Desperate times call for desperate measures."

She didn't see that she'd crossed a line. All of a sudden I wasn't so sure this partnership was a good idea.

Hope must have had her phone on vibrate because she suddenly pulled it out of her pocket and looked at the screen. "I have to go," she said. "If anything else happens, call me." She didn't wait for my answer.

I turned around to find Owen standing in the doorway. "You heard," I said. I wasn't even going to pretend that I was thinking out loud. There was no one around.

Owen narrowed his golden eyes.

"She shouldn't have called his father," I said. Owen followed me back into the kitchen. When I sat down he jumped onto my lap. "This was a mistake. I shouldn't have agreed to try to work with her. And I shouldn't have been doing it behind Marcus's back."

Owen wrinkled his nose at me. "Just because he didn't ask me directly what I was doing doesn't mean it was okay."

He seemed to think about what I'd just said as though it was a new concept to him. Or he was waiting for me to stop talking and make another piece of toast. I decided making the toast was a better use of time.

We'd finished eating and Owen was sitting at my feet, methodically washing his face, when there was another knock at the back door. "Mrrr," he said without missing a pass with his paw.

"I heard," I said. I headed out to the porch with a

general feeling of trepidation. I didn't want to deal with Hope again tonight. But it wasn't Hope standing on the steps. It was Elliot Gordon.

"Hello, Ms. Paulson," he said. He was as tall as his son with the same broad shoulders. He had the same wavy hair as Marcus, shorter and combed back from his face.

"Hello, Mr. Gordon," I said, wondering why he was at my door. At my feet Owen leaned his head against my leg.

"I'd like to talk to you," he said. "May I come in?"

I hesitated; what little I knew about the man didn't really make me inclined to like him. On the other hand, even Marcus said his dad was an excellent lawyer. I opened the door a little wider. "Come in, Mr. Gordon," I said. I led the way into the kitchen.

Elliot Gordon looked around, making no attempt to hide his curiosity. "Everett Henderson used to own this house."

"He still does." I leaned against the counter and folded my arms across my chest. "Why are you here?" I asked. "I don't think you came here to talk about real estate, but I could be wrong."

"Merow," Owen commented loudly to emphasize the point.

Hercules had come from wherever he'd been all this time. Flanked by him on one side and Owen on the other, I felt a little like Batgirl with Batman and Robin as my sidekicks—after all, Barbara Gordon had a degree in library science.

Marcus's father laughed. "I like you," he said. His

hands were in the pockets of what looked to be a very expensive coat—gray wool and cashmere I was guessing. His feet were slightly apart and the look in his eyes—which were dark brown, not blue like Marcus's—reminded me so much of Marcus it made my chest hurt. His expression grew serious. "My son is a suspect in a murder. I don't intend to let him be arrested."

"Neither do I," I said.

"So you're willing to help me." He didn't phrase the words in the form of a question.

I shook my head. "No, but I'm willing to let you help me." I waited. I could hear my heart going thump, thump, thump in my ears.

"There isn't any point in arguing with you, is there?" he said, and I saw a hint of a smile pull at the corners of his mouth.

"No," I said. "But if you want to, I'll listen."

He laughed again. "Fine," he said. "I'll help *you*."

I didn't think for a moment that he intended to "help" me. I knew when I'd been played, but that was okay. If that's what it took to get Marcus out of this mess it was *more* than okay.

I made coffee and we sat at the table. Elliot took off his coat. Underneath he was wearing a charcoal gray suit with a crisp white shirt and a gray-and-blue-striped tie loose at the neck.

"How much did my son tell you about me?" he asked.

"I know you're a lawyer. I know you wanted him to go to law school." I also knew it was more than "wanting" Marcus to go to law school. Elliot had planned for the two of them to practice law together. He'd been furious when Marcus decided to become a police officer, calling it a waste of his son's brain. He'd refused to attend his son's college graduation.

Owen and Hercules had moved to sit on either side of my chair, still in sidekick mode. Hercules seemed to be following the conversation intently; Owen looked a bit bored. He'd yawned twice.

Elliot leaned down and held out his hand to the little tabby. I shook my head. "You can't pet him," I said. "He used to be feral. He doesn't like to be touched by strangers."

"He seems friendly," Elliot said.

"He is friendly," I said. "Just don't touch him."

I looked down at Owen, who seemed intrigued by the watch Elliot was wearing. "Owen," I warned.

The cat looked up at me with his best innocent expression fixed on his face.

My cell phone buzzed then. It was Marcus. The knot that had been in my stomach since the restaurant loosened. "Excuse me," I said to Elliot. I got up and walked into the living room.

"Hi," I said. "Are you okay?"

"I'm fine," Marcus said. "I'm sorry everything took so long."

"So they didn't . . . keep you?"

"No, they didn't arrest me. I'm fine. I promise."

I leaned against the door frame because my legs suddenly felt wobbly. "Is Brady with you?" I asked. I could hear what sounded like traffic in the background.

"Yeah," Marcus said. "He's coming out to the house. I need to fill him in on the background to all of this, but I can stop in if you want me to."

I did want him to, but I didn't think it was a good time for a confrontation with his father. From the kitchen I heard Owen give a yowl of aggravation. "Talk to Brady," I said. "I'm fine. I'll see you tomorrow."

"All right." He hesitated. "I, uh, have to track my father down. I don't think there's actually much chance he left."

"That can wait until tomorrow as well," I said. I was uncomfortably aware that now I was the one keeping a secret.

I heard him blow out a breath. "You're right. I'll see you in the morning."

"Love you," I said. "Good night."

I looked down to see Hercules standing in the doorway. One ear was turned to the side, making him look a little apprehensive, which I was pretty sure he was. "It's okay," I said.

I walked back into the kitchen, wet a clean dishtowel under the tap and handed it to Elliot without saying a word. Owen was sitting next to the refrigerator, his tail whipping across the floor, a sure sign that he was irritated. I leaned down and smoothed the fur on the top of his head. "It's okay," I said, keeping my voice low. "I think you left a chicken under the sofa. Why don't you go get it?"

He glared at me, making grumbling noises, but he headed for the living room.

I went back to the sink, washed my hands and got

my first-aid kit from the cupboard. It was actually a Christmas cookie tin that I'd repurposed. I set it on the table.

Elliot had wrapped the dishtowel around his hand.

"Let me take a look," I said.

Owen had left two long scratches on the back of Elliot's left hand. They didn't look too deep. The cat was capable of doing a lot worse. He *had* done a lot worse.

"Are you going to give me a cookie to make me feel better?" Elliot asked.

I didn't say anything. I took the top off the cookie tin and got out a gauze pad and a bottle of peroxide. I cleaned the scratches, put on a bit of antibiotic ointment and a square adhesive bandage.

"Aren't you going to say 'I told you so'?" Elliot said as I washed my hands again.

"I thought that was self-evident."

He laughed. "You're not what I expected."

I took my seat again. "Is that a compliment?" I asked.

He thought for a moment. "Yes."

I smiled. "Thank you."

Elliot gestured at my phone. "That was Marcus."

I nodded. "Yes, it was."

"They finished questioning him."

"He's on his way home."

"He's not coming here?" He raised one eyebrow.

My cup was cold. I got up and stuck it in the microwave. "No. I wanted to talk to you without him here."

"He doesn't want my help."

As I turned back to the table I caught a glimpse of what looked like sadness on his face, what seemed to be the first real emotion I'd seen from the man. "No, he doesn't," I said. "But I do, as long as you're sincere about wanting to help. Don't try to use me to work out what's wrong between you and Marcus. The only side I'm on is his."

"Then we're on the same side," Elliot said.

I hoped that was true. "I know you're here because Hope called you."

"I was coming anyway." His closed hand tapped restlessly on the table.

So he was keeping track of Marcus. I let that go, sat down again and pulled one leg up underneath me. "So how much do you know?" I asked.

"Assume I know nothing," he said. "Tell me everything."

So I did, leaving out the scene with Travis at Eric's. That part of the story wasn't mine to tell and it had nothing to do with Dani's death. Travis had been at a meeting when she was killed.

"The only two people in town who have those same medallions on their key chains are John Keller and Travis Rosen, and they can both account for their time," Elliot said, his mouth pulled into a frown.

I pushed my hair back from my face. "The only one that's missing is Marcus's."

Elliot shook his head as if that didn't matter. "We'll need to find out how many of those key chains were given away in the first place."

"Twenty-one thousand, five hundred," I said.

He narrowed his eyes at me. "How do you know that?"

"I did some research."

"We need to find that squatter," Elliot said. He tapped on the table again.

"Hope was going to see if she could get the police in the Clearwater area to keep an eye out for his van."

"I have some contacts in the state patrol," he said as though I hadn't spoken. That was twice he'd done that, ignored what was said when it didn't fit with what he'd already decided.

"You mean here," I said.

He nodded. "Yes. We don't have any proof that man— What's his name?"

"Ira Kenyon."

"We don't have any proof he's in Florida. We don't even know he left the state at all."

"You're right," I said. "I never thought of that." Hercules came in then from wherever he'd been since the "incident" between Owen and Marcus's father. He jumped up onto my lap, settled himself and then turned to look at Elliot.

"And what about the developer?" Elliot asked.

"He was at a meeting."

"What kind of a meeting?"

Hercules turned to look at me for a moment. I shook my head. "I don't know. Some kind of business meeting." Hope had told me in one of our phone conversations, but I'd forgotten.

Elliot made a sound that was part exhalation, part

annoyance. "How many people were there? There's a big difference between a meeting with two people and one with two hundred."

"Because the more people the greater possibility he wasn't where he said he was."

Elliot nodded. "Exactly."

I could call Lita and see what she knew. "I can find out about the meeting," I said.

"Are John and Travis still here?" Elliot asked.

"For the most part," I said. "They're back and forth between here and Red Wing."

"Good," he said, nodding.

"Not if you're planning on talking to them about Dani's death. They aren't going to tell you anything."

He seemed amused by what I'd said. "Why do you say that?"

"Because I wouldn't talk to you."

Hercules's green eyes darted between the two of us. He seemed to be enjoying the conversation.

"You're talking to me right now."

"And you're not trying to figure out if I might have killed Dani." I raised an eyebrow in classic Mr. Spock style. (No offense to Zachary Quinto, who had some pretty great eyebrows of his own, but I was an old-school *Star Trek* girl.) "For the record, I was at the library, there were more than two people there, but fewer than two hundred."

"You think you should talk to the boys, then?"

I nodded and Hercules gave a soft meow of agreement. "At least let me talk to them first." I stressed the last word.

"Fine," he said.

I wasn't sure that I hadn't just been played again.

Elliot got to his feet and reached for his coat. "I don't suppose there's any possibility you and Marcus would have breakfast with me?" he said.

I set Hercules on the floor and stood up as well. "It's not a good idea. Not now."

"I'm not going anywhere," he said, shrugging into his coat. "I love my son, Ms. Paulson. Despite our differences—and there have been a lot of them over the years—I love him."

"So do I," I said quietly.

He nodded. "Then we have a great deal in common." He said good night and left.

9

Marcus called at five to seven the next morning. I was standing at the counter waiting for the coffeemaker. "Are you up?" he said.

"Yes," I teased. "I had to get up. The phone was ringing."

"Did I wake you?" he said. "I'm sorry."

I laughed. "I'm kidding. I was up. I'm just waiting for the coffee. Owen decided we should all be up at six thirty."

The cat lifted his head when he heard his name, flicked his tail in my direction and then went back to his food.

"Since you made coffee, how about I come and make us breakfast?"

"I'd like that," I said, smiling into the phone even though he couldn't see me.

"See you shortly," he said.

I was wearing an old T-shirt and leggings and my hair was half up, half falling out of a messy bun. I had time to change before Marcus arrived.

Then I heard a knock on the back door. "If that's Elliot, you can deal with him," I told Owen, who murped what sounded like agreement and kept on eating.

It wasn't Elliot, though; it was Marcus. He pulled me into a one-armed hug.

"How did you get here so fast?" I said.

He grinned. "I was already in the driveway."

I tugged at my T-shirt. "I was going to put on something a little less covered in cat hair," I said, brushing a clump of Owen's fur from my knee.

"I like covered in cat hair," Marcus said, pulling me in for a kiss.

A meow came from the kitchen. Marcus laughed. "Hey, Owen," he called.

There was another meow in answer.

Marcus followed me inside.

"What's in the bag?" I asked, pointing to the canvas grocery bag he was carrying. He shot a quick look over in the cats' direction.

"B. A. C. O. N."

Hercules glanced in his brother's direction, stretched and then ambled over to sit in front of Marcus.

"Don't tell me he can spell," Marcus said.

"Apparently he can," I said. "He hasn't mastered subtlety, just five-letter words that pertain to food. And keep in mind that Owen has a nose like a wolf."

Right on cue the little tabby lifted his head. His nose twitched and he turned and made a bee-line for Marcus, pawing the tote he'd just set on the floor.

"Hey!" I said sharply. "Don't do that."

Owen ignored me completely. He raised a paw and tried to reach into the top of the bag.

"Don't do that, either," I snapped. I picked the bag up and set it on the counter.

"Later," Marcus whispered to them. He looked at me. "Got any tomatoes?"

"There's a couple in the fridge."

"How about a breakfast sandwich?"

"Sounds good," I said. After a moment there were two agreeing murps from the floor.

"Sit," he told me, making a shooing motion with one hand. Both cats immediately sat on the kitchen floor and then glared at me as if I was somehow ruining it for everyone by not sitting down right away too.

"I'm just going to get myself a cup of coffee," I said.

Marcus gestured at the chairs. "Sit," he repeated. "I'll get it."

So I sat, watching him get a cup of coffee for me and one for himself. The cats watched the bag with the bacon. "I have to tell you something," I said. "I talked to you father last night."

"Did he plead his case for why he thought he should be my lawyer and not Brady?"

He thought I meant at the restaurant.

"Here," I said.

Marcus was holding an egg and the shell smashed in his fingers. He dropped it in the sink and ran water over his hand. "You let him in?"

I nodded.

"Why?"

"Because I wanted to talk to him. I think he can help."

I watched Marcus take one deep breath and then another before he spoke. "I don't want his help."

I suddenly didn't know what to do with my hands. I pushed at my messy bun with one hand and it went sideways. I pulled out the bobby pins and elastic and shook my hair loose. It gave me time to get my feelings under control a little more.

"I know you don't want his help. And I wouldn't ask you to take it. But I *do* want it."

"Kathleen, you don't know what he's like," Marcus said, frown lines carving deeper into his face.

"He's charming, manipulative, and has no scruples about saying what he thinks you want to hear just so he can do what he was planning on doing all along. And he always thinks he's the smartest person in the room, which he may very well be some of the time, but not all of the time."

Marcus shook his head. "Okay, so you do know my father. What did he want?"

I leaned my elbow on the table and propped my head on my hand. "He wants to help you."

"On his terms." Marcus turned back to the counter and reached for another egg.

I nodded. "Yes, on his terms. Doesn't mean I agreed to that."

He glanced at the cookie tin/first-aid kit that I hadn't put back in the cupboard and then looked at me. "Did you hurt yourself?"

"Merow!" Owen said.

I sighed. "Your father tried to pet Owen. I told him not to."

"He doesn't listen well. Is he all right?"

"He's fine," I said. "It was just the back of his hand. I cleaned it up and put on a small bandage."

Marcus cracked an egg into my red mixing bowl. "Thank you," he said. "But I meant Owen."

At the sound of his name Owen meowed loudly again just in case we were, say, deciding who was getting bacon and who wasn't.

I smiled and shook my head. "No, you don't," I said.

Marcus grabbed a fork and began beating the eggs. "No, I don't," he repeated. "But it's just typical of the things he does."

"He loves you." I shifted in the chair, pulling up both legs so I could lean my chin on my knees.

"I do know that," he said. "And I love him. I just don't always like him."

"So I'll be careful. I'll try not to be charmed or conned by your dad. Can you live with that?"

He sighed and then nodded. "I can live with that."

I smiled. "So maybe you can stop beating the heck out of those eggs."

Marcus finished our breakfast sandwiches—scrambled eggs, cheese, bacon and fried tomatoes. I was glad I hadn't changed after all when a bit of egg fell out of my sandwich, bounced off my T-shirt and landed on the floor.

Hercules immediately put his paw on top—not that Owen was going to go after a bit of egg when he could be eating the extra bit of bacon Marcus had slipped him and I'd pretended I hadn't seen. I had warned Elliot not to try to pet the cat, but that didn't mean I thought it was okay that Owen had gone all Wolverine on the man.

Herc looked up at me with a slightly pained expression on his furry face. The egg had been sandwiched next to the fried tomatoes, which meant he now had tomato on the bottom of his foot.

I lifted my napkin off my lap. "Hold up your foot," I said to him, gesturing with my free hand. He dutifully held up his paw, but not the one that was still firmly on top of that bit of egg, because who knew what one's brother might do if it was uncovered.

"The other foot," I said, nudging it with one finger.

"Merow," he said and his green eyes darted in Owen's direction.

"No, he won't." I leaned forward and put my left hand, on its edge, next to the bite of egg, which had to be pretty soggy by now. Hercules hesitated, then lifted the paw and I managed to wipe it with the napkin in my other hand. He turned it over, licked it a couple of times for good measure and then dropped his head to finally eat the scrap of scrambled egg.

I tried to sit up again but my center of gravity was off. I flailed one arm in the air and then I felt Marcus's hands on my shoulders pulling me upright.

"Thank you," I said, kissing his mouth and only getting about half of it because I was still slightly off balance.

"You're welcome," he said. He got up for the coffeepot.

"You haven't said what happened last night," I said, reaching for my sandwich.

Marcus shrugged. "It was just more of the same, the same questions I've answered three times now. What kind of a relationship did Dani and I have? Did we stay in touch? What did we talk about the day she died? What did we argue about?" He pulled his hand back through his hair. "I've done the same thing myself but only when I had a viable suspect—which I'm not in this case."

"What did Brady say?"

"He thinks it was a fishing expedition. Right now all they have is what looks to be part of my key chain under her body and a so-called gap in my alibi." He set down his fork. "There have to be thousands of those key chains out there."

"Twenty-one thousand, five hundred," I said around a mouthful of bacon, egg and tomato-soaked toast.

He laughed. "I should have known you'd know that."

I reached for my coffee. "Would it bother you if I went to talk to Travis and John? They spent more time with Dani in the last few weeks than anyone else. They might know if she'd had any problems with anyone."

His smile faded and his expression became more guarded. "I'm not sure either one of them will talk to you. Maybe John, but not Travis for sure."

"But I thought things were better between you two."

"They were for a while, but as far as Travis is concerned things were good until Dani and I reconnected. He said he knew I didn't have anything to do with her death but he just couldn't stand the sight of my face."

I got up and put my arms around his neck. "I'm so sorry. He's just saying those things because he's hurt." I kissed him and sat back down again. "I keep meaning to ask you: How long did your dad live here when he was a kid?"

"He was about twelve when his family moved here and they were still living here when he left for college at seventeen. I don't think my grandparents moved until the year after that."

I took another bite of my sandwich. I could feel two sets of kitty eyes watching my every move even though Marcus had already given both of them a tiny bit of bacon. "He never came back here to live after that?"

Reaching for his coffee, Marcus shook his head. "No. We came here in the summer for a lot of years when I was a kid. If you go past the marina and stay on Main Street there are half a dozen little houses near the water."

"I know where you mean."

"You could rent those in the summertime back then. That's where we'd stay. Always in the very last one." He smiled at the memory. "There were two little bedrooms under the eaves with a shared closet between them. Hannah and I would open our closet doors and we could lie in bed and talk to each other."

He got up for more coffee, refilling my cup before he topped up his own. "We'd come for three weeks. My father would take the middle week off but at some point he'd have to go back to the office, maybe for the day, maybe for the rest of the week. It never changed."

I ate the last bite of my sandwich and then pulled up both feet so I could rest my chin on my knees. "Did you ever actually consider going to law school?"

His mouth twisted to one side for a moment. "Yes," he said.

"So what happened?"

"I told you that he wanted me to go to law school and go into practice with him and I didn't want to."

I nodded.

"I didn't tell you why."

I reached for my coffee. "So tell me now," I said.

"I took Business Ethics and Leadership in my third year. The professor had started offering these workshops on financial literacy for student athletes—on his own time, for nothing; he wasn't making a cent. I volunteered to help, and before you tell me what a great guy that makes me, I got extra credit for it."

"Okay."

Again Marcus smiled at something he'd remembered. "A prosecutor from the district attorney's office came and talked about get-rich-quick investments that people who suddenly have a lot of money can get caught up in. After, we went out for a beer. I talked to the guy for two hours about what he did."

I smiled across the table at him. "You were hooked."

Marcus nodded. "I was twenty-one. Putting the bad guys behind bars seemed like a pretty great way to make a living."

"You dad didn't agree."

"No, he didn't." He turned his mug in slow circles on the table. "He told me I could work in the prosecutor's office for a year. I could make connections that would help when I joined him. I didn't want to make connections. I wanted to make the world a better place and, yes, I know how idealistic that sounds."

"Idealism isn't bad," I said.

Marcus gave me a wry smile. "Tell that to my father. I knew if I went into law I'd always be Elliot Gordon's son—never my own man. So I decided to be a police officer. He took it as a personal slight. The Christmas after I graduated from the police academy he gave me a study kit for the LSATs. He said I was wasting my potential."

I shook my head. "I'm sorry," I said softly.

"You know what's funny?" He leaned down to give each cat a couple of fish-shaped treats that he must have palmed when he got up for more coffee.

"What?"

"In a way I owe my father. If he hadn't reacted the way he did over me wanting to work in the DA's office I probably never would have become a police officer, and I think I'm better at that than I would have been as a lawyer."

I smiled. "I think you would have been a good lawyer. I think you would have been good at anything you set your mind to."

"And you're not biased," he teased.

"I'm not," I said with mock seriousness. "I'm just looking at the facts the way any good reference librarian would."

Marcus laughed.

"You know what else is funny?" I asked. "The fact that you didn't even try to hide what you were doing." I tipped my head in the direction of the boys, who were both happily eating.

"A little treat isn't going to hurt them." Owen lifted his head, looked at me and gave a sharp meow as if to say, "What he said."

"No, but Roma might if she finds out how often you give them a little treat. She swings a mean broom."

Marcus shook his head at me. "I want a rematch. I still say Roma cheated."

He was referring to a broom hockey match to

benefit the animal shelter that both he and Roma had played in during last year's Winterfest. Marcus had captained one team and Brady Chapman the other. Roma—who was on Brady's team—had swept in the winning goal and managed to trip Marcus with the other end of her broom in the last seconds of the game.

"Roma did not cheat," I said, getting up to take my dishes to the sink. "Your legs are too long for broom hockey."

He reached out and snagged me with one arm, pulling me down onto his lap. "My legs are too long?" he said. "Really? And what else is wrong with me?"

I frowned and pretended to think about it. "Your shoulders are too broad," I said, putting both hands on them. "Your hair is too thick." I reached up with one hand and pulled my fingers through his dark waves. "And your lips are too kissy."

He leaned in and kissed me. "Umm, I can see that you're suffering," he said.

A loud meow came from the floor at our feet. "You don't need any more treats," I said.

Owen—because it had been him voicing his opinion—meowed again. "Let me rephrase. You're not *getting* any more treats." I kissed Marcus one more time. "You neither. I need to get ready for work." I stood up and set my dishes on the counter. "Are you going to help Eddie this morning?" I asked.

Marcus got to his feet as well. "I'm going to go see my father. Maybe I can convince him to go home."

"Maybe," I said. I didn't think it was likely. "In his defense I think he really does want to help."

Marcus pulled a hand back through his hair. "He can't seem to understand that I don't always want that help. It's hard to get out of the man's shadow, because he casts such a big one."

10

About five minutes after Marcus left Abigail called. "I found a great glow-in-the-dark skeleton I thought we could hang in the gazebo for Spookarama. Do you want me to bring it with me?"

"Please," I said. We talked for a minute about how we were going to handle handing out treats during the Halloween party and then I said good-bye and headed upstairs to change.

The first thing I did when I got to the library was call Lita. I had no idea what time she got to work, but no matter how early I called the office she was always in.

"Good morning, Kathleen," she said. "I'm glad you called. I heard Marcus was invited to the police station to answer some questions. How is he?"

"He's fine," I said. "But, uh, that's why I called." I paused and took a deep breath. "I need a favor and it's for him in a way."

"Everett instructed me over a week ago to make sure anything Marcus needs he gets, which I would have done anyway." I could feel her smile coming through the phone. "Tell me what I can do."

"Ernie Kingsley was at a meeting the day Danielle McAllister was killed. I need to know everything about it. How many people were there? Could Ernie have gotten there late? Did he leave early? Who saw him?"

"In other words you want to know how much of an alibi his alibi really is?"

I turned slowly from side to side in my chair. "I'm not saying he killed her, not deliberately. I just want to be one hundred percent certain he's not involved."

"Give me a couple of hours," Lita said. "I'll call you back. I know Ernie's assistant, Nora. He's here today to give his pitch to the business coalition, so she'll have a minute to talk."

I hung up and leaned back in the chair. There was a squeak somewhere in the back mechanism. I sat for a minute, making it squeak like the floor in a horror-movie haunted house while I organized my thoughts.

Whatever Marcus said to his father—which he was probably saying right now—I didn't think the elder Gordon was going to leave town. But I wasn't sure if I could trust him, or if I should. I was already having reservations about Hope. I needed to know more about Elliot Gordon, at least as a lawyer if not a person. I knew I couldn't call Marcus's sister, Hannah. He didn't want her to know what had happened, not yet.

I wondered if Brady knew anything about Elliot.

I'd noticed that the older man had seemed to recognize the younger's name when Marcus had called him at the restaurant. I'd already asked for one favor. Maybe I'd get lucky with a second.

The phone rang several times before Maggie answered. "Hi, Mags," I said.

"Hi," she said. "Are you at home or the library?"

"Library."

"Good. How about coming for pizza tonight? I feel like cooking."

Marcus and I hadn't made any plans because normally I was at tai chi on Thursday night, but class had been canceled again because now Oren was painting the stairwell up to the studio. As far as I knew Marcus would be at Eddie's.

"I'd like that," I said, shifting my weight sideways in the chair so the squeak would stop. "Any chance Brady will be there?"

"Do you want him to be there?" she asked. Her voice sounded a little hollow.

"What are you doing?" I asked. "Your voice sounds odd."

"Downward Dog. So what about Brady?"

"Marcus's father showed up last night. I just wondered . . . I just wondered if Brady knows anything about him, what he's like as an attorney."

"Somehow I think he does," Maggie said. "I'll ask him if he can join us."

"Thanks," I said. "Is there anything you want me to bring?"

"Just yourself."

* * *

Lita called me back about eleven thirty. "Phone, Kathleen," Susan said, holding up two fingers.

I nodded to show I'd heard her and pointed over my head as I headed for the stairs so she'd know I'd take the call in my office.

"I'm sorry this took so long," Lita said. "I had to wait for one person to call me back."

"I'm impressed you managed to find out anything this fast," I said, sitting on a corner of my desk.

"Well what I found out was that there were fifty-two people at that meeting in Red Wing. It was at the Anderson Center. They didn't finish until after eight thirty. I talked to five different people. They all saw Ernie."

So Kingsley couldn't have had anything to do with Dani's death. According to Hope the medical examiner estimated she'd been killed between five and eight.

"Thanks, Lita," I said. "It was a long shot anyway."

"I wasn't finished," she said.

The hairs rose on the back of my neck. "Okay," I said slowly.

"Every one of those five people remember seeing Ernie because he was late getting to the meeting. He seemed a little jumpy and disheveled."

"Did anyone happen to notice what time he walked in?"

"Yes, as a matter of fact two different people did. It

was ten after six," Lita said, a self-satisfied edge to her voice. "Does that help?"

Ten after six. Given the approximate distance from the lake to Red Wing, even if he'd stuck to back roads, Ernie Kingsley would have had enough time to kill Dani and make his meeting at just about the time he walked in.

My heart started to race. "Yes, it does," I said. "Thank you so much."

"Any time," Lita said. I could tell from her voice that she was smiling on the other end of the phone. "If you need anything else, anything—"

"I'll call you," I finished.

I hung up the phone. So now what? I couldn't just walk up to the developer and ask him if he killed Dani. What had Lita said earlier? *"He's here today to give his pitch to the business coalition."* I leaned back and pulled a stack of papers on the side of my desk a little closer. What I was looking for was a press release from the town. It was third in the pile, an invitation to a presentation by developer Ernie Kingsley on the proposed Long Lake development. The pitch was aimed at the downtown business community. All stakeholders were urged to attend. When she'd read the word "stakeholders" Ruby had threatened to show up in a black cape with a hawthorn stake and a garlic necklace.

It occurred to me that maybe I could show up as well in my role as head librarian. I could talk to Kingsley and at least see how he responded when I brought up Dani's death. I decided not to call Hope or Elliot. I didn't want the developer to know what I suspected and I didn't think either one of them could be subtle.

I went back downstairs to talk to Susan. "Do you mind if I take the early lunch?" I asked. "I thought I'd head over to the presentation about the development. If it really is going to bring more money to town I'd like to get a little of it for the library."

"Sounds good to me," Susan said.

I found a parking spot on the street just one block up from the community center. Thorsten was at the door.

"Hi, Kathleen," he said. "You here for the dog and pony show?"

I smiled. "I've heard a lot of rumors. I thought it would be a good idea to get the facts."

He gave a snort of derision. "Don't think you're in the right place for that."

I walked around smiling and saying hello while I looked for Ernie Kingsley. There were a lot more people in the small room than I'd expected and it was hard to see over everyone's heads. I stood just to the side of the door to the hallway and looked around. I caught sight of Ruby near the middle of the room, no cape, stake or fragrant necklace in sight. And then I caught a glimpse of Ernie Kingsley just coming in the door on the other side of the room. I took two steps in his direction and I was grabbed from behind. A dark-suited arm wrapped around me and pulled me into the hall.

I jammed my elbow back hard, making very satisfying contact with the person's diaphragm. He—I knew by the strength in the arm it was a man who had grabbed me—let go. I whirled around, mouth open to scream, and discovered Simon Janes half doubled over, trying to get his breath. "What did you do that for?" he managed to gasp out.

I stared at him wide-eyed and more than a little aggravated. "What did I do that for?" I gestured at the door with one hand. "What did you do *that* for?"

Simon straightened up. There was a fine sheen of sweat on his forehead. "What exactly were you going to do once you were face-to-face with Ernie?" he asked.

"None of your business," I retorted.

"I can pick you up and have you in the parking lot in less than a minute," Simon said, straightening one sleeve of his suit jacket.

I made a fist, folded my arm and held up my elbow. "I can hit a lot harder than I just did. And I can scream loud enough to be heard in the back row of the Stratton Theatre—from here."

"He won't tell you anything," Simon said flatly.

"I wasn't going to walk up to him and say, 'Hey, did you kill a woman out at Long Lake?'"

He almost smiled. "I didn't think you were that stupid. But if he gets even a hint of what you suspect he'll surround himself with a flank of lawyers and you'll lose your chance to find out whether Ernie was involved or not."

I felt something sour at the back of my throat. He was right. "I can't just do nothing, Simon," I said, making a helpless gesture at the door with one hand.

"Twenty-four hours."

I frowned. "What do you mean?"

"Give me twenty-four hours. If you'll wait that long I'll get you a meeting with him if you still want it."

"How do I know you won't just go warn him about what I suspect?"

"Oh c'mon, Kathleen." He held up both hands in exasperation. "I know you don't know me very well but I think you know me better than that."

I wanted to believe him. I wanted to trust him. "What do you mean by you'll get me a meeting if I 'still want it'?"

Nothing changed in his expression. "If by tomorrow at this time you still feel you need to talk to Kingsley I will make sure you get a meeting with him. You have my word."

I crossed my arms over my chest. "So I just trust you." I didn't bother trying not to sound skeptical.

He smiled then. Mia had exactly the same smile. "Yeah. You just trust me."

If I tried to go back into the meeting Simon was perfectly capable of causing a scene—and would. I had nothing to lose by waiting for a day. And something, some instinct I couldn't explain, told me I could trust Simon.

"All right," I said. "Twenty-four hours." I squinted at him. "And if you ever grab me like that again I won't hold anything back."

He grinned and one eyebrow went up. "I'll keep that in mind."

"C'mon in," Maggie called when I knocked on her apartment door that evening. I'd stopped at the house to change and had left two very disgruntled cats at home.

The aroma of sausage and oregano met me on the stairs. Maggie was at the stove. And Roma was sitting on the sofa.

"Hi," I said. She got to her feet and wrapped me in a hug. "I didn't know I was going to get to see you, too."

"I can't say no to Maggie's pizza," Roma said. "And I wanted to make sure that you were okay. I'm sorry I was gone when all this was going on."

"I'm all right," I said. "There wasn't anything you could have done and truthfully, some days I was glad to just spend some time with Lucy and the other cats."

"What about Marcus? Is he okay?" I could see the concern on her face.

"He is. In fact, he made breakfast for me."

Roma and Maggie exchanged a look and grinned. "Ooooo," they exclaimed like a couple of fourteen-year-olds.

"Don't start," I warned.

Roma immediately clasped her hands primly in

front of herself and tried not to look Maggie in the eye. Maggie pressed her lips together and attempted to be serious but it didn't exactly work. I could see the laughter in her green eyes.

It was so good to spend time with them. Somehow, just being in the same room with them made everything I'd been worried about seem a little less, well, worrisome.

"What can I do, Mags?" I asked. There was flour in her hair and on her hands and a dab of sauce on her chin. And as usual when she made pizza there wasn't a bare bit of counter space in the kitchen.

"Sit and talk to Roma," Maggie said, turning back to the cast-iron skillet on the stove.

"We can clean up later," Roma said, quietly settling onto one corner of the couch.

"I heard you." Maggie frowned down at the contents of the pan.

"We know." Roma smiled. It was good to see her smile. I knew how much she missed Eddie. I'd tried very hard to support her decision even though I wished she'd change her mind and say yes to his proposal, but after close to five months I was afraid that might never happen.

I sat next to her on the sofa. "How are you?" I asked. "I know Eddie's moved into his new place."

She nodded. "I told him to go back to Minneapolis, to go home." The way she felt about him was written in every line on her face, just the same way it was with him. "He said as long as I was here this was home."

"You haven't changed your mind." I didn't phrase it as a question because I already knew the answer.

Roma shook her head. "Nothing's changed." She moved to shift the pillow behind her. I noticed that once again she was wearing the antique rose gold locket Eddie had bought her. Maybe there was hope for the two of them after all.

"Syd's coming in a couple of weeks," Roma said. "She has three days off school and she's going to spend a night with me."

"I'm glad you still get to see her."

"That's her mom as much as it is Eddie." She gave me a half smile. "She's really trying to get us back together. Syd, I mean. She told me this breakup could scar her for life and affect her ability to have a healthy relationship when she's an adult."

I smiled. "What did you say to her?"

Roma sighed softly. "I told her it was complicated. She said that was what adults said whenever they were doing something stupid."

"She loves her dad and she loves you, too," I said.

"And I love her. I'm so glad I still get to be part of her life." She looked away for a moment and then her eyes met mine again. "Do you think it's selfish of me to stay in Syd's life? Is it going to be too awkward when Eddie meets someone else?"

"You don't have a selfish bone in your body," Maggie interjected. She was at the sink. I had no idea what she was doing. Not dishes, because it seemed like every surface in the small kitchen was covered with dirty ones. "And it's not like there's so much love in the world that there isn't enough room for a little more," she added.

I nodded. "What Maggie said. It's not selfish. It's loving." I reached over and gave Roma's arm a squeeze. I didn't say that I didn't think Eddie *was* going to meet someone else. When Roma had decided she couldn't marry Eddie because she was older than he was, she'd told Maggie and me she didn't want us to feel we had to take sides. I'd promised her that we'd do our best not to, but if it came down to that we were one hundred percent on hers.

Roma leaned sideways to see what Maggie was doing in the kitchen. "Could we please do something?" she asked.

Maggie opened the oven door, slid the pizza inside and then poked her head in to check something.

"I guess it's not too early to set the table," she said, her voice echoing a little from inside the oven. She pulled her head out and brushed off the front of the denim apron she was wearing.

Roma was already getting the placemats. I got up and started clearing off the table.

"These are nice," Roma said, holding up the woven placemats. "Where did you get them?"

Maggie turned to look at her and smiled. "They are nice, aren't they? You know the big barn, Hollister's, about a mile past you?"

Roma nodded.

"That's where I got them. Brady was with me and he bought an old Lime Ricky bottle."

"You mean the place with the American flag weathervane?" I said, wondering why there were chocolate chips on the table if we were having pizza. "I thought they were a vegetable stand."

"They are," Maggie said. "They have the best corn and potatoes. Oh, and honey. But then the barn is like a flea market, plus Gerald—he's the father—always has a few old vehicles for sale. People use them mostly for off-roading."

"I almost forgot," Roma said as she folded napkins to put at each place. "Did you talk to Oren?"

"He thinks Ira might have gone to Florida." I moved over to the sink and began running some hot water so I could wipe the table and the counter.

Maggie opened the dishwasher and started putting spoons in the utensil rack. "You mean Ira who's been living out by the lake?"

I nodded, adding soap to the hot water in the sink. Even though Maggie had a dishwasher I knew she didn't put her good glasses in it and I could see four of them in various places around the kitchen. "There's no sign of him out at the lake. Or anywhere else for that matter."

"Kath, you don't think Ira had anything to do with the death of Marcus's friend, do you?" She turned and peeked at the pizza through the oven window. For Maggie, pizza-making was as much an art as collage or painting.

"I don't know," I said. "Not deliberately, but maybe by accident."

Mags shook her head emphatically. "Ira doesn't have that kind of energy."

Roma gave me a look. Maggie was a very spiritual person. I'd heard her make that kind of comment about someone before. And in my experience she was usually pretty accurate in her assessment of people.

"Should I set a place for Brady?" Roma asked.

I rinsed my cloth and went to wipe the table for her. She smiled a thank-you.

Maggie had picked up a plastic spatula and was scraping at some bits of dough dried to the granite countertop. "He has a meeting. He'll be here later."

Roma finished setting the table and helped Maggie scrape dishes and load the dishwasher. I washed all the glasses and Maggie's big saucepot, and the kitchen was pretty much cleaned up by the time the oven timer beeped.

Maggie reached for her oven mitts and peered through the window in the oven door. "They look like they're done," she said. She tipped her head in the direction of the counter by the sink. "Kath, would you grab the platter for me?"

The pizza was delicious as always—sausage, mushrooms, tomatoes and chewy mozzarella on a thick crust with just a hint of olive oil and a dusting of cornmeal on the bottom. As good as the pizza I'd had at the hotel with Simon had been, this was better. The resolution I'd made to just have one slice was very quickly broken.

Like we usually did, we moved into the living room for dessert. Roma had made lemon pudding.

"This is really good," I said, scraping the bottom of my bowl.

Roma smiled. "The recipe is easy. I'll e-mail it to you."

"There's more," Maggie said. She got to her feet, took the small glass dish from my hand and walked over to the kitchen. "Roma, what about you?" she asked.

Roma shook her head, "I'm good, thanks."

Maggie came back with more pudding for both of us, handed me my dish and sat down again, stretching her long legs onto the footstool.

"What happens now as far as the investigation goes into the death of Marcus's friend?" Roma asked. "Do the police have any suspects other than Marcus—which is ridiculous, by the way?"

"They're looking for Ira; at least I assume they are. And Hope has been doing what she can."

Maggie licked her spoon and gestured at me with it. "Marcus's friend, is her brother Dominic McAllister by any chance?"

I nodded. "Yes."

"That's kind of odd," she said. I waited for her to explain but she ate another spoonful of pudding instead.

Roma glanced at me and smiled. "Odd how?" she asked.

"Remember last year when that group of artists in Minneapolis wanted to buy the old shoe factory and turn it into studio space with a café on the main floor? They were going to reinforce the roof and put solar panels up there and a garden so the building would be completely self-sufficient."

"I remember that," I said. "But it didn't work out. The building was torn down and some developer is building a condo high-rise." I looked at my bowl, wondering where exactly my second serving of pudding had disappeared to.

"Not some developer," Maggie said. "Dominic McAllister."

"So his sister's an ardent environmentalist and he's not," Roma said.

Maggie nodded. "Like I said, odd."

I heard a noise behind us then and a voice called, "Hello."

Brady.

"C'mon up," Maggie called. She turned in the direction of the stairs. Her smile got a little wider.

Brady Chapman had his father's smile and the same strong arms and huge hands. He'd started to go gray very early but the salt-and-pepper hair didn't make him look old at all. He wore it short and spiked a bit on top.

Maggie got up and took his jacket from him and I noticed the smile that passed between them. Even though she kept insisting the relationship with Brady wasn't serious I could see that it seemed to be heading in that direction.

"How was your meeting?" she asked.

"Long but worth it, I think." He smiled at Roma and me. "How was the pizza?"

"Wonderful as always," Roma said. "We saved you a piece." Her eyes darted in my direction. "We did, didn't we?"

"I made two," Maggie said.

Brady dropped onto the arm of Roma's chair. He looked over at me. "Maggie said you wanted to ask me about Elliot Gordon?"

I'd told Maggie and Roma about Marcus's dad arriving the night before while we were eating. "He showed up on my doorstep last night."

One eyebrow went up but Brady didn't say anything.

"I really do believe he wants to help Marcus and I don't think he's leaving any time soon." I stopped. Now that Brady was here I wasn't sure how to continue. It seemed petty to say I wasn't sure if I could trust him. But it seemed as though Brady could read my mind.

"You want to know if you should give him all your trust." It was a nicer way of expressing my reservations.

"Yes."

Brady made a fist with one hand and cupped it with the other. "I really only know Elliot by reputation. I don't know him personally and I've never faced him in court, so keep in mind what I'm telling you is secondhand."

I nodded, leaning forward a little and propping my elbow on the arm of the sofa. "He argued a case in front of the Supreme Court when he was only twenty-eight and won against a far more experienced and seasoned litigator."

"Wow," Roma whispered.

"We studied the case when I was in law school. My professor said Elliot was a cross between F. Lee Bailey and Johnnie Cochran with some Perry Mason thrown in."

I remembered the man's somewhat melodramatic arrival at Eric's Place. The description seemed accurate from what I'd seen so far.

"So he's good at what he does?"

"Very good," Brady said. I noticed Maggie was leaning against him, although I wasn't sure she was aware of that. "He also has a reputation for stepping over or on people who get in his way."

I nodded.

"Has this helped at all?" he asked.

"It has," I said. "Thanks."

Maggie put a hand on Brady's leg. "Want a slice?" she asked.

He nodded and then held up two fingers. "Two, maybe?"

They moved into the kitchen. Roma touched my arm and I shifted in my seat to face her.

"I have a suggestion. I don't know if it will help."

"What is it?"

"Do you remember when we were trying to find out how Tom—my father—died?"

"I remember," I said. It had been a very painful time for Roma, finding out that the biological father she'd thought had abandoned her had really been dead for almost all of her life.

"The key to figuring that out was learning more about him as a person. Maybe that's true for Dani as well."

Some of the things I'd learned about Tom Karlsson were ugly, but they had ultimately led to his killer. Maybe I did need to find out more about Dani the person.

I nodded slowly. "Maybe it is."

11

It was unseasonably warm the next morning. I took my coffee outside. Owen came to sit on the wide arm of the Adirondack chair. He was washing his face when suddenly his head came up. His ears twitched and he turned his head to look at the side of the house. "Mrrr," he said.

I waited and after a moment Elliot Gordon came around the side of the house.

I got to my feet. "How do you do that?" I said to Owen. He'd already resumed washing his face and ignored me.

"Good morning," Elliot said. He was wearing jeans and a close-fitting black sweater with black leather shoulder and elbow patches. And he was carrying a large manila envelope.

"Good morning," I said. I held up my mug. "Would you like a cup of coffee?"

"I would, if it's no trouble."

"It's already made." I gestured to the door. "Come into the kitchen."

I got Elliot a cup of coffee, refilled my own and we sat at the table. He slid the envelope across the table to me.

"What is this?" I asked.

"Everything I've been able to find on the McAllister family."

I pulled out a sheaf of papers. There were notes in fine, neat handwriting made in the margins of some of the pages. I suspected this was research done by a legal assistant.

"Can you give me the short version?"

"American Land Trust, the organization Danielle McAllister worked for, is funded by her grandmother."

I frowned, flipping through the pages. "Are you sure?"

He didn't say anything and when I looked up the expression on his face told me he was just going to ignore my question.

"The money is filtered through a number of different corporate entities," he said.

"Which means it's not common knowledge—or something the family wanted to be common knowledge."

"I think that's a safe assumption," Elliot said, adding cream to his coffee.

"Do you think Dani knew?" I asked.

He nodded over the top of his coffee cup. "Based on when the organization was formed and when she went to work for them I don't see how she couldn't."

"The McAllisters have a lot of money."

"Old money," Elliot said. "There's a difference, you know, between old money and nouveau riche."

"Old money brings tradition, prestige, influence, connections," I said.

He nodded, taking another sip of his coffee. "Exactly."

I remembered the story Maggie had told me about Dani's brother. "Dominic McAllister is a developer. I'm not trying to imply developers don't care about the environment."

"McAllister doesn't," Elliot said flatly.

"I'll take your word on that," I said. I took a sip of my own coffee. "So if environmental concerns aren't at the top of Dominic McAllister's priorities, why did the family secretly fund an organization that seems to be at cross-purposes to their day-to-day business?"

"Not the family. Matilda McAllister."

Hercules wandered in from the living room, glanced at us as he passed the table and went to sit in front of the door to the porch. I got up and opened it for him, grateful that he hadn't just walked through the way he often did.

"Dani's grandmother," I said as I retook my seat.

"She controls the family trust and has money of her own," Elliot said. "Dani has always had her grandmother's favor and ear."

I sighed. "Which also means access to her money."

"Something some other family members haven't been happy about."

I stretched one arm up over my head. "So are you

suggesting someone in her family killed her over that?" I sounded skeptical because I was.

"Rumor has it that Matilda has the ear of the governor, not to mention several other powerful people in the State House."

I tried to follow the logic through. "So if Dani could find any reason to stop the project at Long Lake, no matter how flimsy, between pressure exerted by the coalition and her grandmother's influence the project would have been scuttled."

It gave Ernie Kingsley even more of a motive. I thought about my deal with Simon. I was going to hold him to his promise to set up a meeting with the developer. As far as I was concerned I definitely still wanted it.

"Kingsley-Pearson is leveraged to the hilt. If this project folds the company will go under." Elliot's face hardened.

"You think someone from the company could be involved," I said.

"I think neither one of us wants my son to be accused of something he didn't do." He had a great poker face. I wouldn't want to play cards with the man.

"That's true," I said.

"You doubt my intentions."

I shook my head. "No, I don't. I believe that you care about Marcus and you want to help him. But as my friend Burtis says, I didn't just fall off the turnip truck. You didn't just come out here to share information. You could have done that over the phone. So tell me what else you want."

He leaned back in his chair and crossed one leg over the other. "I want you to give this information to my son's lawyer. If I give it to Marcus I'm not sure he'll even look at it. "

"I can do that," I said. I picked up the papers and put them back in the envelope.

"You and Burtis are friends," Elliot said. "How did that happen?"

"He saved my life. He and Marcus. And my cats like his turkey jerky."

"Next time you see him tell him I said hello."

I nodded. "I will. And just so you know, he still lives in the same place."

He smiled but didn't say anything.

After Elliot left I went out to the porch and sat down next to Hercules, who was looking out the window. "Interesting man," I said.

He wrinkled his nose at me almost as though he was agreeing.

I looked at my watch. I'd been mulling over Roma's advice to learn more about Dani. I'd told Marcus I wanted to talk to both John and Travis. "Maybe now is a good time," I said to Hercules.

He jumped down and headed for the kitchen door, meowing at me without even looking back.

I'd made oatmeal chocolate chip cookies after I'd gotten home from Maggie's. Now I put a dozen in a bag to take to Travis. Hercules was sitting by my shoes.

"Want to come with me?" I asked.

"Meow," he said, eyeing the bag with the cookies, whiskers twitching.

"No, these are for Travis," I said. "Do you still want to come?"

I couldn't help grinning as he cocked his head to one side, seemingly considering the question. "Mrrr," he said after a moment of thought.

I gestured at the door. "Let's go."

We drove out to the Bluebird Motel first, Hercules on the passenger seat beside me, looking through the windshield and making little noises from time to time as though he were giving directions.

Even though Ruby wanted to sell the piece of land her grandfather, Idris, had left to her, she'd given John and Travis permission to access it, so if Travis wasn't at the Bluebird I'd head for Wisteria Hill.

"I don't want that development to be built if it's not the right thing for the town and the land," Ruby had told me when I'd said I thought it was good of her to let John and Travis on the property. "I'd rather hang on to the land." She'd grinned at me. "Maybe I'll build a tree fort and go live out there."

I was hoping it was early enough that Travis would still be at the motel, and when I pulled off the highway I saw his rental car still in the lot.

"I won't be very long," I said to Hercules.

He looked pointedly from me to my cross-body bag. How did he know I had a tiny container of fish-shaped crackers in there? A friend of Roma's owned a small cat food company and Owen and Hercules had been taste testers—happily—several times for his new products.

"Stay in the truck and I'll give them to you when I come back." I patted the bag.

He sighed and laid down on the seat, putting his head on a small paperback book on the history of Minnesota that Abigail had gotten for me for a quarter at a flea market.

I picked up the bag of cookies and got out of the truck. I knocked on the door of Travis's motel room, expecting him to ask who it was. Instead, after a moment, he opened the door. His hair was disheveled. There were dark circles under his eyes and a couple of days of stubble on his cheeks. Everything about him, even the way he was standing, was so profoundly sad I knew I couldn't ask him any questions about Dani. I knew it would be wrong to take advantage of his grief like that.

"Hi, Travis," I said. "I just came to see how you were, if you need anything." I suddenly felt a little silly standing there with the bag of cookies. I held them out to him. "I, uh, made these for you."

He didn't take the bag. "Did you come to plead Marcus's case?" he asked in a voice edged with snark. "Are you going to tell me we should grieve together?"

I shook my head slowly. My heart ached for him, my chest actually hurting. "No," I said. "I just came to see if I could do anything for you. Not make you feel worse. I'm sorry." I turned to go.

"Have the police figured out who killed her?" Travis said.

I turned back around to face him. "Not yet."

He closed his eyes briefly. "She came here because *he* was here. She wanted to talk to him."

Dani knew Marcus was in Mayville Heights? "How do you know?"

He swallowed and his face tightened. "I went looking for her, after the restaurant that morning. She was on her phone talking to someone. I heard her tell whomever she was talking to that now she'd have the chance to talk to him. Then she said, 'No more secrets.'" He pulled a hand across the stubble on his chin. "She wouldn't talk to me. She wouldn't tell me what the hell she was talking about. She wouldn't let me apologize."

The bit of conversation Travis had overheard didn't prove anything. I sighed. "I'm sorry." The words seemed inadequate but I didn't know what else to say.

"Secrets, Kathleen," Travis said bitterly. "All these years later and the two of them are still keeping secrets."

I noticed he was still referring to Dani in the present tense. Marcus had done that a few times as well.

"I know," I said.

"You know?" He narrowed his eyes at me.

I let out a long slow breath. "I know there's something they were keeping from everyone. I don't know what it is."

Travis's mouth worked before he spoke. "You're okay with that?"

I looked away for a minute and then met his gaze again. "Marcus told me it wasn't his secret to tell. Which means he's protecting Dani. I don't expect you to ever be friends again with Marcus after what happened, but you know whatever else he is, he's deeply loyal to the people he cares about. Whatever his reason is for keeping this secret, he thinks it's important. I know he'd do the same thing for me if I needed it."

He looked at me for what felt like a long time. Then he cleared his throat and inclined his head in the direction of the room behind him. "I have a coffeemaker. You want a cup?"

I nodded. "I'd like that."

Travis and I sat at the small round table just inside his room. He told me more about Dani, his face lighting up as he related the story of how they met in high school when he skidded down an icy stretch of sidewalk outside the school and she caught him. As he had before, he talked about Dani in the present tense, as though she wasn't gone.

Very quickly I realized I wasn't going to learn anything from Travis that would tell me more about who Danielle McAllister had been as a person. His memories were colored by how he felt about her. There was nothing critical or negative in them and while I'd thought more than once since her death that I probably would have liked Dani if I'd had the chance to get to know her, I knew that no one was quite as perfect as Travis described. It struck me that he had been a little obsessed with her.

Still, it seemed to help him to talk. "If I hear anything about the investigation, I'll let you know," I said when I got up to leave.

"Thank you," he said. It seemed like there was

something else he wanted to say so I waited for a moment without speaking. Finally he spoke, looking past me as he did. "Tell, uh, tell Marcus that Dani's family is having a service for her a week from Sunday. Maybe . . . maybe we could, uh, drive up together."

I nodded. "I'll tell him."

Hercules was sitting on the driver's side when I opened the truck door. He looked up expectantly at me. "Let me get in," I said. He moved over about a foot. I took the little box of crackers out of my bag and shook three of them onto the seat.

"Ready?" I asked after he'd eaten them. He made a quick pass at his face with a paw then moved over a few inches and gazed out the windshield. He was ready.

I got home in lots of time to change for work, make a sandwich and start dinner in the slow cooker before I left for the library. It was a quiet morning and I was arranging a display of Halloween-themed books when Simon Janes walked into the building just before lunch. He nodded to Mary, who was at the desk proofreading the mock-up of the poster advertising Spookarama, and walked over to me.

"Good morning, Kathleen," he said with a smile.

I smiled back at him. "Good morning."

"Could we talk somewhere private?" he asked.

"Sure," I said. I led him over to one of our meeting rooms. Once I'd closed the door he handed me the brown envelope he was holding.

"What is it?' I asked.

"Ernie Kingsley is a lousy businessman and a first-class ass, but he didn't kill anyone."

"How do you know?" I said, my heart sinking.

Simon indicated the envelope. "Look inside."

I lifted the flap. The only thing inside was a photograph. Looking at it, I realized it was a screen capture from a security video. The black-and-white image was of Kingsley and a young woman who barely looked eighteen wearing red stilettos, red fringed bikini bottoms and nothing else. She was giving him a lap dance.

I looked at Simon. "Where did you get this?"

"From a club just outside of Red Wing," he said. "Look at the time stamp in the corner."

I looked at the number on the bottom right-hand side of the picture.

"He was there for more than an hour," Simon said. "I saw all the footage." His hands were jammed in his pockets, feet apart. He looked uncomfortable.

I did the math in my head. "He didn't kill Dani. There's no way he had time."

"No, he didn't."

I looked up from the picture. "You knew. That's why you said you'd get me a meeting with him if I still wanted one."

"I suspected," he said. "I'd heard some talk—he wasn't exactly discreet. It wasn't that hard to find out for certain."

I handed the photo and envelope back to him. "Thank you," I said.

"I'm sorry it wasn't the answer you were looking for."

I sighed softly. "I just want the truth."

Simon slipped the photo back into the envelope. "In my experience that's not always so easy to find."

There were even fewer people in the library in the afternoon than there had been in the morning so I was able to spend some time in the workroom doing some of the simpler repairs to our pile of damaged books. I left the more complicated work—including the sticky picture book from Tommy Justason—for Abigail, who had just taken a book-repair workshop in early September.

I was staring at a copy of *Where the Wild Things Are*, wondering how a piece of purple bubble gum had gotten wedged down between the spine of the book and the dust jacket, when there was a knock on the half-open door behind me. I turned around to find John standing there smiling at me.

"Hi," he said. "Mary was downstairs. She told me to come up. I hope that was okay."

I stood up and rolled my neck from one shoulder to the other. "Yes," I said. "I could use a break. I've been hunched over so long I'm beginning to feel like Quasimodo."

He was carrying a small white paper bag with handles. He offered it to me. "I just came to thank you for all your help, not just for letting me use the herbarium. You introduced me to Rebecca and Maggie. And I know you went out to check on Travis this morning."

"You didn't have to do this," I said. "Thank you." The bag held apples from Hollister's.

"They're Honeycrisp," he said. "Good for eating and cooking, so I was told."

"I'm sorry about everything, John," I said, setting the apples on the table.

"Me too." He swiped a hand over his neck. He seemed subdued, even given everything that happened.

"You didn't find what you needed, did you?"

He shook his head. "The bats are on Wisteria Hill land. There's no evidence of them in any caves on Ruby Blackthorne's property or on the land around the lake. And it's probably a good idea that you don't ask me how I can be sure about that last bit."

"So the development will go ahead?"

John shifted restlessly from one foot to the other. "Barring some kind of last-minute Hail Mary, yes." He looked down at his feet for a moment. "I feel like I let her down."

I knew he meant Dani. "I know how hard you looked for something, anything, to use to stop the project."

He laughed but there really wasn't any humor in the sound. "I thought about faking something, you know. Capturing a few bats somehow and relocating them. Looking for some plant and—" He shook his head. "I know how stupid that sounds. Dani would have said, 'Have you lost your mind, John-Boy?' I wanted to finish what she started, but not like that."

"It was a good decision," I said.

"I keep thinking that if she were alive she would have been able to find something." He smiled. "We met in middle school, you know. In the rock club— Dani and thirteen geeky boys. We all spent more time looking at her than we did at rocks. Sometimes I wish we could just go back there and do things just a little bit different." He shook his head. "I have to get going. I need to return the journals to Rebecca."

"Take care of yourself, John," I said.

He nodded. "You too, Kathleen."

Marcus called while I was on my supper break. He'd stopped in at the house to check on Owen and Hercules and return my stepladder. I told him about my visit with Travis and relayed his message.

"I'll call him," Marcus said. "Or maybe it would be better to just go see him. Thanks." We made plans to check out a flea market after the library closed the next afternoon and I hung up.

I was no closer to figuring out who Dani was as a person. I wanted to know the real woman, not the idealized version that Marcus and his friends had told me about.

The evening was just as quiet as the rest of the day had been—sometimes Fridays were that way—and I was home a few minutes earlier than usual. I pulled on my sweats, grabbed my laptop and sat at the kitchen table. I'd just turned on the computer when a furry paw poked its way around the basement door and the rest of Owen followed. He looked surprised to see me.

"I live here," I said. He padded over to me. I picked him up and he planted his two front paws on my chest and peered at my face. "How was your day?" I asked, as I scratched behind his left ear. He made a rumbling sound of satisfaction low in his chest. After a moment he turned to look at the computer screen.

"I wanted to see what else I could find out about Dani," I said. "Roma pointed out that if I knew more about her as a person maybe I'd be able to figure out why someone killed her."

Owen wrinkled up his gray tabby face. I wasn't sure if it was because he didn't think much of the idea or because I'd mentioned Roma. He'd had his shots just a couple of weeks earlier and he was still nursing a grudge at her over that.

It took an hour before I found what I was looking for. Owen sat on my lap and watched the screen intently, pawing at the air occasionally as though trying to tell me what to click on next. In the end it was luck as much as it was my good research skills and his suggestions.

American Land Trust had created a memorial page for Dani on their website. As I read the comments I began to get more of a sense of the woman. She had a great sense of humor and a penchant for playing pranks on her friends. She was a big Minnesota Wild fan and it struck me that she would have gotten a kick out of meeting Eddie.

The remembrances were all heartfelt, but one comment made my throat tighten. It was one sentence: *The light has gone out of my world.* Tanith Jeffery. Dani's best friend, maybe?

It was an uncommon name, Tanith—the Phoenician goddess of love, I remembered reading somewhere, because those kinds of facts stuck in my head.

And maybe in the end it wasn't luck. Maybe it was that tiny piece of information that twigged something in my brain.

Tanith Jeffery was a jewelry designer, I learned. I found several photos of her eating ice cream and standing, arms linked with three other women, smiling into the sun at Twin Cities Pride. After that it took some leaps, but everything began to make sense.

I went into the living room and called Marcus. "I need to talk to you," I said.

"I'm just leaving Eddie's. I can stop in on my way home."

"Okay," I said. "I'll see you soon."

I went out to the porch to wait for him. Owen had disappeared again.

Marcus saw me as he came around the house. He waved and then stepped inside the porch, leaning down to kiss me. "What are you doing out here?" he asked.

"Waiting for you," I said, "looking at the stars, thinking."

"So what did you need to talk to me about?"

"Sit, please." I gestured to the bench by the window. I sat next to him, turning so I was facing him. "I know that there was nothing going on between you and Dani when you were in college," I said. I couldn't see his face very well in the moonlight that was coming through the window, but it seemed to me that he blanched a little. "Her grandmother was—is—extremely conservative. I think the day Travis caught you two kissing outside her dorm room you were covering for Dani so he wouldn't find out there was a girl in her room—a girl she was involved with."

For a moment he didn't say anything, then he sighed softly. "I wanted to tell you, but like I said, it wasn't my secret to tell."

I nodded. "I know."

"She wasn't sleeping with Travis. That's why he was so angry. He thought we'd done what they weren't doing." His arms were propped on his legs and his hands hung between his knees. "She really did try to end things with him. Like I said, he was pressuring her for one more chance and her grandmother, who was like mother and father to Dani after her parents died, was pushing her to try to work things out. Dani adored her grandmother but the woman has very rigid beliefs. If she'd known the truth . . ." Marcus shook his head. "I don't think Dani wanted to take the chance of losing the only family she had left. You saw for yourself what Travis can be like when he's angry. He would have gone right to her grandmother."

"Does John know?" I asked.

Marcus shook his head. "How did you find out?" he asked.

I told him about the comment Tanith Jeffery had written online. "It seemed pretty clear she and Dani were close. When I did a little digging I discovered that Tanith was gay. After that it was good research skills and a bit of luck."

Marcus still looked puzzled. "What do you mean?"

"I found a photo of a dinner at which Tanith Jeffery received a design award. She was at a table of what I take were her friends. Dani was one of them. The look on her face . . . It just didn't feel like much of a leap to think they were involved."

I reached over and linked my fingers through his. "I'd seen the same look on the face of one of my sister's friends when Sara won an award for volunteering at the Boys and Girls Club. It was a mix of pride and love. When I told Sara she thought I was crazy, but I turned out to be right."

Marcus leaned back until his head was against the wall. "Her grandmother was funding American Land Trust."

"I know."

He smiled at me in the near darkness. "I should have guessed you'd figure that out as well."

"I didn't," I said. "Your father did. I have everything he's come up with so far. I think you should give it to Brady."

The smile disappeared. "My father?"

I nodded. "He's trying to help."

"I went to see him. I told him to go home."

I leaned over and kissed his cheek. "That's not going to happen."

"Yeah, I'm starting to see that," he said.

"Do you think Dani was afraid that if her grandmother knew who she really was she'd cut off the money?" I asked.

He nodded. "Her biggest worry was losing what she had left of her family, but yes, she was afraid that if her brother found out he'd use the information against her. He had no idea their grandmother was basically funding everything Dani did. Dani said he wasn't exactly the tree-hugger type."

"Did she know you were here—in Mayville Heights? Or was meeting you at Eric's just something that happened by chance?" Travis, at least, seemed to believe Dani had come to town to see Marcus.

Marcus turned his head to look at me. "I wondered about that, you know. She said she needed to talk to me but she hadn't known I was here. It was just a coincidence."

"What did she want to talk about?" I asked.

He put his arm around my shoulder and I leaned against him with my head on his shoulder. "I wish I knew," he said.

12

Marcus stayed for a little longer then he headed home. I went upstairs, ran a bath and tossed one of Maggie's herbal soaks into the water. I was brushing my hair when the phone rang. It was Brady Chapman.

"I'm sorry to bother you, Kathleen," he said, "but Maggie is helping Ruby chaperone some kind of overnight thing at the high school and I didn't think it was a good idea to call Marcus with this." He sounded . . . rattled, which was really unlike Brady.

"What's wrong?" I asked.

"It's my father. And Elliot Gordon."

"What about them?"

"They're at the bar at the St. James Hotel. Right now they should just be wrapping up their rendition of 'Sweet Home Alabama.'"

I started to laugh. "I'm sorry," I said. "You're not kidding, are you?"

"I really wish I was," he said drily. "The manager

called me. If I pick them up in the next half hour she won't call the police. The problem is, I'm in Minneapolis. I couldn't get Lita, either."

"I'll go get them," I said, kicking off my fuzzy slippers.

"Thank you," Brady said. "Like I said, I didn't think it would be a good idea to call Marcus."

"I agree." I felt a little guilty. After all, I had, in a way, suggested to Elliot that he get in touch with Burtis. "Don't worry. I'll get Elliot up to his room and I'll take your dad home."

"I know my father's reputation," Brady said. "But the truth is, he doesn't drink very much himself."

I laughed again. "Then he'll probably just sleep it off and wake up with a really big headache in the morning. Don't worry about this. I've been around my parents' theater friends all my life. This won't be the first time I've had to rescue someone who had a bit too much. At least they're just singing Lynyrd Skynyrd. Be grateful they're not reenacting Hamlet and Laertes's duel with real swords."

"I owe you, Kathleen," Brady said.

"No, you don't," I said. "I'm on my way."

I pulled on my jeans and a sweater, yanked my hair back into a ponytail and grabbed my purse and keys.

Brady must have called the hotel manager back, because when I walked into the hotel a woman came from behind the front desk and walked over to me. "Ms. Paulson," she said, offering his hand. "I'm Melanie Davis."

She was about my height, and curvy with smooth brown skin and gorgeous dark eyes. I'd heard Lita mention her name.

"I'm here to get Mr. Chapman and Mr. Gordon," I said.

"I think they're just finishing their encore," she replied drily. She led the way to the bar. The hotel had been experimenting with live music on Friday and Saturday nights but I didn't think this was what they had in mind.

Burtis Chapman and Elliot Gordon were an incongruous pair at best. Burtis made me think of something carved from a block of stone, strong and solid. His face was lined and weathered from so much time spent outdoors. He'd lost most of his hair—all that was left were a few white tufts that were generally poking out from under his ubiquitous Twins ball cap.

I knew that not all of Burtis's business dealings were on the up and up, but he had a generous soul and he was deeply loyal to the people he called his friends. And that was more than enough for me and had been long before he'd helped rescue me from a burning building.

I had no idea that Burtis could sing. Or Elliot, for that matter. They were rocking out to Bob Seger's "Old Time Rock and Roll." The jazz trio—guitar, bass and snare drum—looked like they were having just as much fun.

"They're good," I said softly. The manager gave me a look that told me I shouldn't have said that out loud.

I wasn't the only one who liked what I was hearing.

The song ended and people began to clap enthusiastically. Burtis and Elliot bowed, acknowledging the applause. I made my way over to them, skirting around the tables. Burtis smiled when he caught sight of me.

"Kathleen, girl, what the hell are you doing here?" he asked.

"I thought you might need a limo driver," I said.

"Are you tryin' to say I'm too drunk to walk home?" he asked. I knew he wasn't angry. I could see a devilish gleam in his eyes.

"Yes, I am," I said.

He laughed, a deep booming sound that seemed to bounce off the walls. "Well, you're right." He turned to Elliot, gesturing at me with his free hand, his other arm still around Elliot's shoulders. "That son of yours is a fine man," he said. "And he's a damn fine police officer, which I know you don't wanna hear but I'm gonna say it anyway. But he was dumb as a glass of water when it came to her. Almost screwed it up big-time."

"I'm parked out front," I said. "Let's go."

"You tryin' to shut me up or change the subject?" Burtis asked.

I smiled at him. "Either one will work for me." I put my arm around Burtis's shoulder, which had the effect of making me feel as though I'd just joined a very odd Vegas kick line.

"Shotgun," Elliot said then.

"You can't call shotgun," Burtis countered.

"The hell I can't," Elliot retorted. "I just did it."

"I'm not riding in the back like an old dog."

"If you can't run with the big dogs you better stay on the porch," Elliot said.

The words hung between them for a moment, then they both laughed at some joke I didn't get.

At least we were moving in the direction of the door. "First of all, no one is riding in the back," I said. "And second"—I looked at Elliot—"you're not coming with us." I pointed at the ceiling. "You're going to bed."

Burtis smirked at him.

"I called shotgun," Elliot said. "We have a verbal agreement." He had a little trouble getting the word "agreement" out.

"We can outrun him, Kathleen." Burtis winked at me.

"We're not running anywhere," I said firmly. "You"—I pointed at Elliot—"are going to bed. "You"—I moved my finger to Burtis—"are going home."

"I'll sue," Elliot said.

"You can't sue your boy's girlfriend," Burtis said.

I wondered just exactly how much they'd had to drink.

"The hell I can't!" Elliot straightened up and adjusted the collar of his shirt. "Don't you know who I am?"

"Don't you?" Burtis asked.

They laughed again like it was the funniest thing either one of them had ever heard.

I tried to steer them toward the elevators but they were bigger and stronger and since we were still linked arm in arm I found myself on the sidewalk with them before I quite knew what happened.

Burtis slapped the passenger-side fender of the truck with one hand. "They don't make 'em like this anymore," he told Elliot.

"How did you two get here?" I asked.

"That depends," Elliot said, "on whether you believe in evolution or creationism."

"You forgot aliens," Burtis said.

Elliot nodded solemnly. "Or aliens."

The preschoolers at story time were easier to manage than those two. "I mean did you two have a car?"

"I have an Audi," Elliot said, holding his head up with a decided amount of pride.

"La-di-da," Burtis replied. "I have a truck." He smacked the fender again with his big hand and looked at me. "Open up, girl."

I unlocked the passenger door and Burtis hauled it open. "Get in, Elly May," he said to Elliot.

"I called shotgun." Marcus's dad crossed his arms petulantly over his chest, his feet planted wide apart. The effect he was going for was ruined because he was swaying slightly. I had the feeling if I poked him with my finger he'd topple over.

Burtis dropped his elbow down on the hood of the truck, forearm upright, fingers spread apart. "Let's go a round," he growled. "I can still take you."

"Nobody is taking anyone anywhere except me," I said, stepping between them. I pointed at Elliot. "Get in the truck. In case you didn't notice there's only one seat so you're both riding shotgun." He climbed in without saying another word. I was glad because I had no way to actually make either one of them do anything.

"Get in," I told Burtis. He was still leaning over the front of the truck, ready to arm wrestle. I pulled my phone out of my pocket and held it up. "Don't make me call Lita." I fervently hoped he wouldn't call my bluff because, like Brady, I had no idea where she was.

"Yes, ma'am," he said, hanging his head and climbing in next to Elliot.

I walked around and slid in on the driver's side, leaning over to make sure they were both belted in safely. They smelled like this foul cough medicine that my father bought on the Internet from Canada. He swore by it but I thought it smelled like a mix of paint thinner and old-fashioned liniment.

"What were you two drinking?" I asked.

"Jäger Bombs," Burtis said.

"We were taking a stroll down memory lane," Elliot added.

"What is a Jäger Bomb?" I asked, thinking as I did that I was probably going to regret the question.

"First you need beer," Burtis said.

Elliot nodded in agreement.

"Then you need a shot glass of Jägermeister."

Elliot nodded once again.

"You drop your shot glass in your beer and bottoms up." Burtis pantomimed the action.

"And then you're bombed," Elliot added.

They elbowed each other and laughed.

"Kathleen, did you know this man is my oldest friend?' Elliot asked.

"Oldest friend?" Burtis said. "I thought I was your only friend."

"Oldest friend, only friend, tomato potato," Elliot said.

"So how did you two get to be friends?" I asked, shooting a quick glance in their direction.

"Well, he stole my woman," Burtis began.

"Don't start that," Elliot said. "She wanted me." He raised a finger in the air and hit the roof of the truck.

"The hell she did," Burtis retorted.

Elliot shifted sideways to look at him. "Well, her tongue wasn't in my mouth to check my fillings."

"I laid you out before. I can do it again," Burtis warned.

"You're slow, old man," Elliot retorted.

"Well you're soft, pretty boy." I didn't need to look at them. I could hear the smirk in Burtis's voice.

"Mary Connolly still got those great legs?" Elliot abruptly asked.

"Oh yeah," Burtis said. "She works for Kathleen down at the library. You should go see her."

"You mean Mary Lowe?" I said, slowing down as the car in front of me turned.

"She used to be Mary Connolly," he said. He nudged Elliot with his shoulder. "That is one kick-ass broad. I'll take you out to The Brick. She dances. Think feathers."

I knew about Mary's dancing. I decidedly didn't want to think about feathers.

Burtis started to sing then, doing the intro to "Sweet

Home Alabama." Elliot closed his eyes and kept time on the dashboard. They sang all the way out to the Chapman homestead, finishing just as I pulled up in front of the old farmhouse.

"Thank you for the ride home, girl," Burtis said, leaning forward to smile at me around Elliot.

"I'll walk you to the door," I said.

"Don't be a damn stranger, Elly May," Burtis said to Elliot.

I came around the truck and walked him up the steps to the wide veranda that ran the length of the front of the house. He patted his pockets, found his keys and fished them out. I unlocked the front door and folded the key ring back into his hand.

"He's a good man," Burtis said, jerking his head in the direction of the truck.

I smiled at him. "Go to bed," I said.

To my surprise he leaned down and kissed the top of my head. "Sleep tight," he said.

When I got back in the truck Elliot's head was against the back of the seat. His eyes were closed. And he was snoring. I shook his shoulder. If he got into too deep a sleep I'd never be able to get him out of the truck and up to his room once we got back to the hotel.

He didn't move. I poked him with my elbow. "C'mon, Elliot, wake up," I said. He just kept on snoring.

Great. Now what?

I started the truck and pulled down the driveway. Elliot snored in a steady rhythm beside me, sleeping the sleep of drunks, fools and angels, as my mother would say. How was I going to wake him up and get him into the hotel?

I turned down the hill. I knew there was a length of clothesline and a couple of bungee chords in the back of the truck. I couldn't come up with any way to use them to get Elliot up and into the hotel that wouldn't draw way more attention to us than I wanted—and that would work. I could only think of one thing to do.

The snoring had gotten louder when I pulled into the driveway. I left Elliot in his seat, shut off the engine and walked around the back of the house. A light was on in the kitchen. That was good.

I banged on the back door and after a moment Marcus opened it, Micah at his feet.

"Kathleen, what are you doing here?" he said.

"Your father's in the front seat of my truck, snoring," I said, rubbing my hands together. It was getting cool now at night.

He frowned at me in confusion. "My father?"

I nodded.

"Why?"

"I was taking Burtis home. Your father called shotgun, not that there was actually anywhere else for him to sit."

"Hang on a minute." He held up both hands like he was about to surrender. "My father and Burtis were . . . ?"

"In the bar at the St. James."

"Why were you driving them anywhere?"

This was taking longer than I'd intended. "Because Brady is in Minneapolis, Maggie is in a lockdown at the high school with Ruby and I have no idea where Lita is." I looked over my shoulder. "I'm sorry about bringing him here, but it was that or leave him in the truck all night covered in a blanket."

"Show me where he is," Marcus said, resignation in his voice.

We walked back around the house and I pointed at the truck. Marcus leaned in on the driver's side and took Elliot by the shoulders, shaking him. Then he pulled his dad along the seat and eased him out, putting one arm behind the older man and one in front of him for support. I slammed the truck door and went around to Elliot's other side to help support his weight. We got him all the way around the house and inside.

"Living room," Marcus said.

We eased Elliot onto the sofa and I grabbed a plaid throw blanket from the back and covered him.

Marcus looked down at his father. "How much did he have to drink?"

"A lot," I said. "If it helps, they seemed to be having a good time, especially when they were singing."

Marcus turned his head slowly to look at me. "Singing?"

"Lynyrd Skynyrd in the truck on the way out to Burtis's place. Bob Seger in the bar at the St. James."

He exhaled loudly. "Okay. That settles it. I can never go in there again."

I put my arms around his waist and leaned up to kiss him. "Did you know your dad and Burtis were friends when they were young?"

He shook his head. "I had no idea. Neither one of them ever said a word about it."

He walked me out to the deck. "I don't suppose I can convince you to stay, can I?"

"No," I said. "I've heard enough seventies' rock for one night." I planted a kiss on his mouth and went back to the truck.

I didn't sleep very well. I kept dreaming that Elliot and Burtis had decided to take their music on the road and I had somehow gone along as their road manager. I was down in the kitchen making blueberry pancakes before six o'clock Saturday morning. Owen wandered in, yawned and sat down next to his dishes.

"Good morning, sunshine," I said as I got his breakfast. He grumped at me and avoided making eye contact. Some nights Owen stayed up for hours roaming the house doing who knew what. Then in the morning he was a cranky grump and I had learned to give him lots of space. Hercules came in just as I finished making the pancakes. He sniffed the air and murped inquiringly.

"Pancakes for me, cat food for you," I said. He seemed okay with that.

We both lingered over breakfast. Hercules took his time eating and making sure he looked good to face the day. I'd brought Abigail's twenty-five-cent book in from the truck and I picked it up and read the back cover as I finished my second pancake.

Owen, on the other hand, ate, washed his face and

then headed for the back door. I let him outside so he could do his morning circuit of the property. He grunted in my direction, which I took as "Thank you" but may not have been. The sky was low and dull and that, combined with the ache in my previously broken left wrist, told me that we were in for rain.

When I stepped back into the kitchen I found Hercules sitting on my chair, bits of paper at his feet. Abigail had bookmarked several places in the slim paperback that she thought might interest me. Hercules had just pulled all but one of those bits of paper out of the book.

"What did you do?" I asked, hands on my hips. For some reason the cat looked quite pleased with himself. "That was bad. Very bad."

Hercules frowned as though he couldn't understand my attitude. I picked up the book. The one piece of paper left was marking a place close to the beginning. I opened the book to see what Abigail had wanted me to check out. The text, illustrated with a couple of old maps of Minnesota, talked about how the state got its name. Minnesota was named for the Minnesota River, from the Dakota Sioux word for sky-tinted water.

"Sky-tinted water, I like that," I said to Hercules, who tipped his head sideways and blinked slowly at me a couple of times. "And I probably would have been interested in the other things Abigail marked, even though you don't seem to think so."

Hercules jumped down from the chair, walked over to his water dish and peered down at it. It was still about half full. "Mrrr?" he said. He looked back at me.

"No, I think sky-tinted water means water that's outside, like a lake or a river. It reflects the color of the sky, which is one of the reasons lakes and rivers look blue. That's just plain, clear water in your dish." I was explaining reflection to a cat.

At least he seemed to be considering what I'd said. "Thank you for the place name lesson," I said. Then I leaned down so my face was inches from him. "But next time stay away from my books."

Hercules licked my chin and then sat down, looking expectantly at me. He seemed to be waiting for me to do or say something. I had no idea what.

I sat down at the table again, speared the last bit of my pancake and ate it. Then I looked at Herc still looking at me. "I don't suppose you know where Ira Kenyon is?" I said.

He shook his head, flicked his tail in annoyance and took a step backward, bumping his dish and sending a tiny splash of water onto the floor. Hercules yowled and jumped at the same time, all four feet going in different directions like a feline version of Riverdance.

"It's okay. I've got it," I said. I grabbed a rag from under the sink and wiped up the water. Then I got a second cloth to dry Hercules's feet. He complained the entire time. Hercules hated having wet feet, so much so that Maggie had actually bought him a pair of boots—which is how I learned that he hated looking like a dork more than he hated wet feet.

I refilled the water bowl and set it closer to the side of the refrigerator so he wouldn't spill it again. "There," I said. "There's your water, clear because we're all out of sky-tinted."

And then, suddenly, I remembered something Maggie had said while we were talking about the development. She'd pointed out that right now this end of the lake wasn't even any good for swimming thanks to a very late algal bloom.

"The clear water is on the other side," I said aloud.

"Merow," Hercules agreed and began to clean his paws.

"Ira Kenyon didn't go to Clearwater in Florida. He went to clear water on the other side of the lake." No. That was too easy. On the other hand, it wouldn't be hard to check.

I looked at Hercules, who was now happily ignoring me, cleaning his front left paw. He'd tried awfully hard to draw my attention to water, in the name of the state and in his dish. Had he been trying to tell me something? More than once it had seemed to me that Owen and Hercules were playing detective in their own unique way.

I waited until seven thirty to call Hope. "I know how ridiculous this sounds," I said, explaining my leaps of logic while leaving out the cat's role in the process.

"I've seen cases solved with thinner hunches," Hope said. "I'll go out there and look for him. I'll call you later."

I was on the back steps shaking the mat from the

porch when I spotted Rebecca coming from her house carrying a beautiful golden-orange chrysanthemum. I walked across the grass to meet her.

"Good morning," she said, holding out the plant.

"Is this for me?" I asked.

Rebecca smiled. "It's for the library. Abigail is going to put it on the table in the reading corner. She said you're decorating for the Halloween party."

I nodded. "She told me she was going to see what she could scrounge to brighten up that spot."

"Well, I'm one of the scroungees," Rebecca said.

I took the plant from her. "Did John come to see you?" I asked.

She nodded and her smile faded. "Yes, he did. He told me that he couldn't find anything that would stop the development. I was hoping for a different outcome."

"You and me both."

"The day you introduced us at the library I really believed we had a chance." She adjusted the yellow scarf at her neck. "It's not that I'm against progress. It's just that I don't want to see a beautiful piece of land destroyed." She raised her eyebrows slightly. "Everett called me a tree-hugger."

"I'm sure he meant it as a compliment."

"If I thought that going out there and chaining myself to one of those trees would stop this whole thing I'd do it, but I think Ernie Kingsley would just cut it right out from under my feet."

I smiled at her over the top of the plant. "From what I've heard about the man, you're probably right."

"The day John came out to see the rest of my mother's journals started out with so much hope and it ended in such a dark way."

That was the day Dani had been killed and we were still no closer to figuring out who her killer was.

Rebecca leaned sideways to look at Hercules sitting on the step. "Are you coming over?" she asked the cat.

"Merow," he said.

"All right, then. See you tomorrow." She smiled at me and headed back across the lawn. Half the people I knew talked to my cats like they were people. At least it made it seem a lot less odd now when I did it.

Marcus called me mid-morning at the library to cancel our flea market plans. "I'm sorry," he said. "Brady thinks the prosecuting attorney may be going to take everything to the grand jury sometime in the next couple of weeks."

I drop into my desk chair as my stomach flip-flopped. "How can they do that when you haven't done anything wrong?"

"The prosecutor doesn't want it to look like he's treating me any differently than he would anyone else."

"So he'd do this to any other person who's innocent?"

"Kath," he said gently.

I sighed. "What did Brady say?"

"That's why I have to cancel. He wants me to meet him at his office so we can go over everything."

"Go," I urged. "Call me when you're done and we'll do something."

"Ummm, I like the sound of that," he said.

My face got warm. "How's your dad?" I asked, partly to change the subject.

Marcus laughed. "Last time I checked he was sitting at the kitchen table with a bottle of aspirin and an entire pot of coffee. Is it wrong that I might have laughed?"

"Yes," I said, "but I probably would have done the same thing."

I heard some kind of crash in the background. "I've gotta go," Marcus said. "Everything will be okay. I love you."

"I love you, too," I said. I wanted to believe everything was going to be okay. But it seemed to me that it was going to need a nudge or two.

13

Hope called as I was getting into the truck after the library had closed at lunchtime for the day. "Are you still at the library?" she asked.

"I'm just about to head home."

"Do you mind if I stop in for a minute?"

"No," I said. I didn't have any plans anymore. "Did you find Ira?"

"Yes," she said. "I'll tell you all about it when I get there."

When I pulled into the driveway Hope pulled in right behind. I grabbed my briefcase and got out of the truck. "So Ira was there, on the other side of the lake?"

She nodded. "Living in his truck just back from the water in a little clearing in the trees. He's only been there a couple of days. He knows someone with an apple U-pick up north and he's been working there. Ira's actually a pretty interesting man."

"You don't think he killed Dani."

She shook her head. "No. His right arm is basically useless. I suspect he had a stroke at some point in the past. There's no way he would have been able to pick her up, let alone throw her over the embankment. And I took a look at the truck. It's banged up in places but nothing recent and nothing that makes it look like it hit someone."

"It was a long shot anyway," I said with a small sigh.

"Hey, I'm impressed that you figured out where he was. If you ever want to give up being a librarian . . ." She grinned.

"I'll go work for Burtis Chapman," I said, "because I'd make a lousy detective."

"I think you're pretty good at it."

My stomach growled loudly then. "Have you had lunch?" I asked.

"I thought maybe I'd head over to Fern's," Hope said with a shrug.

"I have soup and brownies," I said. "And cats who will at least pretend to listen while you talk about your day."

"Sounds good to me," she said.

Owen was in the kitchen lying on the floor on his back, chewing on the head of a funky chicken. He lifted his head to look at us and I thought he looked just a little buzzed on the catnip.

"Should I start looking for the body?" Hope asked.

"It's probably under the fridge," I said.

"Do you know why he bites the heads off?"

"He likes to chew on them and suck on the beak

part. Roma thinks he was separated from his mother too soon." I washed my hands and reached for the placemats and napkins.

"Just let me wash up and I'll do that," Hope said.

I left the things on the table and got the soup out of the fridge and a pot from the cupboard so I could heat it up for us.

"You found Owen and Hercules at Wisteria Hill, right?" Hope asked as she set the table.

"More like they found me," I said, "but yes."

"It's beautiful out there. I know the resort is supposed to bring money and jobs but I can't help thinking I'd rather have the trees than an ugly glass-and-metal building."

"You haven't heard?"

Hope was folding a napkin into some kind of triangular shape. She looked up at me. "Heard what?" Then before I could answer she made the connection. "Ah crap. Marcus's friends didn't find anything. Did they?"

I opened the cupboard for a couple of bowls. "No. It doesn't look like there's any way to stop things now."

"I guess I shouldn't be surprised given that John Keller was doing all the work since Danielle McAllister's death."

"Wait a minute," I said. "What do mean?" Hercules had come in and was sitting by the table. He murped a soft inquiry as well. Owen was still engrossed in his chicken.

Hope smiled down at the little tuxedo cat and waggled her fingers at him.

"I think I told you that I did some background checking on both John and Travis Rosen."

I nodded.

"Turns out he used to work as a lobbyist for a consortium of construction companies."

"Doing what?"

"Making a case for the kind of thing he's working against now."

I started filling our bowls. "Maybe he had a change of heart and that's why he went to work with American Land Trust."

Hope shrugged. "I know it makes me sound cynical but in my experience those kind of things don't happen very often."

I set a steaming bowl in front of her. "This smells good," she said. "Chicken noodle is my favorite, although at my house it generally comes out of a can."

I took the place opposite her. Out of the corner of my eye I saw Owen drop the chicken head, stretch and head for the table. "You could make this," I said. "The slow cooker does most of the work. If you decide you want to let me know and I'll show you what I do."

"Seriously?" Hope asked, spoon halfway to her mouth.

I smiled. "Absolutely."

We ate in silence for a couple of minutes, then Hope set down her spoon. "Kathleen, how much do you know about Dani McAllister?"

"I only met her once," I said. "Marcus and the others told me some stories about her, but that's about it." There was something about the slight frown on her face that made me curious about her question. "Why do you ask?"

"I don't know if this matters and I'm not even sure it's something I should pursue . . ."

"But . . ."

"I think Dani was gay."

I set my own spoon down, hoping nothing in my expression gave me away. "Have you asked Marcus?"

She shook her head, making her dark curls bounce. "No. It's none of my business unless it has something to do with her getting killed, and so far I haven't found any evidence of that. I don't want to air her personal life because if she was gay she kept that information pretty private. But we are running out of possibilities for what happened to her."

I got up and started the coffee to buy myself a little time. "What makes you think you're right?"

"She had a book of essays in her backpack written by women sharing their experiences coming out. It just made me wonder." She suddenly stopped, closed her eyes for a moment and shook her head. "I have a book about decomposition in my backpack," she said. "What does that say about me?"

"That you're a good detective," I said. I hesitated for a moment. "And you're right about Dani."

"How did you find out?"

I explained about my online research and Marcus's confirmation, without saying anything about his and Dani's so-called secret.

Hope crumbled a cracker into her bowl. "I think it's

sad that Dani felt she had to hide who she really was from everyone."

I nodded. "Me too." No matter how crazy my family may have made me over the years, I knew they loved me unconditionally. I couldn't imagine how Dani had to have felt, thinking that she'd lose her grandmother's love just by being honest.

"Do you know the woman's name? The one you think might have been involved with her?"

"Tanith Jeffery."

"I should get in touch with her." I didn't answer right away and Hope looked up from her soup. "You don't think it's good idea."

I sighed. "It's just . . . what would you say?"

"Well, I'm not going to say, 'Hey, you think your friend was killed because she was gay?' if that's what you're worried about, Kathleen."

I didn't know what to say, so I didn't say anything.

Hope looked away, smoothing a hand over her hair. "I'm sorry," she said. "I know that's not what you were thinking."

"I wasn't," I said. "It just seems to me that this woman cared about Dani. I don't want to see her get hurt for no good reason."

Hope nodded. "I get that. I do. In police work we ask a lot of people a lot of questions and, yeah, sometimes those questions stir up some painful emotions. But sometimes they help us catch the bad guy, and for the people we talked to, that's worth it."

It took no time, using her cell phone, for Hope to find Tanith Jeffery's number. "Okay, I'm going to put this on speaker so you can hear both sides of the conversation, but please stay quiet." She glanced down at the cats. "You too." Owen yawned and headed for the basement. Hercules sat up straighter, his green eyes on the phone in Hope's hand. "We good?" she asked.

I nodded. Hercules murped softly.

Hope punched in the number and I pulled up both legs and hugged my knees. Tanith Jeffery had a voice that reminded me of singer Bonnie Raitt. Hope explained who she was and why she was calling.

"I've been debating whether or not I should call you," Tanith said. "It wasn't common knowledge but . . . Dani and I were a couple. I feel as though I've been doing my grieving in secret."

"I'm so sorry for your loss," Hope said. "Is there anyone you can think of who might have wanted to hurt her?"

"I've been asking myself that question since she . . . since it happened. And I can't think of anyone. Everyone liked her. I know people always say that when someone dies but it's the truth."

Hope and I exchanged a look. The pain in Tanith Jeffery's voice was raw.

"Ms. Jeffery, are you familiar with Travis Rosen?" Hope asked.

"Dani's college boyfriend, yes. He replaced the engineer who was helping with the field research on the project she was opposing. She'd been trying to find the right time to tell him about us. It was . . . it was hard for her. I don't suppose there's any way you'd know if she did."

"I'm sorry," Hope said. "I can't answer that."

I was impressed with her kindness. I could hear the empathy in her voice and I was sure Tanith Jeffery could as well.

"What about John Keller?" Hope asked.

"Yes," Tanith said slowly.

I had my chin propped on my knees but I raised my eyes to Hope's. Like me she'd heard the change in the other woman's voice.

"How do you know him?"

"They work together." She cleared her throat. "Worked, I mean."

It was still there in her voice, a tiny bit of reticence.

"Ms. Jeffery, is there anything I should know about Mr. Keller?" Hope asked.

"They'd known each other since they were twelve or thirteen," Tanith said.

Hope rubbed her shoulder with one hand. "Just for a minute, don't think of me as a detective. Think of me as another woman. Is there something you'd *want* me to know about him?"

She exhaled slowly. "It's really just a feeling."

"So what's the feeling?" Hope asked.

"I thought there was just something a little off about him. Dani didn't agree with me, by the way."

"Off how?"

Tanith sighed again. "It was just little things, really. For instance, they were in touch with each other a few times a year but he didn't tell her he was applying for the foundation job until he got it. Why would someone

do that? Why wouldn't you mention you know someone at a place where you want to get hired?"

"Did he give any reason for that?"

"He said he didn't want to take advantage of his
friendship with Dani."

Hope leaned forward and propped an elbow on
the table. "Was there anything else?"

"He moved into her neighborhood. She said she'd
see him at the grocery store, at the gym, getting coffee. He just seemed to be everywhere."

I looked at Hope. Her mouth was pulled into a
tight line. I wondered if she was thinking what I was
thinking: that John's behavior was more than odd. It
sounded creepy.

"Detective Lind, do you think it's possible that
John Keller had anything to do with Dani's death?"
Tanith asked.

"I don't know," Hope said. "But I promise you I'm
going to find out." She gave the woman her cell number, urging her to call if she thought of anything. Then
Hope ended the call and set the phone down on the
table.

My stomach was churning. "He talks about her in
the past tense," I said slowly.

Hope gave her head a little shake as though I'd in-
terrupted her train of thought. "What do you mean?"

"When Marcus or Travis talk about Dani they do
the same thing as Tanith Jeffery just did. They talk
about her in the present tense. Like she's not gone."

"That happens a lot."

"Not when John's talking about her."

That got me her full attention. "Are you sure?"

I nodded.

Hope picked up her cup, realized it was empty and set it down again. I got up and got the coffeepot, pouring a refill for both of us.

"He has an alibi," she said. "He was with Rebecca. I talked to her myself."

I added cream and sugar to my cup. I wasn't sure what to say. Hope was a good detective. It didn't feel right to pick up the phone and check with Rebecca. I glanced down at Hercules, who looked pointedly toward the backyard. I knew what his vote was.

"Go ahead," Hope said.

I frowned at her over my coffee. "I don't know what you mean."

"Call Rebecca."

"I believe you," I said.

She pulled a hand through her dark curls. "I appreciate that. Call her anyway. It's better if you do it than if I do."

"Murr," Hercules said at my feet.

Hope smiled. "See? He agrees with me. Call Rebecca."

I reached for my cell phone on the counter.

"I've been thinking about your mother's journals," I said when Rebecca answered.

"You're thinking John might have missed something."

"Something like that."

"I'm sorry, dear," she said. "But I think you're grasping at straws. That young man was so excited to see those notebooks. He took them and went right back to his motel room. He couldn't wait to start reading them." She sighed. "I wish he'd been able to find something that helped in them."

I put my free hand palm down on the table and swallowed before I spoke again. "John took your mother's books back to the motel?"

"Yes, but he took very good care of them and he brought them all back."

"That's uh, that's good," I said.

"Do you want me to bring them over?" Rebecca asked.

Hope was watching me. I couldn't read anything from her expression.

"No," I said. "If John didn't find anything, I don't think I would." I thanked her and hung up.

Hope put her head in her hands. "I didn't ask the right question," she said. "I asked her if Keller had come to her house to see her mother's journals. I didn't ask if he stayed." She lifted her head and looked at me. "That was stupid."

"You thought you had it covered."

"But I didn't," she said.

"Where did he get the car?" I asked, dropping one leg and curling the other underneath me. Hercules saw that as a sign to jump up onto my lap.

Hope looked blankly at me. "What car?"

"Dani was hit by a car and then the killer put her body over the side of that embankment. Dani and the two men had two vehicles. On the day of the murder she had one and Travis had the other. Where did John get a vehicle if he ran her down?"

I felt as though my brain at the moment looked like the kids' game Mouse Trap and all I needed to happen was for all the little pieces to fall into place so the trap would fall down on the killer. On John, because now I was certain that's what he was. "You know that they had no permission to be on the actual property that was going to be part of the development other than that little piece Ruby owns?"

"Right."

Hercules nuzzled my hand and I began to stroke his fur. His attention was still on Hope. "I think John was actually on the lakeside property. He alluded to having been there. It's rough, hilly, boggy-in-places terrain. Could some kind of cut down Jeep or truck have caused the injuries that Dani had?"

"It's possible," Hope said. She rubbed at the creases in her forehead. "I'd have to see it to be sure. That still doesn't answer the questions though; how *did* John get a vehicle?"

"The big red barn."

"You mean Hollister's? The place that sells the vegetables?" I could see the skepticism on her face. I would have felt the same way if not for the conversation I'd had with Maggie and Roma the night Maggie made pizza.

"They have a little under-the-table side business selling old vehicles for off-roading—I'm guessing they're not licensed, either. I know John knows the place because he brought me a bag of apples from there as a thank-you for all my help."

Hope got to her feet.

"What are you doing?" I asked.

"I'm going to drive out there and see what I can find." She pulled her keys out of her pocket.

I stood up as well and set Hercules on the floor. "You're not going to call Detective Foster?"

"And tell him what? John Keller has a hole in his alibi and we think he's the killer because the victim's girlfriend thought there was something off about him?"

"I'm going with you, then," I said.

"You're not a detective."

"And you're not on this case."

We stared at each other for a moment. "We're taking my car. It has four-wheel drive," Hope finally said.

I grabbed a hoodie and my phone. Hercules followed us. I stopped in the porch and bent down to his level. "You can't go with us. Stay here." I wanted to say "No walking though the door" but with Hope standing there I couldn't. He immediately looked at Hope.

She shrugged. "Does he get carsick?"

"No," I said, "but on occasion he will try to give directions."

"What the heck," she said. "Let him come. Maybe he'll bring us good luck."

"Are you sure?" I asked.

She nodded. "We're just a couple of women driving

around with our cat, looking for a little piece of land to buy to build a getaway, maybe plant some flowers, make a fire pit, explore the woods in some kind of off-road vehicle."

I smiled at her. "You're good."

She smiled back. "I didn't get the badge for sending in two box tops and answering a time-limited skill-testing question."

14

The big red barn was up the road a little from Wisteria Hill. Unlike Roma's place, which was set back from the road, the barn and the old farmhouse were easy to spot. The farm stand was out by the road with the barn off to the right and the old house on a slight slope of land to the left. Both the old house and the barn had a list to one side, as though they'd gotten tired of standing upright over the years.

Hope pulled in next to a couple of cars. "Look at the pumpkins, check out the squash and apples. Watch. Listen. That's it."

"Stay here, please," I said to Hercules as we got out of the car.

There were a couple of ladder-back chairs by the end of the vegetable stand. Hope walked over to them and tipped her head on one side as though she was trying to picture them arranged somewhere. Gerald Hollister spied her and headed in her direction. I made my way over to the bushel baskets, arranged on a couple of long low tables. Two other women were checking out pumpkins. And I realized I knew the woman waiting on them. Her son was one of the new first-graders added to our Reading Buddies program.

I could get bits and pieces of Hope's conversation with the old man, and she wasn't getting anywhere. He offered the two chairs to her for way more than I knew they had to be worth. And when she mentioned she'd heard he might be able to help her with an off-road vehicle he told her flat out whoever had told her that was steering her wrong.

Hope took it all in stride, shrugging and saying it must have been someone else. She pointed at the old barn and asked if Hollister had any more chairs. He told her no—another lie, I was guessing.

Meanwhile the two women had found their pumpkin at last. Bella Lawrence—Lawrence because she wasn't married to her boy's father, the old man's son—came up quietly behind me.

"Hello, Ms. Paulson," she said in her soft voice. Then she pointed at a basket of apples. "Haralson are good if you looking to make pie," she added in a slightly louder voice. "So are Honeycrisp."

"What about these?" I asked, moving over to the end of the makeshift table as far away from Hope and the old man as I could get.

Bella shook her head. Her long dark hair was pulled back in a braid, and her face, devoid of any makeup, made her look like a teenager—too young to be the mother of a six-year-old. "Those are SnowSweet. Good for eating, not for pie."

She lowered her voice again. "The old man is lying to your friend," she said. "I know she's a police officer. She talked to Duncan's class when they toured the fire station."

Neither one of us was any good at undercover work it seemed.

"Please don't tell him," I whispered.

She smiled. "What he doesn't know doesn't hurt him. Anyway, I owe you. You should hear Duncan read now that he's in your Reading Buddies. He isn't going to be stuck here, that's for sure."

I picked an apple from the top of one of the baskets and pretended to be considering it just in case the old man was looking our way. "So he does have some off-road vehicles?" I said.

"A truck and an old Jeep."

"Has anyone used either one of them lately?"

Bella picked up the basket of apples directly in front of me. "Good choice," she said. She led me around behind the mound of pumpkins. "You know that thing planned for the lake? The resort?"

I nodded. "He doesn't want it to happen. He figures the county'll make him fix this place up and come after him for tax on all the stuff he's selling. This guy came looking for something off-road." Her eyes met mine. "I listen because it's good to know things. He said he could stop the development from happening but he didn't want anyone to know he's been over on that land."

I described John.

"That's him," she said. She took a pumpkin from the pile. "Is that everything?" she asked.

"It is," I said. "Thank you."

Bella dumped the apples into a paper bag and I paid her for everything. As she handed the bag of apples to me she bent her head close to mine. "If you want to look at that Jeep it's parked in a lean-to out to the back of here. Head that way." She pointed down the road. "Watch for a peeling green post and some yellow tape around a tree. That's the road you want." She straightened up and gave me a practiced smile. "Thanks for coming. Stop by again."

I set the apples and the pumpkin on the backseat. Hercules immediately stuck his nose in the bag.

Hope slid behind the wheel with a fake smile plastered on her face.

"Turn right," I said.

She glanced at me, eyes narrowed, but put on the right-turn blinker. "That was a waste of time," she said once we were on the road. "And why did you want to go this way?"

"Because John did rent an off-road vehicle from Gerald Hollister and I know where it is."

"How do you do that?" Hope asked, shaking her head, a smile starting to spread across her face.

"Do what?" I said, keeping my eyes glued to the side of the road. I was watching for a post with peeling green paint and a piece of yellow flagging tape tied around a tree.

"Get people to tell you things."

"Bella Lawrence is living with Gerald's son. Her little guy is in Reading Buddies and she doesn't like the old man very much."

"In other words she was happy to help you."

"And throw a bit of a monkey wrench into in his plans as well." I caught sight of the green post. "Up there," I said, gesturing at the road ahead. "There's a gravel road. Turn off."

We pulled off the main road onto an unpaved track. Hope stopped and put the car in park. "Okay, where are we going?" she asked, turning toward me.

"Bella told me that Gerald rented a cut-down Jeep to John so he could get around the property out by the lake. He agreed to keep it quiet because it's to his advantage." I explained what Bella had told me about her almost father-in law's position on the development.

"So why are we on a dirt road in the woods?" Hope asked.

"Because the Jeep is at a lean-to at the back end of Hollister's land, according to Bella."

I pointed at the road ahead through the windshield. "If you follow this it turns and runs behind Hollister's land and Wisteria Hill. I came out here this summer to pick blueberries with Roma."

"If we could get a look at that Jeep and there's damage—"

"It shouldn't be that hard to link the vehicle back to John," I said.

She nodded slowly. "I don't imagine the old man

will be so tight-lipped when there are murder charges involved." An impatient meow came from the backseat. Hope grinned. "I think that means 'Get moving.'"

"I think you're right," I said.

We drove by the back of Hollister's property the first time and had to double back. I remembered Roma pointing out where his property and hers met, noting the remnants of a ramshackle fence in the scrub and bushes close to the road.

"Watch for a broken-down fence," I said. Hercules moved to the driver's side of the car and looked up at the window. But it was Hope who spotted the weathered wood and sagging barbed wire.

"There!" she said, pointing through the windshield. She pulled the car off the road as far as she could onto the narrow shoulder then turned in her seat and looked at me. "I think you should stay here."

"Not a chance," I said, unfastening my seat belt. "I'm going to get out of the car, climb over what's left of that fence and trespass on Gerald Hollister's property. Being an officer of the law, you're going to come after me, because I'm breaking the law. *And* as an officer of the law, if you happen to find evidence of one crime while you're trying to stop another—" I held up my hands. "Who can find fault with that?"

She gave me a wry smile. "A lot of people can, Kathleen. Your scenario has more holes than my old rain boots."

It was raining now, a steady drizzle that made me wish I had my own rain boots.

"I know," I said. I took a deep breath and let it out.

"Just stay here, Hope. I'll go look for the Jeep, I'll take photos with my phone and bring them back for you to look at."

She was shaking her head before I finished speaking. "No way."

"Then I guess we're both going," I said. I looked over my shoulder at Hercules sitting in the middle of the backseat. "Guard the car," I told him.

"Mrr," he said as if he'd understood, which I knew was a definite possibility.

Hope and I got out and walked across the dirt road. There was a narrow shoulder that dropped down steeply to a wide, muddy ditch. The fence began on the other side. There were bushes and spindly trees growing up, through and around it.

We made our way down the bank and through the mud, which sucked at our shoes. Up close the fence was taller than I'd expected. The wire was barbed. I couldn't see any way to get a handhold or foothold over.

"We're not getting over this, are we?" Hope said.

"No," I said. "That barbed wire may be old but that doesn't mean it won't tear your skin apart." I walked alongside the fence, hoping I'd find a break in it somewhere, but it just continued around the corner and into the dark, damp woods. I turned and headed back to where Hope was standing. "This isn't going to work. The fence continues into the woods. We could spend hours walking and not find a way to get over safely."

Rain was dripping off the edge of her hood onto her face and she swiped at it impatiently with the heel of her hand. "Then you're just going to have to give me a boost over and I'll take my chances with that barbed wire, because I'm not leaving without finding that Jeep."

"I have an idea that might work better," I said.

"You're not going to suggest we send Hercules in with the camera, are you?" she asked.

I shook my head and water sprayed off my jacket. "Nah, he wouldn't go. Hercules hates getting his feet wet. I think we might be able to get to this piece of land through Roma's. I don't think this fence goes all the way around on the section where the properties abut. I know those woods a lot better, too."

"All right," Hope said. "Let's go."

We went back to the car and Hope drove slowly down the woods road and turned back onto the main road toward Wisteria Hill.

"What are we going to tell Roma we're doing out here?" Hope asked.

Out of the corner of my eye I saw Hercules's head swing around toward me when he heard Roma's name.

"She's not here," I said. "She's over in Red Wing helping the vet there with a surgery. She won't be back until later tonight."

Hope glanced at me as the car reached the top of the driveway. "Seems like we got lucky."

"Let's hope it keeps up," I said.

Hope and I got out. Once again I'd told Hercules to guard the car. He'd climbed into the front and was sitting on the passenger side, watching us through the side window. It was still raining and I had no worries about him leaving the vehicle.

Hope looked around. "Okay, which way?"

I pointed at the carriage house. "There's a path around the side that leads across a field and into the woods. If we stay close to the brook there's a place where the water is low that we can cross and then we should be on Hollister's land. If we keep heading back that way we should come on the lean-to."

"Let's do this," Hope said.

We made our way around the weathered old carriage house and across the overgrown field behind it. The embankment had been graded and reinforced with a rock wall and it was fairly easy to climb up to the top. I pointed through the trees that stretched ahead of us. "Can you hear that?" I asked.

Hope pushed back the hood of her jacket. "That's water, isn't it?"

I nodded. "That's the brook. If we follow it back about half a mile there's a place I'm pretty sure we can get across."

The trees provided some cover from the rain as we walked. "How did you get to know all this area so well?" Hope asked.

"Mostly Roma, a little bit Maggie and Rebecca," I said. "Roma convinced me to join her group of volunteers who take care of the feral cat colony back before she even owned Wisteria Hill. I started spending more time out here and I just started exploring. Then Rebecca began teaching Maggie about the uses for different plants and when they came out here to look for some of them I'd usually come with them." I smiled at the memory of walking through these woods with Rebecca, who would point out tiny plants I'd never noticed before. "Rebecca grew up out here. Her mother worked for the Hendersons."

"I like her," Hope said. "Rebecca, I mean."

I nodded. "I don't think there's anyone who doesn't. Owen and Hercules are crazy about her. She buys Owen those catnip chickens. It's like she's his catnip chicken dealer."

Hope smiled. "Sorry. I don't think that's a crime." She put out a hand to steady herself as the ground began to slope downward. "Can I ask you how you picked their names? Is there some literary connection?"

"There is for Owen," I said. "His name comes from *A Prayer for Owen Meany*. I was reading it when I first got the cats and he kept sitting on the book. Now I realize it was probably to get my attention."

"What about Hercules? That's Roman mythology, not Greek, right? Hercules is named for the guy who did the twelve labors."

"Right," I said.

"Okay, that was a lie," she said.

I looked over at her. "No, it wasn't. Hercules is the son of the god Zeus and a mortal woman."

She waved a hand dismissively. "Oh, I don't doubt that. What I meant was you're lying about naming your cat after him."

"How did you know?" I said.

"You answered too quickly."

I laughed. "I'll remember that next time I want to fudge the truth. No, Hercules isn't exactly named for the son of Zeus. He's actually named for Kevin Sorbo. He played Hercules in a TV series back in the nineties."

"So why didn't you name Hercules Kevin?" I could see she was trying not to laugh.

"So I could avoid having conversations like this one."

Hope did laugh then. "How's that working out?"

Just then we came level with an area where the brook widened and the water was much shallower. Several large rocks made a bridge of sorts to the other side. "I'm pretty sure this is the spot," I said.

The rocks were wet and slippery but we both made it across safely.

My shoes were oozing water. So were Hope's. "Are they your new running shoes?" I asked, pointing to her neon-yellow-and-green footwear. Hope was training for another triathlon. Marcus had convinced her to buy new shoes with fancy inserts that had been custom made in Minneapolis.

Hope looked down at her feet. "I knew spending all that money on these things was a bad idea." She looked around. "Which way do we go?"

"That way," I said with a confidence I didn't completely feel. I pointed more or less northwest. If Hope thought I was lying again she kept that to herself.

We walked for another twenty minutes or so. Hope was the first to spot the lean-to up ahead of us in a small clearing. A rough road curved away from it off to the far left side. The lean-to looked more like a section of an old barn left after the other half had collapsed. I had my fingers crossed as we made our way closer, and then I spotted it.

"The Jeep is there," I said to Hope.

"Stay here," she said, holding up one hand.

I stopped where I was while she made her way carefully closer, bending low to study the front end of the vehicle. Finally she turned and looked at me. "There's front-end damage, Kathleen," she said, and I could hear the excitement in her voice. She pulled her phone out of her pocket. "I'm going to take a couple of pictures and we can get out of here."

"I don't think so," a voice said, and John Keller stepped into the clearing.

15

Hope's hand moved almost imperceptibly.

"Don't even think about it," John said, gesturing with the gun in his right hand. "I can shoot your gun right out of your hand. In fact, I can shoot you in the hand before you can even get the gun out, and then shoot Kathleen in the hand just because she really irritates me."

Hope held up both hands, palms facing John. "Okay. No gun. But you know this isn't going to work."

"Do they teach you to say that the first day of cop school? Because I have to say it's pretty lame."

"Gerald Hollister may be willing to lie about renting you that Jeep," I said. "But when they find our bodies out here, shot to death, he won't keep covering for you."

John smiled at me like he was a teacher and I was his star pupil. "Very good, Kathleen. However, you missed two key points. One, your bodies aren't going to be out here and two, I'm not going to shoot you, as tempting as that might be."

"So what are you going to do?" I asked.

His wet hair dripped onto his face but he didn't seem to notice. "Right now I'm going to get Detective Lind's gun." He looked at her. "Pull it out nice and slow. Two fingers. Try anything funny and I'll shoot Kathleen."

Hope took out her gun as John had directed.

"Toss it over here," he instructed. "If you throw it too far or too short, like I said before, I'll have to shoot Kathleen."

"I thought you said you weren't going to shoot us," I said. My stomach clenched but I tried very hard not to let him hear the panic I was feeling.

John nodded. "Good point, Kathleen. I did say that. Shooting you would mess up my plan, but I will do it if I have to." He gestured at Hope with the gun. "Throw it, and remember, accuracy counts."

Hope lobbed her gun in his direction and it landed on the ground at his feet.

John crouched to pick it up and tucked it in his waistband. I couldn't help hoping it would somehow discharge and shoot him in the foot. "Now toss me your cell phones."

I looked at Hope. "Do it," she said.

I threw my phone underhand at John. He caught it in midair. "Nice," he said to me. Hope tossed her phone over as well. It landed once again at his feet. John picked it up and put both phones in his pocket. "We're going to take a little walk." He looked at me. "Back the way you came."

That meant back in the direction of Wisteria Hill. Back in the direction of help.

"You too, Detective," I heard John say.

We trudged through the trees as the rain came down, soaking through my jacket. My shoes and jeans were already wet. I promised myself a warm pair of socks and a huge cup of hot coffee when we got out of this. I wasn't going to think about the possibility that we *wouldn't* get out of this.

"Why did you kill her?" I heard Hope ask behind me.

I turned and looked back over my shoulder. Hope had stopped walking and was looking at John.

"You think I don't know you're trying to stall," he said. "Wherever you went to school, you should ask for your money back."

"If you're going to kill me I'd at least like to know why I'm going to die," I said.

"You think I want to do this?" he asked.

"No, you probably don't." My hands were shaking and I stuffed them in my pockets so he wouldn't see. "And I know you didn't want to kill Dani. You loved her."

"Yes, I did," John said. He lifted the gun so it was in line with my midsection. "Walk."

We continued in silence for a while, John directing me when he thought I was trying to veer from the path. We were headed back to Wisteria Hill but I had no idea why.

"She didn't see that you were the best person for her," Hope said. "Not the other two. You."

"I loved her." John's voice was low and filled with emotion. "Why couldn't she see how good we could have been together?"

"I know," Hope said.

I slowed my pace a little so she could close the gap between us, hoping John wouldn't notice.

"No, you don't," he said.

"Marcus doesn't see how good we could have been together," Hope said.

I looked back at her but she wouldn't meet my gaze. John had stopped walking. Hope and I did as well. "You and Marcus?" he asked. "Stop screwing with me."

"I'm not." Hope's voice was laced with something. Longing? Pain? I wasn't sure. She started moving again and so did I.

"Did you tell him?" John said suddenly.

"Not in so many words," she said. "But . . ." She let the end of the sentence trail away.

"But what?"

I heard Hope sigh behind me. "It doesn't matter," she said flatly.

"But what?" John asked even more insistently.

"But he should be able to see that I'm the one who loves him the best. How can he not see that?"

"She was the same way." He meant Dani, I knew. "Travis heard her talking to someone on the phone about coming here to see Marcus. I knew what it meant. She'd been secretive for a while. I knew she was going to try to get back together with him."

"You told her how you felt," Hope said.

I couldn't hear their footsteps, I realized. I took a chance on turning around again.

Hope was facing John, hood pushed back, rain dripping from her hair. "We have history," Hope said. "Why doesn't that mean anything?"

"She said I didn't really know who she was at all." John gestured again with the gun.

Hope moved closer to him, taking a tiny step as she nodded at his words. She was going to rush him, I realized. I wasn't a police officer but I knew he'd shoot her before she ever got the chance to get his gun. Hope was strong and fit, but John was bigger.

"I knew her better than anyone. Who helped her pass organic chemistry? Who cleaned up the mess when she screwed Marcus? You know what she did? She told me to get out of her life and then she just walked away. I just . . . I was just trying to catch up with her. I didn't mean to hit her." He gestured with his gun hand again and his voice got louder in the silence of the rain-soaked woods. "It was her fault. She just should have loved me.

I looked at Hope and thought of Owen. She had the same coiled energy as he did, ready and watchful in the backyard before he launched himself on a squirrel or a bird. I had no way to stop her. At least I could help distract John.

"Love isn't an obligation," I said. "Being deeply loved by someone gives you strength, while loving someone deeply gives you courage. Lao Tzu said that."

John took several steps closer to me so he was less than an arm's length away from Hope. "Want me to shoot her?" he asked. His eyes never left my face but I knew he was directing the question at Hope.

"It won't change anything," she said.

My heart pounded in my ears and my chest was so tight I couldn't breathe. The gun was level with my head. If John decided to pull the trigger anyway I was dead. Then, finally, he lowered his arm.

And Hope made her move.

John had seen it coming. Somehow he'd seen it coming. The hand holding the gun arced sideways and caught her on the side of her head. She staggered and he kicked her right leg out from under her. Her arms flailed in the air as she tried to get her balance but her foot caught in a protruding tree root and she went down. I lunged to catch her but I was too late.

I bent over Hope. Her eyes were closed and there was blood in her hair on the right side of her head. I felt for a pulse, grateful to feel her heart pounding even faster than mine. I reached in my pocket, pulled out a couple of Kleenex and pressed them against the gash on Hope's head.

"Get her up," John ordered.

"She's unconscious," I said, not looking at him. I was so angry I was afraid I'd do something stupid and get us both shot. Every minute longer was another minute I could use to figure a way out of this.

"Then carry her or drag her. I don't care." He spit out each word.

My anger boiled over. "Neither one of those is going to happen," I snapped. If he hadn't had the gun I would have hit him. "So either you wait until she comes to or shoot us, because those are the only two choices you have. And if you shoot a police officer they will hunt you down like a rabid dog until someone puts a bullet in *your* head." I was breathing hard and I could feel flecks of spit on my lips.

Hope's eyes fluttered and opened. "Way to build a rapport, Kathleen," she rasped.

Rain had soaked the tissues pressed to her head. I took my hand away. It didn't seem to be bleeding anymore but the skin was already swelling and darkening.

I helped Hope sit up slowly. Her eyes rolled and for a moment I thought she was going to pass out again.

"Move," John barked.

"Wait," I retorted.

"I'm all right," Hope said. "Give me a hand."

I helped her get to her feet. She grimaced as she put weight down on that right foot. "Let me look," I said. I bent down and rolled up the bottom of her jeans. Her ankle was already swelling. I probed carefully with my fingers and Hope sucked in a sharp breath.

I stood up and wiped my hands on my wet jeans, which really didn't do any good. I looked at John. "Her ankle might be broken. It's sprained at least. She can't walk. Just leave us here and go."

"I can walk, Kathleen," Hope said. "Let it go." There was warning in her eyes.

"Let me help you," I said. I put my arm across her back, taking as much of her weight as I could, and we started moving again.

It was slow going. The rain continued to fall and the ground was slippery and uneven. I concentrated on putting one foot in front of the other and not letting Hope fall. Her breathing came in ragged gasps. I glanced over at her. She was gritting her teeth and pain was etched in the lines on her face.

She caught me watching her. "Hunt you down like a rabid dog?" she whispered, and her mouth pulled into a semblance of a smile.

"Best I could do in the moment," I said.

"If you get a chance to get away—" she began.

"—I'm taking you with me," I finished.

"You two planning some way to best me?" John was right behind us, so close I fancied I could feel his breath on the back of my neck, which in reality was impossible because I had my hood up.

"Yes," I said.

Hope pressed her lips together. "You're so bad at this," she said.

"You set Marcus up," I said. I wasn't trying to stall. I needed to hear John confirm everything. I needed to stay angry so we'd stay alive.

"Yes, I set Marcus up." John's voice was smug.

"You hacked his phone. You made it look as though he'd sent those texts to Dani."

"And they say the Internet is a waste of time," he said.

I swallowed the lump in my throat. "What I don't get is how you planted the key chain?"

He laughed but there was nothing humorous about the sound. "That was just a spur of the moment thing.

The drive-in logo broke off my keys. Then I realized I could leave it there and all I had to do was get one from Travis or Marcus to replace mine and send the police in another direction. That night at Marcus's house when I used his bathroom I saw his keys on his dresser. Since he had taken Dani away from me again, it just seemed like poetic justice."

I didn't say anything. It was clear something was broken in him.

We kept walking. I lost all concept of time. We could have been moving for five minutes or two hours. Hope's face was pale and wan and the rain had washed a trail of blood from her hair down the side of her face. Not only was I fairly sure she had a broken ankle, I thought she had a concussion, too.

I looked around, trying to get my bearings. We were on Ruby's property, I realized finally, not that far from the old camp, which meant we weren't that far from Wisteria Hill. The thought gave me hope. I shifted a bit more of Hope's weight onto me.

"Where are we going?" I said. I could feel John, still no more than a step behind us.

Ding, dong, bell,
Pussy's in the well.
Who put her in?
Little Johnny Flynn.

He recited the children's nursery rhyme in a sing-song voice.

A well? Was there a well somewhere on this land?

All I could think of was a dark, cold, small space. I bit down hard on my tongue so I wouldn't vomit. Or scream. I was claustrophobic.

"Stop!" John ordered. We stopped walking. Hope sagged and I lost my grip on her. She dropped to the ground. I bent down to help her up.

"Leave her," he said.

I turned to look at him. I wasn't a violent person. I believed that words were better for solving problems that fists, but in that moment if John Keller hadn't had a gun I would have taken a swing at him and not lost a moment's sleep.

He was using one foot to scrape wet leaves off of something on the forest floor. It was some kind of plank square: the cover to the well, I was guessing, based on the weathering of the wood.

An iron ring was bolted to the middle of the wooden cover. Eyes and gun on Hope and me, John bent down and pulled the cover up. I smelled dampness and dirt and must.

Panic rolled over me like a wave. I squeezed my hands into tight fists. *Roma will come home*, I told myself. *She'll find the car and Hercules. Someone will find us.*

I made myself look at John and fought to keep the panic from carrying me away. We were going to get out of this.

He laughed. The ugly sound wrapped around the trees.

"What's so funny?" I asked.

"Your stupid Pollyanna optimism," he said. "You still think you're going to get out of this."

I bent down and helped Hope to her feet again. Her skin was even grayer, if that was possible.

"I know where the two of you parked," John said. "The lake is very deep, you know."

I bit down on my lip so hard I drew blood. Hercules could get out of Hope's car. He didn't like the rain but he knew the property. *He'll be safe,* I said silently. *And we will get out of here.*

John grabbed Hope's arm, pulling her away from me. She staggered and he took advantage of her momentum, pushing her down into the open hole. On instinct she grabbed at the ground, her hands clawing the mud, looking for something to hold on to. All she got were handfuls of wet leaves and pine needles. She fell back into the darkness.

"Now you," John said, pointing the gun at me. I had a fleeting thought that being shot would be better than climbing down into that dark, tight hole. But Hope was already down there and I couldn't leave her there alone.

I walked to the edge and sat down, dangling my legs in the hole. I couldn't see Hope and I had no idea how far she had fallen, how far I would fall. Was she already dead? Had the fall broken her neck? Would the same happen to me? I flashed to my father as Henry the Fifth in Shakespeare's play of the same name as Henry spoke to his army. I could hear my father's voice in my head and I whispered the words along with it: "Stiffen the sinews, conjure up the blood, Disguise fair nature with hard-favoured rage." And then I jumped.

16

I landed on some kind of wooden platform twelve, maybe fifteen, feet down. The fall knocked the wind out of me and I lay there, trying to get my breath. Above us John pulled the wooden cover over the hole. I stifled a scream. It came out like a whimper.

I'd never been in a place so dark. I put a hand out and felt packed earth. It felt as though the ground itself was pushing back. Tears rolled down my face—or maybe it was rain dripping from my hair. I felt around slowly, carefully, for Hope, *Please don't let her be dead* running on repeat in my head. My hand touched something that felt like fur. I yanked it back and did let out a small scream. I heard a moan behind me. "Hope?" I said stretching out my trembling arm.

My hand connected with her shoulder. "Kathleen?" she managed to gasp out.

"Yes," I said. I found her other shoulder and helped pull her into a sitting position. She leaned against me.

"We're going to get out of here," I said. "I just need a minute to think."

I looked up over my head. The air was stale but there were small spaces between the planks that made up the well cover. We were getting some air. We could breathe as long as the smell from whatever was decomposing down here didn't overcome us.

"How far down?" Hope asked.

"I'm not sure," I said. "Fifteen feet, maybe less. This isn't a well. It's a spring or something. I'm guessing it's been partly filled with gravel. We can get out. It's not that deep."

She didn't answer me. I shook her gently. She groaned.

What had I learned about head injuries in first aid? "You have to stay awake," I said, giving her shoulders a squeeze. "I'm going to get us out of here but your job is to stay awake."

"Okay," she said after a moment. Her voice was weak but she was with me for now.

I touched the wall of the well. *Please God, let it be dirt and not brick*, I thought.

Dirt.

Yes.

The dirt was packed hard and dense with twisted tree roots, but maybe, just maybe I could scrape out enough of a handhold to make it to the top. I felt for a spot about waist-height and tried to make a hole using just my hands. The earth felt like a mix of rocks and clay compacted together, with the tree roots surrounding it all like a net or a web.

"We're trapped," Hope whispered.

I choked off a sob and dropped back down beside her. I swiped away the tears that were running down my face with one dirty hand. "No!" I said. "We are not dying down here. We're getting out and getting Hercules and I'm going to punch John Keller right in the nose and I'm going to like it. And then I'm going to have a bath and a whole pan of brownies."

Hope made a strangled sound and for a moment I thought she was choking. Then I realized she was laughing. "You are . . . Pollyanna," she said.

I sniffed and swiped at my eyes again. "Pippi Longstocking," I said. "That's who I wanted to be when I was a kid."

"Who . . ." Hope's voice trailed off.

"She's the main character in a series of children's books. You'll like them. When we get out of here I'll check them all out for you."

She didn't answer. I nudged her shoulder again. "You have to stay awake, Hope," I said.

"I am," she whispered after a moment.

"I need something to dig with." I felt around the wooden platform, trying to stay away from the spot where I'd touched whatever was rotting down here.

There was water underneath us. Just as air was getting down to us through the spaces in the boards above us that water would come up through the spaces in the dirt and gravel below us. I had to get us out now. I had to find something to dig with. It occurred to me that if I took my sneaker off could I use the sole as a shovel. I wasn't sure it would work.

I untied my shoe and pulled it off. It was so wet a small stream of water poured out. "Okay, cross your fingers," I said to Hope. I pressed the sneaker's upper against the sole and dug at the well wall with it. The wet shoe slipped out of my hand and fell onto the wooden platform. I swore and bent down to retrieve it.

"You said a bad word," Hope rasped.

"I'm sorry," I said. My fingers brushed the dead whatever it was. I recoiled, felt around a little more and caught the end of a shoelace.

Hope laughed, the same half-strangled sound as before. "You're so . . . nice. Not like me."

I turned the shoe around and attacked the wall with the heel end. "You're a nice person," I said.

"No," she mumbled.

The heel of the shoe didn't work any better than the toe had. I beat on the wall in frustration. I was standing in water now, I realized. It was rising rapidly.

"What's wrong?" Hope asked, struggling to get to her feet. Her ankle wouldn't hold her and she collapsed onto the ground with a groan.

I made a grunt of frustration. "I was trying to use my shoe to dig with but it won't work. The sole is too rubbery."

"You need . . . insoles," she said.

"Wait a minute," I said. "Are you wearing yours?"

"Yes." Her voice got a little stronger. "Yes."

I squatted down, felt for Hope's leg and found her left foot. "I'm just going to take this shoe off," I said. "I don't want to take the other one off because your ankle is swelling and I'm afraid we won't get it back on."

I stripped the insole out of Hope's running shoe, picturing it in my mind because I couldn't see it. The curve of metal was held between two pieces of leather. This might just work. I put Hope's shoe in her hands. "Cross your fingers," I said.

She caught my fingers and gave them a squeeze. Her grip was weak. "Thank you," she said.

I stood up and attacked the wall with the heel end of the insert. Dirt fell onto my arm. "It's working!"

"Yay . . ." Hope's voice petered out.

I felt behind me with one hand. I touched the top of her head. "No, no, no. You have to stay awake. I can't do this by myself."

"It's . . . wet."

"I know," I said. "But I'm going to get us out. Just don't go to sleep on me."

I dug awkwardly with my makeshift trowel. It was slow going and it still felt like the ground was pushing back, trying to fold around us. I started to breathe hard. Were we running out of air? "Talk to me, please?" I asked, my voice as shaky as I suddenly felt.

"You afraid of . . . the dark?" Hope said.

I started to dig again.

"Closed spaces," I said, grunting with the effort it took to dig. I moved my foot, guessing there must be two inches of water at my feet now. Rain slid down my face. At least that's what I told myself it was.

I dug what I hoped was a good enough handhold and then reached farther up the wall and began digging again. And I kept talking to Hope, telling her stories, asking questions, trying not to let panic overwhelm me.

Finally I had four steps etched into the wall, the last at the limit of my reach. I crouched down next to Hope. She was sitting in several inches of water. I felt for her arm and put my hands on her shoulders. "We're going to get out of here," I said. "I need you to stand up. I'm going to climb up and push the cover out of the way. Then I'm going to help you up. Right now I need you to stand up so I can show you where to put your hands and feet."

I helped her to her feet and had her feel the wall for the small indentations I made. They suddenly seemed very small.

"When you run a marathon what do you tell your-self when you're facing those last few miles?" I asked.

"That . . . I'm . . . crazy."

I smiled even though she couldn't see it in the darkness. "Okay, three crazy miles to go," I said. "See you at the finish line." I felt for my two handholds and put one foot in the bottom indentation I'd made. It slipped out but I kicked my foot in hard and the second time it held. The wall of the cistern was wet and slippery. I hugged it with my body, lifted my right arm and pulled myself up a little higher. Finally after what seemed like an eternity I was right below the wooden cover.

I pushed up with one hand. The cover moved maybe a couple of inches and cold dirty water poured onto my face. I spit and shook my head and pushed again. The wooden square moved a little more this time. I took a deep breath and pushed one more time, groaning with the exertion, and this time the cover lifted and slipped to the side. There was just enough space for me to fit my hand, but that was enough. I pushed, the wood sliding over an inch at a time, but it moved. And finally there was enough space for me to get my arm up over the top. I felt around for the iron ring, grabbed it tightly and flung my other arm out of the hole, grabbing at the ground. For a moment I was suspended by one arm, my body weight pulling at my shoulder. Then I caught a tree root and held on for dear life. I kicked my legs out from the wall of the cistern and used the momentum I'd gained to push back against it when we reconnected, pulling with every last bit of my strength. And somehow I got the top half of my body up onto the wooden cover. I kicked my legs again, rolled hard to the right and I was out.

I lay there for a moment like an overturned bug, rain falling on my face. Then I rolled to my side, got on all fours and pulled the cover all the way back from the opening of the hole. I crouched at the edge but I couldn't see anything. Or anyone.

"Hope," I called.

She didn't answer.

I leaned closer, bracing myself with my hands on either side. "Hope," I yelled again.

What if she'd collapsed? What if she was lying facedown in that water right now? Just looking onto that yawning opening made me shake, but if I had to go back down into it again then that's what I was going to do.

And then I heard her. "Kathleen."

I pulled the scarf I was wearing under my jacket

off my neck. I tied a slipknot at one end and tightened the loop. I looked around for somewhere to brace my feet. The trunk of a nearby tree was going to have to do. "I'm dropping my scarf down to you," I said. "Put one wrist through the loop and pull it tight. I'm going to pull and help you up."

I hung as much of the top half of my body down in the hole as I dared, planted my feet, toes down in the mud, against the tree and let the scarf down, swinging it a little so Hope could find it. Given the length of the scarf, Hope's height and my long arms, this should work. *Please let the math be right,* I prayed. Finally I felt her grab the scarf.

"Keep your weight on your left foot as much as you can," I called. "Ready?"

After a moment I heard her voice. It may have been weak but I could hear the determination. She began to climb. I pulled and I prayed and somehow by some miracle we did it. One of Hope's hands was close enough to grab, and then the other, and we screamed with the effort but together we got her over the top. She was on her stomach in the mud and I was on my side and the rain pelted us like tiny stinging fists, but we were out.

It wasn't until I sat up that I realized Hope had passed out. I felt for a pulse and leaned my face close to hers. Her heart was beating and she was breathing. She was just unconscious. Somehow I had to get her down to Wisteria Hill.

I could make some kind of sled and drag her, I decided. I looked around for a couple of long, sturdy branches, thinking I could tie my raincoat to them and drag her. Off to my left for a moment I thought I saw a wink of light. I shook my head. It was just a trick of my overloaded brain. Then I saw it again. A bobbing light. I wasn't dreaming or hallucinating. A voice called my name. "Kathleen!"

I stood up and waved my arms over my head. "I'm here," I shouted, relief making my whole body shake.

The light bounced again and turned in my direction and Elliot Gordon came out of the trees, trailed by a very wet black-and-white tuxedo cat. I pressed my hand to my mouth and sobs shook my body.

Elliot caught me by the shoulders. "Oh my God, Kathleen, are you all right?" he said. He was soaked to the skin, his hair plastered to his skull.

I nodded. "Hope's unconscious," I said, gesturing behind me.

"Hang on," Elliot said. He moved past me, crouching to check Hope.

I kneeled on the ground and gathered Hercules into my arms. He craned his head up and licked my chin. "I'm so glad to see you," I said, half laughing, half crying. I unzipped my jacket and put him inside, zippering it around him, holding him against me with one hand. Even wet he was better than any electric blanket.

"Can you take this?" Elliot said, holding out the flashlight he was holding. "I'll carry her."

He had a gash near his eye, angry and red, I realized.

"What happened?" I asked.

"Don't worry," he said with a hint of a smile. "It wasn't your cat. I had a small altercation with a tree branch. I'm okay." He was still holding out the light.

I took it from him, swinging it to look down into the cistern. The water had to be chest-height now. I could make out the remains of what looked to be a raccoon on the bottom. My hands trembled and I turned the light away.

Elliot looked at me, horror etched on his face. "Keller put you down there?" he asked.

I nodded. "It's not as deep as it looks." Then I realized what he'd said. "Wait a minute. How did you know it was John?"

Elliot wiped the water from his face with one hand. "Long story," he said. He glanced at the scarf still wrapped around Hope's wrist but didn't say anything else. He just untied the sodden fabric and handed it to me. I stuffed it in my pocket.

Elliot slid his arms under Hope's limp body and stood up. He gave me a look I couldn't quite fathom. "Let's get out of here," he said.

Hercules poked his head out of the front of my jacket and meowed his enthusiasm for the idea.

"John Keller killed Dani," I said to Elliot.

He nodded. "I know."

I frowned at him. "What do you mean, you know? And I don't understand how you found us."

"Your neighbor, Rebecca. You talked to her about John's alibi—or, I should say, lack thereof. She came back to talk to you and when your truck was there and you weren't she called Marcus. He was with Brady

Chapman. When they heard Rebecca's story Brady called Detective Foster. They got John before he could leave town." His face tightened. "He wouldn't tell them where you were. Everyone has been looking for you."

"He set Marcus up," I said. "He left his own key fob from the drive-in with Dani's body and then took Marcus's the next time he was at the house. He hacked his phone to make it look like Marcus and Dani were texting."

Elliot nodded, his lips pulled into a thin, tight line. "How did you know we were out here?"

He inclined his head in the direction of the ramshackle camp. "Burtis and I and some other guys we knew used to play poker there. I was driving around trying to figure out where you might be and it occurred to me that Keller had been out in these woods and he'd likely seen the old building."

I pushed my wet hair out of my face. "Okay, but I don't understand how you ended up with my cat."

Elliot looked over at Hercules and smiled at the little cat, who it seemed to me smiled back at him. "The old carriage house on Everett Henderson's property. I was walking across the field behind it and there he was, heading for the woods. I knew then that I was on the right track. There was no other reason for him to be out here in the rain."

I leaned forward and kissed the top of Hercules's head.

Hope was still unconscious. I reached over and felt for her pulse again. It was steady and strong.

"She'll be okay," Elliot said. "Help's coming. I couldn't

get my phone to work at first, but I had a signal just before I found you."

I looked up at him. I could see so much of his son in his face. "You saved us," I said in a voice choked with emotion.

He smiled and shook his head. "I think you pretty much did that yourself."

17

We made it the rest of the way through the trees. It took both of us to get Hope down to the field behind the carriage house but we managed. As we came around the old building I heard the scream of sirens. A black truck I recognized as belonging to Burtis skidded to a stop with a spray of gravel at the top of the driveway. Brady was driving and Marcus was in the passenger seat. He was out of the vehicle before it had even stopped moving.

Hercules squirmed in my jacket. I undid the zipper and set him down as an ambulance crested the top of the driveway followed by Roma's SUV. And then I ran to meet Marcus, throwing myself into his arms.

Elliot headed for the ambulance. I reached out to touch his arm as he went by and he smiled at me.

Marcus took my face in both hands. "Are you all right?" he said. I could see the fear in his blue eyes.

I nodded, suddenly unable to speak. Roma had parked her car and was heading toward us.

"Kathleen," she said, and I could see tears running down her face.

I kissed the palm of Marcus's hand and then I turned to hug Roma. "We didn't know where you were," she said. "We thought you were . . ." She didn't finish the sentence. Instead she gave me a wobbly smile and brushed the tears away. Then her eyes narrowed and she caught one of my hands. "You're hurt," she said.

For the first time I noticed that I'd scraped the skin off the palms of both of my hands. After what we'd just been through it didn't seem like a big deal. I shook my head. "I'm all right. That's just from getting out of the well." I pointed at Hope. "I think her ankle is broken and she has some kind of head injury."

The paramedics had Hope on a stretcher and they were both bent over her. Elliot was walking toward us with a bottle of juice in his hand.

"He put you in a well?" Marcus said. His free hand clenched into a tight fist and he tightened his grip on me with the other.

Roma closed her eyes for a moment. "The old cistern on Ruby's property."

I nodded. "What saved us was that as far as I can tell it's partly filled with gravel. It was only about twelve feet or so deep."

"Only?" Roma said softly.

"What saved them was Kathleen," Elliot said. He handed me the juice. "Drink," he ordered.

I did. No glass of orange juice had ever tasted as good.

"She got both of them out of that hole in the ground," Elliot told Marcus and Roma.

Hercules was at my feet and he meowed loudly, unhappy, I was guessing, at being left out of everything. I bent down and picked him up again. "Hercules was in Hope's car. He somehow managed to get out when John took it." I looked at Marcus. "Your father found him here. He came looking for us. Hope was unconscious. He carried her out. I wouldn't have been able to do that."

Elliot gave us a small smile. "Somehow I think you would have managed."

Marcus turned to his father. "Thank you . . . Dad," he said. He swallowed a couple of times and then wrapped his father in a hug. Elliot's eyes were bright as he hugged his son back.

One of the paramedics was coming toward us. As he got closer I realized it was Ric Holm. He'd come to my rescue before.

He smiled at me. "Hi, Kathleen," he said. He raised an eyebrow. "We have to stop meeting like this."

"Her hands need to be cleaned and bandaged," Roma said. She caught my free arm and held it out so Ric could see.

I gestured at Elliot. "Look at his face first, please. He took a branch in the eye."

Elliot held up a hand. "I'm fine. Take care of Kathleen's hands first. They're going to get infected."

Ric laughed and shook his head. "Both of you, stop being noble." He caught my fingers and rolled my hand over for a closer look. "We're going to have to pick some splinters out," he said. "How did you do this?"

"A wooden cover over a well."

He winced and turned to check the side of Elliot's face, probing gently with his fingers. "I can clean that but you should be checked out by an eye doctor just to be safe."

Elliot opened his mouth, to object I felt certain.

Marcus nodded. "I'll take care of that, Ric."

Elliot turned to look at his son.

"Don't start, Dad," he said. "You won't win this one."

Ric raised an eyebrow at Roma. "We're getting ready to transport the other patient. Can you give me a hand?" He looked at me. "That okay with you, Kathleen?"

Roma was a certified first responder as well as a vet and this wouldn't be the first time she'd taken care of me. I smiled. "It's fine."

We walked over to the ambulance. Hope was wrapped in a couple of blankets on the stretcher under the care of the other paramedic in attendance. Her eyes were half open and as I came level with her one hand reached out and touched my arm. "Kathleen," she said in a low voice.

I stopped and leaned over her. Hercules meowed softly. Hope managed a small smile. "He got out of the car," she said.

I nodded. "He's pretty resourceful."

"So are you," she said. "You saved us."

"We saved ourselves," I said.

"You're the right person for him," she said, and I knew she was referring to Marcus.

I nodded. "And you're the right partner."

She closed her eyes and I gave her hand a squeeze before Roma led me away to the back of the ambulance.

I sat down on the tailgate and set Hercules beside me. Ric looked down at the cat. "This isn't the one who . . . ?"

I shook my head. "No. That was Owen. This is Hercules." At the sound of his voice the cat looked up at Ric and meowed. His fur was matted in some places and sticking up in others.

"I take it the same hands-off policy is in effect, though," Ric said, climbing into the back of the ambulance.

"Yes," Marcus and Roma said as the same time. Hercules looked at them, all green-eyed innocence.

Ric handed supplies to Roma, who was pulling on a pair of plastic gloves. He jerked his head in Elliot's direction. "Have a seat, sir," he said. He reached over my shoulder and handed a small plastic bag to Marcus. "Turkey jerky."

"Thanks," Marcus said, "but I'm not hungry."

Ric laughed. "It's not for you. It's for the cat."

Hercules meowed loudly just in case Marcus was wondering which cat. Marcus pulled a piece of jerky out of the bag and set it down in front of Herc, who murped a thank-you and bent his head to eat.

Elliot was still standing. I slid sideways to make room for him and indicated the space. He sat down with a sigh. "I'm fine," he muttered.

Once my hands were cleaned and bandaged and

the gash on Elliot's face had been attended to they took Hope to the hospital. Elliot and I were allowed to go home after Marcus reassured Ric that he'd make sure both of us saw a doctor in the morning. Wisteria Hill was crawling with police officers.

"Roma is going to drive you," Marcus said. "I'm just going to fill the guys in and I'll be right behind you."

Brady was standing off to the side. "I'm going to take your father down to the hotel to get some clean clothes," he said.

Elliot was standing a few feet away from us, looking in the direction of the woods. I wondered what he was thinking about.

"Elliot, come back to the house once you're cleaned up," I called.

Marcus nodded. "Please, Dad," he said. He pulled his keys out of his pocket and stripped one off the ring, handing it to Brady.

"Take Dad back to my place," he said. "It's faster and we're the same size."

Maggie was waiting at the house, sitting on the back steps. She wrapped me in a hug and unshed tears sparkled in her eyes. "I'm so glad you're okay," she said. She winced as she caught sight of the bandages on my hand. "You are okay, right?"

I nodded. "I could use a shower."

She smiled. "That we can do."

Maggie looked down at Hercules, waiting patiently on the step to be let in instead of walking through the door. She pulled something out of her pocket. It was a small can of sardines.

"Maggie," I said.

She looked at me. "He was walking in the rain, Kathleen. He was coming to help you. In. The. Rain." Indignation was in her voice and her stance.

"Merow," the cat said, just a little self-righteously it seemed to me, and to Maggie's delight he actually lifted one paw in the air.

I reached down and stroked his fur with my fingers. "Maggie's right," I said. "You're a hero. You can have all the sardines you want."

Roma wrapped my hands in a couple of plastic bags and I managed to shower and get cleaned up. Maggie helped me get dressed and dried my hair.

"How many sardines did you give him?" I asked.

"I didn't count," she retorted as she brushed my hair. Then she stopped, put both arms around my shoulders and hugged me fiercely. "I'm so glad you're all right." There was a catch in her throat.

"I am, Mags," I said. I held up my hands. It looked like I was wearing fat fingerless gloves made of gauze. "Roma went a little overboard with the bandages, I swear."

Maggie sat next to me on the bed. "I can't believe John tried to kill you and Hope and that he did kill Dani. I thought he was a nice guy."

"You and me both," I said.

Roma had heated up the last of the soup. Elliot and Brady had arrived and Elliot and I sat at the table each with a bowl. Hercules jumped onto my lap and breathed sardine breath in my face. After Owen had determined that I was okay he had turned into Maggie's shadow.

There was a knock at the back door. "I'll go," Brady said.

He came back after a minute with Rebecca. She took one look at my hands and her face paled. "Oh my word, Kathleen," she said. "What did that awful young man do to you?" I pushed back my chair and went over to her, giving her a hug.

"He didn't do anything that a little antibiotic cream and a few days won't heal," I said.

"I'm so sorry, dear," she said. "I should have said something earlier." Her expression was troubled.

I shook my head and patted her shoulder awkwardly with one hand. "You don't have anything to apologize for. Because of you the police caught John. Because of you Dani gets justice."

"Because of me you were hurt. And Hope."

"No," I said firmly. "Because of John Keller. Not you."

I noticed then that she was carrying a small bag. "Is that for me?" I asked.

That at least got a smile out of Rebecca. "Lemon tarts," she said. "They're still a little warm."

I peered at the bag. "Can I have one right now anyway?"

The smile got a little bigger. "You can have two," she said. And then she reached into her pocket and pulled out a tin of sardines. "And these are for Hercules."

I laughed and hugged her again. "I love you," I whispered against her ear.

"I love you, too," she whispered back.

Brady had made coffee and we sat around the table eating Rebecca's lemon tarts. The conversation turned to the development.

"I wish after all of this that it wasn't happening," I said.

"Oh, that's right. You don't know," Rebecca said.

I narrowed my eyes at her. "Know what?"

"To use my mother's expression, Ernie Kinsley was cooking the books. The IRS got a tip. He's being investigated and someone else has bought the land as of a couple of hours ago. The development—at least this one—is history." She smiled.

I looked across the table at her. "Everett?" I said.

Rebecca shook her head. "No. Oh, he would have if he'd had the chance. He's come around to our way of thinking when it comes to that development idea at least. But someone else with deep pockets beat him to it."

Maggie raised her cup of tea. "A toast to our mysterious benefactor with deep pockets." We clinked cups and mugs and there was another knock at the door. I got to my feet.

"I'll go," Maggie said, shaking her head at me. She headed for the porch and I trailed her because I was feeling restless. I need to move around.

Simon Janes was at the door with a take-out order of food from Eric's. "Come in," I said, gesturing to the kitchen.

He shook his head and handed the two paper shopping bags to Maggie. "I can't stay."

"I'll stick these in the fridge," Maggie said, heading for the kitchen.

"You're all right," Simon said. He didn't phrase it as a question.

I held up my hands. "Just some scrapes."

"And Detective Lind?"

"She has a broken ankle and a concussion but she's okay." Brady had called the hospital and thanks to some connection he had there had gotten an update on Hope.

"You bought the land," I said.

"I'm sorry, what land?"

I looked at him without speaking. Finally he smiled and gave an offhanded shrug.

"Why?" I asked. I had an idea of what that land must have cost. I also had an idea about who had tipped off the IRS.

His eyes never left my face. "I know a good thing when I see it and when I do, I go after it." There was something uncomfortably intimate about the moment.

Simon smiled then. "Take care of yourself, Kathleen," he said, and then he left.

Roma came out to the porch. "Maggie said that was Mia's dad."

I nodded.

"That was nice of him, bringing that food."

"He's a nice man," I said. *And a complicated one*, I added silently.

I went back to the table and ate another lemon tart.

Rebecca came and gave me one more hug. "I have to go," she said. "I think you're in good hands, but if you need anything . . ."

"I know where you are," I said.

Marcus arrived as Rebecca was going out the door. She gave his arm a squeeze and said, "Take care of our girl."

"I absolutely will," he said with a smile, wrapping me in his arms. His clothes were damp.

"Why didn't you go home and change?" I said.

"Because I didn't want to spend one more minute away from you," he said. "I hope it's okay that Eddie's going to get me some dry clothes. I don't want to make it hard for Roma."

"It's okay," I said.

Maggie got a bowl of soup for Marcus and by the time he'd finished it Eddie had arrived with his dry clothes. "Go take a shower," I told Marcus, patting his face with my padded hands.

He leaned down to kiss me. "I won't be long."

"I'm really glad you're okay," Eddie said to me.

"Stay," I said.

He looked over at Roma, who was making a fresh pot of coffee. She couldn't stop hovering, watching me, feeding me, trying to make me sit down.

"It's okay," I said. "Stay. Please?"

Eddie sighed softly. "All right."

There was an empty chair at the table next to Elliot and I sat down beside him. Roma immediately came over. "Is there anything you want?" she asked.

"Marry Eddie," I said.

She just looked at me. I could see how close to the surface her emotions were. I took her hand awkwardly with my two bandaged ones. "You're one of my best friends and you know I love you, don't you?"

She frowned. "Of course I do."

"I learned something today," I said. "I learned that no one has the right to tell another person who they're supposed to love. And that includes you. You don't have the right to tell Eddie who he should love. And by the way, that's still you." She tried to pull her hand away but I wouldn't let her. "You love Eddie and he loves you and the rest doesn't matter. Life is too short to waste happiness."

"What if it turns out to be a mistake?" she asked in a shaky voice.

Elliot had been listening to the conversation. "Then you do everything in your power to fix it," he said.

"You asked what I wanted," I said. "This is what I want."

"Me too," Roma said softly.

I let go of her hands. She looked across the room "Eddie," she said.

He turned to look at her.

Roma took a deep breath and let it out. "Eddie Sweeney," she said. "I love you. Will you marry me?"

Eddie looked at her, stunned.

I bunched up my napkin and threw it at him. "Hey," I said. "This is the part where you say yes."

"Yes!" Eddie said, a huge grim splitting his face. He grabbed Roma and swung her around, almost taking out Maggie and my toaster oven.

Elliot tipped his head to one side. "Nice work, Ms. Paulson," he said.

He held up his hand and we high-fived—very gingerly. Marcus was in the kitchen doorway. He smiled at both of us. I smiled back and nudged Elliot with my shoulder. "You too, Elly May," I said.

If you love Sofie Kelly's
Magical Cats Mysteries, keep reading for
an excerpt of the first book in Sofie Ryan's
New York Times bestselling
Second Chance Cat Mysteries . . .

THE WHOLE CAT AND CABOODLE

Available now!

Elvis was sitting in the middle of my desk when I opened the door to my office. The cat, not the King of Rock and Roll, although the cat had an air of entitlement about him sometimes, as though he thought he was royalty. He had one jet-black paw on top of a small cardboard box—my new business cards, I was hoping.

"How did you get in here?" I asked.

His ears twitched but he didn't look at me. His green eyes were fixed on the vintage Wonder Woman lunch box in my hand. I was having an early lunch, and Elvis seemed to want one as well.

"No," I said firmly. I dropped onto the retro red womb chair I'd brought up from the shop downstairs, kicked off my sneakers, and propped my feet on the matching footstool. The chair was so comfortable. To me, the round shape was like being cupped in a soft, warm giant hand. I knew the chair had to go back down to the shop, but I was still trying to figure out a way to keep it for myself.

Before I could get my sandwich out of the yellow vinyl lunch box, the big black cat landed on my lap. He wiggled his back end, curled his tail around his feet and looked from the bag to me.

"No," I said again. Like that was going to stop him.

He tipped his head to one side and gave me a pitiful look made all the sadder because he had a fairly awesome scar cutting across the bridge of his nose.

I took my sandwich out of the lunch can. It was roast beef on a hard roll with mustard, tomatoes and dill pickles. The cat's whiskers quivered. "One bite," I said sternly. "Cats eat cat food. People eat people food. Do you want to end up looking like the real Elvis in his chunky days?"

He shook his head, as if to say, "Don't be ridiculous."

I pulled a tiny bit of meat out of the roll and held it out. Elvis ate it from my hand, licked two of my fingers and then made a rumbly noise in his throat that sounded a lot like a sigh of satisfaction. He jumped over to the footstool, settled himself next to my feet and began to wash his face. After a couple of passes over his fur with one paw he paused and looked at me, eyes narrowed—his way of saying, "Are you going to eat that or what?"

I ate.

By the time I'd finished my sandwich Elvis had finished his meticulous grooming of his face, paws and chest. I patted my legs. "C'mon over," I said.

He swiped a paw at my jeans. There was no way he

was going to hop onto my lap if he thought he might get a crumb on his inky black fur. I made an elaborate show of brushing off both legs. "Better?" I asked.

Elvis meowed his approval and walked his way up my legs, poking my thighs with his front paws—no claws, thankfully—and wiggling his back end until he was comfortable.

I reached for the box on my desk, keeping one hand on the cat. I'd guessed correctly. My new business cards were inside. I pulled one out and Elvis leaned sideways for a look. The cards were thick brown recycled card stock, with SECOND CHANCE, THE REPURPOSE SHOP, angled across the top in heavy red letters, and SARAH GRAYSON and my contact information, all in black, in the bottom right corner.

Second Chance was a cross between an antiques store and a thrift shop. We sold furniture and housewares—many things repurposed from their original use, like the tub chair that in its previous life had actually been a tub. As for the name, the business was sort of a second chance—for the cat and for me. We'd been open only a few months and I was amazed at how busy we already were.

The shop was in a redbrick building from the late 1800s on Mill Street, in downtown North Harbor, Maine, just where the street curved and began to climb uphill. We were about a twenty-minute walk from the harbor front and easily accessed from the highway—the best of both worlds. My grandmother held the mortgage on the property and I wanted to pay her back as quickly as I could.

"What do you think?" I said, scratching behind Elvis's right ear. He made a murping sound, cat-speak for "good," and lifted his chin. I switched to stroking the fur on his chest.

He started to purr, eyes closed. It sounded a lot like there was a gas-powered generator running in the room.

"Mac and I went to look at the Harrington house," I said to him. "I have to put together an offer, but there are some pieces I want to buy, and you're definitely going with me next time." Eighty-year-old Mabel Harrington was on a cruise with her new beau, a ninety-one-year-old retired doctor with a bad toupee and lots of money. They were moving to Florida when the cruise was over.

One green eye winked open and fixed on my face. Elvis's unofficial job at Second Chance was rodent wrangler.

"Given all the squeaks and scrambling sounds I heard when I poked my head through the trapdoor to the attic, I'm pretty sure the place is the hotel for some kind of mouse convention."

Elvis straightened up, opened his other eye, and licked his lips. Chasing mice, birds, bats and the occasional bug was his idea of a very good time.

I'd had Elvis for about four months. As far as I could find out, the cat had spent several weeks on his own, scrounging around downtown North Harbor.

The town sits on the midcoast of Maine. "Where the hills touch the sea" is the way it's been described for the past 250 years. North Harbor stretches from the Swift

Hills in the north to the Atlantic Ocean in the south. It was settled by Alexander Swift in the late 1760s. It's full of beautiful historic buildings, award-winning restaurants and quirky little shops. Where else could you buy a blueberry muffin, a rare book and fishing gear all on the same street?

The town's population is about thirteen thousand, but that more than triples in the summer with tourists and summer residents. It grew by one black cat one evening in late May. Elvis just appeared at The Black Bear. Sam, who owns the pub, and his pickup band, The Hairy Bananas—long story on the name—were doing their Elvis Presley medley when Sam noticed a black cat sitting just inside the front door. He swore the cat stayed put through the entire set and left only when they launched into their version of the Stones' "Satisfaction."

The cat was back the next morning, in the narrow alley beside the shop, watching Sam as he took a pile of cardboard boxes to the recycling bin. "Hey, Elvis. Want some breakfast?" Sam had asked after tossing the last flattened box in the bin. To his surprise, the cat walked up to him and meowed a loud yes.

He showed up at the pub about every third day for the next couple of weeks. The cat clearly wasn't wild—he didn't run from people—but no one seemed to know whom Elvis (the name had stuck) belonged to. The scar on his nose wasn't new; neither were a couple of others on his back, hidden by his fur. Then someone remembered a guy in a van who had stayed two nights at the campgrounds up on Mount Batten. He'd had a cat with him. It was black. Or black and white. Or possibly gray. But it definitely had had a scar on its nose. Or it had been missing an ear. Or maybe part of a tail.

Elvis was still perched on my lap, staring off into space, thinking about stalking rodents out at the old Harrington house, I was guessing.

I glanced over at the carton sitting on the walnut sideboard that I used for storage in the office. The fact that it was still there meant that Arthur Fenety hadn't come in while Mac and I had been gone. I was glad. I was hoping I'd be at the shop when Fenety came back for the silver tea service that was packed in the box.

A couple of days prior he had brought the tea set into my shop. Fenety had a charming story about the ornate pieces that he said had belonged to his mother. A bit too charming for my taste, like the man himself. Arthur Fenety was somewhere in his seventies, tall with a full head of white hair, a matching mustache and an engaging smile to go with his polished demeanor. He could have gotten a lot more for the tea set at an antiques store or an auction. Something about the whole transaction felt off.

Elvis had been sitting on the counter by the cash register and Fenety had reached over to stroke his fur. The cat didn't so much as twitch a whisker, but his ears had flattened and he'd looked at the older man with his green eyes half-lidded, pupils narrowed. He was the picture of skepticism.

The day after he'd brought the pieces in, Fenety had called to ask if he could buy them back. The more

I thought about it, the more suspicious the whole thing felt. The tea set hadn't been on the list of stolen items from the most recent police update, but I still had a niggling feeling about it and Arthur Fenety.

"Time to do some work," I said to Elvis. "Let's go downstairs and see what's happening in the store."

ABOUT THE AUTHOR

Sofie Kelly is a *New York Times* bestselling author and mixed-media artist who lives on the East Coast with her husband and daughter. She writes the *New York Times* bestselling Magical Cats Mysteries (*Faux Paw, A Midwinter's Tail*) and, as Sofie Ryan, writes the *New York Times* bestselling Second Chance Cat Mysteries (*A Whisker of Trouble, Buy a Whisker*). Visit her online at sofiekelly.com.

Connect with Berkley Publishing Online!

For sneak peeks into the newest releases, news on all your favorite authors, book giveaways, and a central place to connect with fellow fans—

"Like" and follow Berkley Publishing!

facebook.com/BerkleyPub
twitter.com/BerkleyPub
instagram.com/BerkleyPub

Penguin
Random
House